Betrayed

*Also by Arnette Lamb
in Large Print:*

The Betrothal
Chieftain

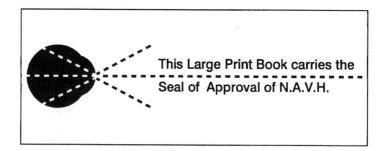

This Large Print Book carries the
Seal of Approval of N.A.V.H.

Betrayed

Arnette Lamb

Thorndike Press • Thorndike, Maine

Published in 1996 by arrangement with Pocket Books, an imprint of Simon & Schuster, Inc.

Thorndike Large Print ® Romance Series.

The tree indicium is a trademark of Thorndike Press.

The text of this Large Print edition is unabridged. Other aspects of the book may vary from the original edition.

Set in 16 pt. Bookman Old Style.

Printed in the United States on permanent paper.

Library of Congress Cataloging in Publication Data

Lamb, Arnette.
   Betrayed / Arnette Lamb.
     p.   cm.
    ISBN 0-7862-0819-8 (lg. print : hc)
    1. Large type books. I. Title.
   [PS3562.A4218B46 1996]
   813'.54—dc20   96-24029

This book is dedicated to the readers who embraced the Highland rogue and encouraged me to write about his daughters. You know who you are, and my gratitude and appreciation defy words.

My very special thanks to Alice Shields, Pat Stech, and Vivian Jane Vaughan for their help and support during the writing of this book.

Prologue

**Rosshaven Castle
Scottish Highlands
February 1785**

Sarah traced the wooden bindings on a collection of children's stories and waited for her father to share his troubling thoughts. To her surprise, Lachlan MacKenzie, the duke of Ross and the once-notorious Highland rogue, fumbled as he filled his pipe. His hands were shaking so badly his signet ring winked in the lamplight. His beloved face, more ruggedly handsome with the passage of time, now mirrored the strife contained within his good heart.

Sadness had begun this winter day, and Sarah wanted desperately to help ease the burden of his loss. She touched his arm. "Agnes and I used to fight for the privilege of doing that. Let

7

me fill your pipe."

His broad shoulders fell, and he blew out his breath. "I'm not your —" Halting, he gazed deeply at her. Affection, constant and warm, filled his eyes. With obvious effort, he forced the words. "I'm not your father."

Although she knew she'd misunderstood, Sarah went still inside. He'd acted oddly five years ago when her half sister, Lottie, had married David Smithson. When another of Sarah's half sisters, Agnes, had left home on an unconventional quest, he'd tormented himself for months. The day Mary demanded her dowry, so she could move to London to perfect her artistic skill with Sir Joshua Reynolds, Papa had ranted and raved until their stepmother, Juliet, had come to the rescue. His fatherly vulnerability was born of his love for all of his children, especially the elders, his four illegitimate daughters: Sarah, Lottie, Agnes, and Mary.

This time Sarah was sure he was bothered by her upcoming marriage to Henry Elliot, the earl of Glenforth, a man whose husbandly abilities he questioned. But Sarah had made her decision and for months had countered

8

Papa's objections.

She must reassure him again. "Just because I'm to wed Henry in the spring and move to Edinburgh doesn't mean I'll stop being your daughter."

His blue eyes brimmed with regret. "Name me the grandest coward o' the Highlands, but I'd sooner turn English than admit the truth of it. Oh, Sarah lass."

Sarah lass. It was his special name for her. His voice and those words were the first sounds she remembered — even from the cradle.

"Tell me what, Papa? That I cannot at once be daughter and wife, sister and mother? I'm not like Agnes, I will not forsake you, but I want my own family."

Always a commanding man, both in stature and in influence, today Papa seemed hesitant. He touched her cheek. "You were never truly my daughter — not in blood."

She stepped back. "That's a lie."

Unreality hung like a pall in the air between them. Of course he was her father. After her mother's death in childbirth, he'd taken Sarah from the hospice in Edinburgh and raised her with her half sisters. It was a tale as romantic as any bard could conjure. Those of noble blood were expected to leave the care of even their legitimate offspring to servants. Not Lachlan MacKenzie. He'd taken his four bastard daughters under his wing and raised them himself.

A stronger denial perched on her lips.

He took her hand. His palm was damp. His endearing smile wavered. " 'Tis God's own truth. I swear it on my soul."

Words of protest fled. Sarah believed him.

Moved by a pain so fierce it robbed her of breath, she jerked free and fled to the shelter of the bookstand near the windows.

On the edge of her vision, she saw him touch a taper to the hearth fire and light his pipe. She felt frozen in place, a part of the room, as natural in this space as the books, the toys on the floor, the tapestry frame near the hearth. This was her place, her home. Her handprints had smudged these walls. Her shoes had worn the carpet. Reprimands had been conducted here, followed by joyous forgiveness.

"You cannot think I do not love you as my own."

His own, and yet not. Bracing her fists on the open pages of the family Bible, she struggled to draw air into her lungs. The familiar aroma of his tobacco gave her courage. "How can you not be my father?"

"I said it poorly." He slammed the pipe onto the mantle and came toward her, his hands extended. "I am your father in all that counts. You are my own, but —" His gaze slid to the Bible. "I did not sire you."

"Who did?" She heard herself ask the question, but felt apart from the conversation.

New sadness dulled his eyes. "Neville Smithson."

Neville Smithson. The sheriff of Tain, a man Sarah had known most of her life. He had lived at the end of the street. She had taught his children to read. Absently, she touched the string of golden beads around her neck. Neville had given her the necklace for her twenty-fifth birthday. Lottie was married to Neville's son, David. Less than an hour ago, both families had stood in the cemetery and laid Neville

Smithson to rest.

His heart, the doctors said. He'd been conducting assizes. He had died in Papa's arms. His unexpected death, which had come as a blow to every household in Ross and Cromarty, now took on a greater meaning to Sarah.

She was neither the love child Lachlan MacKenzie nor one of his bastard daughters. Their illegitimacy was common knowledge, always had been. But in his special way, Lachlan had presented his lassies, as he called them, to the world as cherished daughters — and pity anyone who made sport of it.

Sarah thought of her half sisters. To obscure the details of their births and allay speculation, they all shared a common birthday, even though they had different mothers — a result, he boasted, of his first visit to court as the duke of Ross. "Did you sire Mary, Lottie, and Agnes?"

"Aye, but it changes nothing. In my heart you are their sister and my daughter."

At 10, Sarah had shot up in height. She was of an age with Lottie, Agnes, and Mary, but stood taller than them.

Other differences came to mind. Sarah had always been bookish and quiet. Lottie often swore that Sarah needn't come with them to court, for she'd sooner find merriment in the nearest library. Sarah had been a shy child; as a young woman, she held back, not for lack of gumption, but because her sisters were better leaders than she. They were gone now, each pursuing their own lives. Soon she would do the same.

The timing of her father's admission was curious. "Why did you wait until now to tell me?"

He folded his arms over his chest. " 'Twas Neville's last wish. You were still in swaddling when I took you for my own. He didn't even know about you until you were six, after we came here to live. When I told him, we agreed 'twas best you did not know."

"Why?"

"We feared your life might seem like a lie."

They could have been standing in the dungeon rather than this toasty-warm sanctuary, so cold did Sarah feel. " 'Tis one lie for another, Papa." The endearment burned on her lips. He had often praised her maturity, her sensible nature. But in his heart he must not believe his own opinion of her, for he hadn't trusted her with the truth. Not until now.

Sensible Sarah. She didn't feel sensible in the least.

Betrayal fueled her anger. "Henceforth, how shall I address you? Your Grace?"

Misery wreathed his face, but his will was as strong as ever. "You canna be angry. Your best interests were at the heart of it."

"If a lie has a heart, it beats the devil's rhythm."

"Sarah lass . . ."

As if she could shove his words away, she held up her hand. "I'm not *your* Sarah. My father is — is dead." Anguish stole her breath. Neville Smithson had entrusted his children to her teaching, yet he'd denied her the greatest bond of all — her own blood kin. And now it was too late to look him in the eye and ask why he had not claimed her.

Other ramifications were endless and baffling. "I stand as godmother to two of my own sisters."

"And a fine influence you are on Neville's younger children."

14

Neville's children — her siblings . . . but Lachlan MacKenzie thought of her as his daughter. Sarah didn't know what to think. "But they don't know I'm their sister."

"We'll tell them."

How, she wondered, her pride reeling. But there was no hurt in it for them, was there? Neville's son and heir, David, would surely rejoice and expect Sarah to take his side in his marital disputes with Lottie. What would the younger ones, her godchildren, say? Would they see her differently?

"Did Neville want you to tell them?" she asked.

"There wasn't time. God took him quickly. He spoke of his wife, then of you."

The information neither cheered nor saddened Sarah. She felt numb.

"You were always so different from my other lassies."

That was true, but Lachlan had given each of his children an equal share of his love. To Agnes and Mary, he exhibited great patience. To Lottie, he gave understanding.

To Sarah, he lied. Worse, he had been quick to swear that she was the image of his own mother, a MacKenzie — an impossibility.

Sarah marshalled her courage. "It was all lies. Did you also lie about my mother?"

"Nay. Your mother was Lilian White, sister to my beloved Juliet."

Sarah's stepmother was also her aunt, a situation that had been the cause of great jealousy among her siblings. But all along, Sarah had had an unknown reason to envy them their blood ties to Lachlan MacKenzie. She had been almost six years old when Juliet White came to Scotland to search for her sister's child. After winning the position of governess to four illegitimate girls, she had inspired the passion and won the love of Lachlan MacKenzie. Soon after, she gave him the first of four more daughters and an heir. Three of the girls survived. The children were Sarah's younger siblings.

And yet they were not. Her real siblings lived in the Smithson house at the end of Clan Row.

She glanced at the family portrait on the far wall. Not Mary's finest work, but certainly the most endearing to date,

16

the painting captured the MacKenzies lounging on the bank of Loch Shin. Life had been simple on that day years before.

One sister, Virginia, taken by misfortune, was depicted as an angel peering from behind a rowan tree. The day the family had given up hope of finding Virginia had been the blackest in Sarah's life. Until now.

That sorrow had passed. So, then, would this misery, Sarah pledged. But she must know more about her father. "Did he have any other words for me?"

"Neville loved you. He left you ten thousand pounds."

As a final blow, Lachlan MacKenzie, the only father she had ever known, thought her shallow enough to be bought. Something inside Sarah began to shrivel. She wanted to flee, to cower in the dark and cry until the pain ebbed.

But cowardice was not her way. She was almost three and twenty and would soon embark on a new life as the countess of Glenforth. Therein lay her salvation from the hurtful world that this room, this moment, and this life had become.

You bear the mark of the MacKenzies, Sarah lass.

A lie. No MacKenzie blood flowed in her veins.

In reality she'd been sired by a man who had toasted her every birthday and visited her when she was ill. A sheriff named Smithson, not a duke named MacKenzie. A man buried this morning, a man who sought to buy her forgiveness from the grave.

The cruelty cut her to the bone. "Neville Smithson left me guilt money."

"Nay. You are the same Sarah Mac-Kenzie you have ever been. I would not have given you up, even —" He slapped the Bible. "I wouldn't have given you up."

Even if Neville had asked, she finished the thought. Neville Smithson hadn't wanted her. As a tutor for his children, she'd been acceptable, but not as a treasured daughter.

His fair face rose in her mind, an image as constant as any in her memory. Her father: a fair-minded and honest sheriff with archangel good looks, Neville Smithson, a commoner.

She grasped the necklace he'd given her and ripped it off. A shower of golden

18

beads rained over the rug and scattered beneath the furniture.

"Sarah! 'Tis your favorite."

Scattered. Same as she felt.

"What are you thinking?"

The sound of Lachlan's voice drew her from the stupor her mind had become. "I'm thinking that I must go to Edinburgh and tell Henry." Yes, Henry and a new life.

"I'll go with you."

Denial came swiftly. "Nay. I'll take Rose." Her maid was company enough.

He sighed in resignation. "If Glenforth is unkind to you, or judgmental, I'll make him wish he'd been born Cornish."

The remark was so typical, Sarah smiled. But her happiness fled. It hadn't occurred to her before now that Henry would do anything other than accept the news with good grace. His mother, the Lady Emily, would not be so generous, but Henry usually prevailed in their family disputes.

Sarah would take only her MacKenzie dowry to Edinburgh. Lachlan had pledged the twenty thousand pounds months ago and had put his seal to the formal betrothal. The Smithson money could rot for all she cared; a king's ransom could not make her forgive him.

With Henry's help, she would heal the wounds Lachlan MacKenzie and Neville Smithson had dealt her.

"Take your necklace, Sarah."

"Nay. I never want to see it again."

1

Edinburgh, Scotland
June 1785

"Lady Sarah!"

Two of Sarah's pupils, William Picardy and the lad everyone called Notch, dashed into the schoolroom.

Notch yanked off his woolen cap. The crisp air made his thick brown hair crackle and stand on end. "The king is dead!"

She'd been staring at a blank slate and thinking of the odd turn her life had taken since her arrival in Edinburgh. Notch's shocking statement offered a diversion from her own troubles. "Who says the king is dead?"

Shoving the smaller William out of the way, Notch stepped forward. "The Complement's just come off a warship. Everybody knows the Complement wouldn't come to Scotland for any less of a reason —" His adolescent voice broke, and he cleared his throat. "I say the old Hanoverian's carved his last button, and Pitt the Younger has sent the Complement to give us the jolly news."

The king's Complement was an elite troop of horse soldiers, noblemen all. With great ceremony, the Complement had served English monarchs since the time of Henry VIII. At the ascension of George I, the Hanoverian kings had relegated the crown's cavalry to ceremony and foreign service, preferring a Hessian guard. The arrival of the Complement in Edinburgh certainly meant change, but did not necessarily harken the death of a king.

Notch's fanciful imagination, coupled with his need to impress and rule the younger orphans, was likely at the heart of the rumor.

Sarah intended to get to the truth of the matter. "Did you hear them say the king is dead?" she asked. "You heard one of the soldiers speak the words?"

He slid her a measuring glance, one eye squinting with the effort.

She held her ground. "Who told you?"

He withdrew a little and grumbled, "Didn't have to have it said to me like I was a short-witted babe."

She saw through his bravado, his way of managing alone on the streets of Edinburgh since the age of six. At 11, he was as worldly-wise as a man double his years. But in his eagerness to please, he was still a boy. No matter the reason, he deserved her respect and her guidance.

"No one expects you to predict the fate of kings, Notch. Even bishops cannot do that."

He stared stubbornly at the scuffed toes of his too-large shoes. His black woolen coat had long ago faded to dull gray, and his breeches were patched at the knees. Only his scarf, a contribution from Sarah, was new. That and his recent penchant for washing his face and hands every day.

The other children, four to date, doted Notch's every word. She hoped to make him understand the responsibility he undertook as their leader. He was only a child, but he'd been robbed of his boyhood. She intended to give it back to him.

She leaned against one of the school

desks. "But if you are only speculating about the reasons behind the arrival of the Complement and your theory proves wrong, you shouldn't be made to feel a lesser man because you were merely voicing *your* opinion. You could even learn and discuss the views of others in the matter. Such as Master Picardy here."

Eight-year-old William Picardy clutched his frayed lapels and rocked back on his heels. His blunt-cut brown hair framed a face of near-angelic beauty.

Wondering how anyone could have abandoned this precious child to the streets, Sarah resisted the urge to embrace him. "Why do you think the Complement has come?"

William fairly wiggled with excitement at being addressed. Eyes darting from the school desks to the standing globe to the hearth fire, he considered the question.

"What's it to be, Pic?" Notch tapped his foot. "Are you with me or against me?"

He'd given her a perfect opportunity to broaden the lesson. "It's not a contest, Notch. Neither of you must be right or wrong. Your friendship does not hinge on one of you lording his knowledge over the other. You can learn together."

The expression in his eyes turned aged, wise. "We know our place, my lady. Me and Pic, Sally, and the Odds."

The strength of Sarah's argument waned. The other orphans he spoke of were beholden to him, needed him as much as he needed them.

"I believe . . ." William paused, obviously battling the force of Notch's will.

"Out with it, Pic."

William sighed and said, "The king's upped his pointy slippers."

"There it is." Notch slapped William on the back and sent Sarah a victorious glance.

She gave up the effort to teach them democracy and shared responsibility. Theirs was a precarios existence; safety lay in numbers for orphaned children. Preyed upon and exploited by the very adults whose duty it was to nurture and protect them, the children were wary of "sermon-saying sinners," as Notch called them.

He and the others still didn't know her well enough to trust her. But they

wanted to, and that made Sarah pro-
foundly happy, a rare feeling these
days.

"Have you ever seen the Complement?" William asked.

"Nay," she said. "They've been in service abroad for most of my life."

"She's from the Highlands," Notch reminded him, but in a mannerly tone.
Then he cocked out his elbow and held
his arm in gentlemanly fashion. "William and me thought to have a look at
the king's best. You could come along."

Bowing from the waist, William swept
a hand toward the door. "Smellie Quinn
plugged up the kegs at the Pipe 'n'
Thistle so as *he* didn't miss a sight of
the Complement."

"Gents and ladies is turning out
proper," said Notch.

The less-coy William wheedled, "Do
come with us, Lady Sarah. I promise
we'll have a place in the clean edge of
the lane."

The weekly lesson had ended hours
ago, and if she stayed here alone, she'd
spend the afternoon pondering events
beyond her control and lamenting her
poor judgment.

She reached for her cloak. "Very well,

but only if you stop saying the king is dead — until we hear it from the mayor or the lord provost."

"I give my word." Notch tapped his left fist into his right palm.

"That's the sign of his honor," William offered in awed explanation. "He don't give it lightly."

Sarah thought the gesture meant he'd fight with his fists to prove he was right.

Notch led the way out of the converted storage room and down the winding steps of Saint Margaret's Church. Skirting the confessionals, they exited the side door and stepped into Rectory Close.

Sunshine warmed the spring afternoon, and the ever-present wind whistled around corners. Wooden signs squeaked on rusty chains above the nearby establishments. A cobbler hurried past Sarah and her pupils, his leather apron flapping in the breeze. A portly clerk followed, one hand holding his dusted periwig in place. The sharp aroma of coal smoke, the city's signature smell, filled the air.

"The Pipe 'n' Thistle's got the best view of the road," said Notch, pulling his cap down over his ears. "Sally and the

27

Odds'll have a place for us."

Positioning herself in front of a local tavern in the company of five of Edinburgh's most notorious street urchins with the townspeople looking on wouldn't do Sarah's reputation any good, but considering the string of recent events, another taint would provide small fodder to the gossips.

Let them talk. She'd encountered worse slights in her life. What bastard child did not? Only in her case, the truth of her parentage had hurt a thousand times more than the taunts from society matrons.

"Won't no one pester you, my lady," said William. "Not with Notch along."

Thoughts of her MacKenzie family brought guilt and regret, sorrow and yearning. She needed Lachlan's counsel, but pride held her back. For two months, he'd written to her every Saturday. When she did not reply, he finally stopped. Now she was truly on her own, and the going wasn't as easy as she had thought.

"Gardy-loo!" someone yelled from above.

Driven by instinct, Sarah and her young friends hurried out of the way before a bucket of slops splashed onto the street.

They rounded the corner and turned onto High Street. Standing three deep, the people of Edinburgh lined the well-kept thoroughfare in anticipation of the arrival of the Complement. The magistrate and the collier flanked the stern-faced bishop. Even Cholly, the streetsweeper, paused in his labor. His back bowed, a blanket cape covering baggy pants and a sacklike shirt, the scruffy old laborer leaned on his broom handle. An unkempt beard obscured his face and his eyes were shielded by the brim of a battered hat.

She'd never been close enough to Cholly to engage in a conversation with him, but he was a constant figure in Lawnmarket. Usually within waving distance of her residence, he, too, befriended Notch and his band and kept company with the sedanchairmen.

As they neared the tavern, Sarah spotted the Odds. So named by Notch because their burly size swayed the odds in a fight, the nine-year-old twins were also exact opposites in complexion. Right Odd, the fairer of the two lads, had perched the four-year-old orphan Sally on his shoulders.

"My lady," said Notch, clearing the way through a group of disapproving citizens. "Do you think Lord Tip-o'-the-Hat will turn out?"

Clever, clever Notch, she thought. He had easily grasped the meaning of her lecture on collective reasoning, and he wanted her to know it. He could have asked her opinion on a mundane topic, but that was not his way. The insult to one of the young nobles showing an interest in the now-unattached Sarah was Notch's means of holding part of himself back.

Sarah would have none of it. She liked this lad, for he reminded her of her half sister, Agnes, who was always the first into the pond and the last to admit she enjoyed it. Sarah glared down at him. "You are referring to Count DuMonde."

Before Notch could reply, William wagged the end of his new scarf and smacked his lips in exaggerated kisses. "Shoo-de-bwak! Wee-wee, mah cher-ries!"

"William!" She admonished his mimicry, but couldn't help laughing herself.

Howling, Notch scuffed his friend's head. "Well said, Pic-o'-the-Litter."

the character of Count DuMonde and resigned to the reigning camaraderie, Sarah glanced at the crowd. Like a breeze over a field of heather, anticipation moved through the onlookers. Gleeful smiles and excited murmurs heralded the imminent arrival of the king's Complement.

Sarah felt the anxiety, even as she scanned the faces of the well-dressed women to see if Lady Emily Elliot was among them. Past blaming Henry's mother for the scandalous events of late, Sarah still thought it wise to know the whereabouts of the selfish shrew who had sworn to ruin her.

Upon her arrival four months ago at Glenstone Manor, the Elliot family residence in Edinburgh, Sarah had learned that Henry and his mother were on an extended holiday in London. Rather than stay in the mansion with a staff of servants bewildered by her unexpected presence or return to the Highlands, she'd leased a house in nearby Lawnmarket and awaited the return of the Elliots.

In the past, Henry had encouraged her plans to help the less fortunate, and she had planned to use the leased property for her charity work after the wedding. To ease the loneliness and fill her idle time, she'd begun teaching school in a converted storeroom at Saint Margaret's Church. Those who could not afford private tutors sent their children to Sarah. The orphans came on their own.

But then Lady Emily had come home with shocking news that Henry had been thrown into prison. A demand for both Sarah's dowry and the intervention of the duke of Ross to obtain Henry's release had followed.

Sarah abandoned her plan to confess that she was not a MacKenzie by birth and logically asked the reason for Henry's incarceration. Lady Emily had refused, telling Sarah it was improper for a wife-to-be to ask after the business of her betrothed.

Brows raised in disdain, Lady Emily had tried to end the discussion with, "Rather she should turn over her dowry as agreed and trust her lord and master in the exhausting matter of finances."

Lachlan MacKenzie had worked hard to earn dowries for all of his daughters. Knowing Sarah could manage it herself, he'd given her the money. Upon arrival in Edinburgh, she had entrusted it to the banker, James Coutts.

An affronted Sarah had refused Lady Emily.

The countess's response didn't bear recalling. But she'd carried out her threat to destroy Sarah's reputation, and now only the orphans attended her Sunday morning school. Revenge came with the knowledge that Henry was still behind bars, and Sarah now knew the reasons why he'd been imprisoned.

From atop the shoulders of Right Odd, Sally shouted, "Look! They're coming!"

Over the building exclamations of enthusiasm, Sarah heard the clip-clop of horses' hooves and gladly gave up her search for Lady Emily Elliot.

An instant later, the first came into view, and Sarah understood why the king's Complement commanded so much respect.

The first officer sat atop a magnificent crimson bay horse. Wearing the traditional uniform of blue tabard, white trunk hose, and a chain of office bearing the Tudor rose, he drew every eye. The gusting wind, as much a part of Edinburgh as the biting winter cold, ruffled the white plumes in his helmet.

The horse quivered and tossed its head with tbe urge to run, but the rider held the reins taut and clamped his knees tighter to control the animal.

George II had added knee boots to the nostalgic uniform; George III had commissioned the fur-lined velvet cape emblazoned with a Tudor rose badge.

The entire troop of 13 hand-picked gentlemen, riding three abreast behind the leader, now filled the street. Cheers rose from the crowd, but the officer did not take notice. Chin up, his attention fixed on matters of his own concern, he reminded Sarah of Lachlan MacKenzie when faced with an unappealing yet necessary task. But more than his handsome features and regal bearing, something warm and oddly familiar to Sarah lingered about this dignified military man.

Impossible, she silently scoffed. She was merely attracted to his rugged good looks and commanding air.

"Has the king tucked it in, then?" Notch yelled out. "Is that why you've come to Auld Reekie?"

"Shush!" Sarah grasped the boy's arm. Auld Reekie was the casual name given Edinburgh, a reference to the

36

pungent smoke from so many coal fires.

The first officer turned just enough to spy the bold lad. Then his attention fell on Sarah. To her horror, she felt herself blush beneath his probing gaze. But his slow, sly smile put an end to her embarrassment.

A conceited rogue, she decided. Let the children and the other women admire him. As leader of the most respected collection of horsemen in the Christian world, he was probably accustomed to having women fawn over him. Sarah MacKenzie had better things to do, such as contriving an audience with the mayor of Edinburgh so she could try again to convince him to convert the abandoned customs house into an orphanage.

She turned to leave and almost bumped into her maid, Rose. Garbed in her best dress and matching pink bonnet, Rose looked more like the wife of a prosperous squire than a lady's maid.

"Ain't the sight of *him* a cause for celebration?" Rose grinned like a lovestruck girl. "They say jewels fall from the sky when a gentleman of the Complement kisses a woman."

Sarah should have expected her

saucy maid to turn out. "Then remember to cup your hands if one of them takes liberties with you, so you can catch a few rubies. Simper to your heart's content, Rose. You can even have my place."

Rose executed a perfect curtsy, but her irreverent expression spoiled the polite gesture. "There's cider in the buttery and fresh scones in the pantry. You're as thin as Lottie's manners."

Sarah had heard the comparison often of late, but the dining table was too big and empty, and she couldn't bear to take a tray in her room like some jilted spinster. Knowing that both her good humor and her appetite would return when she sorted out her prospects, she took the remark in the spirit it was intended. Rose was concerned. Unquestionably loyal, she had often braved the wrath of the MacKenzie steward in defense of Sarah and her siblings.

Moving past her maid, Sarah gave a false smile. "Thank you for your observation, Rose. I cannot imagine where I would be without you."

"You'd be home where you belong."

Spoken softly, the admonition bore no

sting. "That's your opinion."

"We all got opinions," Notch said. " 'Cept the dead and buried at Gallow's Foot."

Several hours later, a knock sounded at Sarah's front door. When Rose did not answer the knock, Sarah put down her knitting and hurried to see who was there.

The moment she opened the door, she regretted it.

2

Poised on her threshold, the first officer of the king's Complement now wore a brown velvet coat over an Elliot tartan plaid, pleated and belted in kilt fashion. His sporran even bore a silver crescent, the heraldic symbol of a second son.

She instantly revised her opinion of him. She also knew why he'd looked familiar. Unlike his older brother, this man bore the true face of the Elliots, the same virile image she'd seen in paintings in the halls of Glenstone Manor.

He was Michael Elliot, Henry's younger brother.

Henry. Her pride rebelled at the thought of the scoundrel she'd intended to marry. If this second son had come to Edinburgh to attend her wedding to his brother, he'd wasted a very long journey.

"You're Michael Elliot."

He nodded and clasped his hands

behind his back, drawing attention to the breadth of his shoulders and his thickly muscled neck. "So my nanny told me."

An odd answer and much too personal for Sarah to address. Besides, she'd had enough of the deceitful and greedy Elliots. She was surprised that Henry had not told her of his brother's respected position in the Complement. According to Henry, Michael had merely made a career in the army of the East India Company.

She didn't care if he owned every trading ship in the fleet. "Why have you come here?"

"For two reasons, actually." He eyed her up and down.

Without the helmet and the fancy trappings, there was something rugged about him, something Highland-like, something dangerously appealing to Sarah.

But he was an Elliot. "And the reasons are?"

"I simply had to meet the woman who preferred to wed a toothless and blind draft horse, rather than marry my brother."

Sarah had said that, among other

disparaging remarks, to Henry's mother. The wicked Lady Emily had bullied and insulted Sarah, who replied with logic and sympathy as long as possible. When her patience fled, Sarah had abandoned polite conversation.

Lady Emily had gotten precisely what she deserved. "I do not regret my rudeness to your mother."

Laughter played about his mouth, softening the stern line of his jaw. "At least her memory is better than her manners. My sainted mother also said you were a troublemaker." His voice dropped. "But she hesitated to mention how beautiful you are."

Was the subtle sarcasm in his tone meant for his mother or for Sarah? Probably the latter, considering the poor behavior of the rest of his family.

Bother the Elliots. They could spout compliments until the coal ran out. Sarah was done with them. "You are too kind," she said, meaning in effect that he was a troll to darken her door. "You said you came here for two reasons. Beyond repeating my wish to never set eyes on an Elliot again, what is your purpose?"

Michael felt like a footman sent to

settle the butcher's account. Ignoring her surprised gasp, he moved past her and headed for the hearth. Over his shoulder, he said, "To change your mind, of course."

An ambitious by-blow of the duke of Ross, his mother had said of Sarah MacKenzie. Michael had expected a ruddy-complexioned country lass with backward manners and a sharp tongue. He'd been partially correct, but by the saints, she was a joy to look upon. Gowned in a concoction of saffron-colored velvet and her golden hair glistening like sunshine, she appeared a picture of feminine grace. In opposition to current fashion, her dress was laden with only modest panniers. Her waist was exceedingly trim, so much so the gown fit loosely. He'd stake his share of the next China silk run that she didn't wear a corset.

"Do not expect me to welcome you, and stop staring at me."

"Was I?"

"Yes. You gawk like a shepherd down from the hill in spring."

Michael chuckled, but inside he struggled for something intelligent to say.

Cool disdain gave her a queenly air. "Do you find me entertaining?"

He turned to give his right side a chance to thaw at the fire. "Not at all. I've a Brodie under my command. His Highland speech is not so refined as yours, but the flavor of it is the same. His mother's brother was a shepherd. Brodie tells stories about his uncle's less-than-decorous behavior after a winter spent in isolation." Turning, he treated his left side to a delicious wave of heat. "So I have a basis for comparison of your remark, and I found it humorous." Humor was actually the last trait he had expected to find in Sarah MacKenzie.

"Oh."

Michael nearly preened. "So, if I may respond to your observation, I stare at you because you are uncommonly lovely, and I have been in India for the better part of two decades. Comely Scotswomen are a rarity there." That flattery should melt her reserve and put her on the path to yielding her considerable dowry.

It ignited her temper. Skirts rustling softly, she marched up to him. "Take your pretty words and speak them at a shrine to Siva. I am not for sale."

Good Lord, this MacKenzie lass had a fire in her, and intelligence, too. How else would she know about Hindu goddesses? She'd have her man shirking his duty to find ways to ignite her passions. Never one to shy from a challenge, Michael eagerly moved closer to her flame. "I take it you told the countess as much."

"And more. Good day, sir. I'm sure your regiment misses your guidance."

"You refer to the Complement." Ah, yes. Now he knew where he'd seen those blue eyes. "You were standing beside that young street reiver who asked me if the king were dead."

She gripped his arm just above the elbow and moved to show him to the door. "Notch is not a thief; at least I don't think he steals now. Either way, it's none of your concern. The Complement, however, is, and I wish you well of it, although I'm deeply sorry you brought them here for nothing."

Her hand was surprisingly strong, and Michael planted his feet. He must stall for time, then get back to the business of convincing this woman to hand over her dowry and marry his brother — either one first. "Then this outspoken fellow named Notch did not rob you."

She sighed noisily and withdrew her hand, crossing her arms at her waist. "Of course he did not rob me. Will you please leave? Your brother deserves the disgrace he suffers, and I want nothing more to do with the Elliots."

A belief Michael tended to share, after the brief audience with his mother. But this occasion did not require truth from him. Sarah MacKenzie had made a contract. He would convince her to honor it. Then he'd get on with his new life as a civilian.

If his mother and brother had blackened the family name, Michael would do what he could to rescue them, but he would not allow Sarah MacKenzie or anyone else to question his character. "How can you be certain that you want nothing to do with me when you don't even know me?" A bit of verbal finesse might win his victory. " 'Twould seem my mother was correct, though."

Anger simmered in her eyes. "The only thing the countess of Glenforth excels at is her high opinion of herself and her devotion to a worthless, deceitful son."

46

The room grew warmer, and Michael intended to savor it. He'd been cold to his bones since the ship sailed into the Firth of Forth. India's sunny clime was a lifetime away. "I quite agree and couldn't have said it better myself."

That put a kink in her plans. She leaned against the high back of a tooled leather chair. "You expect me to believe that you dislike your own brother?"

Michael hadn't seen Henry in so long, he wouldn't know him from a well-groomed doorman at Trotter's Club. "Not on our first meeting, of course." He walked around the small sofa and sat down. "But given the chance . . ." He left the vagary to hang in the air while he removed a glove. Patting the place beside him, he finished with, ". . . unless I am convinced that you are a light-headed chit who has committed fraud against the Elliots. In that case, the countess of Glenforth would have just cause to sue for forfeiture of your dowry."

She looked beautifully baffled. "Dementia is an Elliot family trait."

As affable as a merchant on allowance day, Michael reached into his sporran and pulled out a pouch of his favorite treat. Extending it, he raised his brows. "Candy?"

She didn't move. Her expression said, "Get on with it."

After popping a small piece of sugared ginger into his mouth, he stretched out his legs. "If we are demented, then your Highland blood will surely serve us well."

"How many times must I say it? I refuse to wed your brother."

"You could do worse than Henry in a choice of husbands."

"I'm sure I could — in a Turkish debtor's prison."

Michael almost choked on the candy. Beyond curiosity, he didn't care why his brother couldn't meet his financial obligations. He'd simply agreed to this meeting to placate his distraught mother. But he was growing intrigued with Sarah MacKenzie.

"Come now," he began expansively. "My brother withers for want of your affections. He loves you well."

"I do not care a tin farthing what your brother wants or whom he professes to love."

"But you did at one time, else you would not have pledged to become his wife and bear his heirs. Given the smallest chance, he will rekindle your affections. Mother worries that you have simply fallen prey to missish behavior."

"Let me be sure I understand. Your mother, the countess, expresses true concern on my behalf?"

Michael felt a prick of conscience. He did not envy this entertaining and beautiful woman her plight — marriage into the Elliots. But he was only the appointed courier of ill news. Except for funerals and christenings, he'd probably never see her again.

"My mother is ever solicitous of your well-being." For good measure, he embellished the lie. "And she apologizes most sincerely for the cross words you exchanged."

"Cross? She called me an ill-bred, uncivilized ne'er-do-well."

Oh, to be a beetle in the rug during that exchange of feminine fury. "And your reply?"

Color blossomed on her cheeks and she busied her hands pressing out the folds of her skirts. "I called her a pinched-mouth crow."

An apt description, he thought, remembering how his mother's lips had thinned with scorn at the mention of Sarah MacKenzie. "She's deeply sorry for the remark."

"I don't believe you. Had she been sincere, she would have come herself."

A weak truth came to mind. "I offered to come. I wanted to meet the woman who has captured my brother's heart and agreed to wed him."

"She's using you."

That painful reality struck him a blow. He should redeem his brother's gambling markers himself and put Edinburgh behind him. Michael could easily afford it, but he'd sacrificed women and sport to save enough money for his first share in the East India Company. Even in the prosperous years that followed, he'd managed his fortune wisely. Handing even a tuppence of it over to the family that had forgotten him and now used him as a messenger rankled his pride. But it was a small price to pay to be rid of them; the MacKenzies had given their word, and Michael had promised to remind them of it.

"My mother is concerned about her son's happiness." The use of the singular *son* described perfectly his own lack of position in the family. Michael wasn't sure he cared anymore.

"How generous of her."

"Indeed, and you needn't deal with her at all, if you so choose."

"Meaning that I can just hand over my dowry to you."

"And then wed my brother as planned."

"No. Lachlan MacKenzie worked hard to earn my dowry. I'll not see it wasted in the name of male pride."

His respect for her trebled, and he suddenly had a craving to know more about her. "You do not consider the betrothal binding?"

"You mean as a contract?"

She radiated self-assurance. Perhaps Henry had not fallen to misfortune, as Mama had said. Perhaps pride had brought him low. But how, then, had he wooed and won this strong, enchanting woman? "It is a legal document."

Amid a soft rustling of velvet, she strolled to the hearth and stoked the fire. "The law will not enforce it."

A fresh blast of heat warmed his bare knees, and he smiled. "Why ever not? Dowries have been forfeited for lesser reasons than a bride's change of heart."

Replacing the fire iron, she dusted her hands. "Ah, but my reasons adhere to the principle of the maxim."

Maxim? Michael knew little of betrothal laws. Calcutta was hardly a marriage mart for British nobility. But surely a contract was a contract. "Are you certain you've been given good advice by your father's solicitor?"

As if she were a governess addressing a naive charge, she patiently said, "The maxim in both courts and chancery states that a contract that opposes sound policy and is of dangerous tendency to the community is void. I assure you that fulfilling my betrothal to your brother flies in the face of sound *policy* and is fraught with dangerous tendencies to any *community* he inhabits."

Shocked by her passionate and learned discourse on the law, Michael lamely said, "Surely that law applies only to the lower classes."

"Precisely the station of the Elliots." Her smile was pure sarcasm.

Stung and amused at once, Michael didn't know whether to laugh or protest, so he took the soldier's part and challenged. "You cannot swear duress.

You chose him freely."

"If you or any of the Elliots try to hold this troublemaker to the agreement, you will all suffer duress. I shall not be taken lightly."

Michael believed her. *Formidable* perfectly described Sarah MacKenzie. He recalled another of his mother's condemnations. "My mother swears you have a head for manly concerns."

"How delightful," she said, laughing. "Your apologetic mother continues to overstep herself."

Familial loyalty waned and a retreat beckoned. Michael grasped it. "You know her far better than I, but my ready inclination is to agree with you. How did you and the Elliots come to this dreadful pass?"

Surprise lent a wholesomeness to her elegant features. "Ask them. The tale is better told from their part. I doubt you would see my view of it."

She had a lot of pride, this Highland lass. Michael was inspired to learn all of her secrets and listen to all of her opinions.

He moved his feet closer to the fire. "My poor brother languishes in debtor's prison, and my mother has sunk to ranting and raving." Securing the string, he tossed her the bag of sweets. "Not the most pleasant of homecomings for me." Just as she caught it, he lowered his voice. "I've been away a very long time. I'm a stranger here."

Much like a general eyeing a green recruit, she studied him, probably looking for dishonesty. Michael relaxed under her scrutiny; he'd faced inspection for most of his life.

"Do you think to bribe me with sweets?"

When she hefted the bag, as if to throw it at him, he rushed to say, "No. I thought to share the candy with you and seek your advice on several matters." What advice, he didn't know.

She sat in the chair facing him, but ignored the bag in her hand. "What is it you wish to know? The location of a decent cobbler? Whom to choose for a tailor?"

Michael had no intention of alienating her. He'd come here not because his mother had asked him to, because she had not asked — the Lady Emily had commanded. Her audacity had startled him. Prior to the recent order to ship out of Calcutta for Edinburgh, the last direct command he'd received had been from the king, and that was five years ago. In his stunned hesitation, the countess of Glenforth had wrongly judged her younger son malleable.

The fresh scent of Sarah's perfume drifted to his nose and obliterated thoughts of his mother. Sarah smelled of summer rain and spring flowers. He harkened to both the woman and the subject at hand. "Why did you sign the betrothal?"

"I foolishly thought your brother had the makings of a good husband and father. He foolishly coveted my dowry."

A visit to London loomed on Michael's horizon. He would speak with Henry and straighten out this coil, then embark on his new life. In the meantime, he'd enjoy getting to know Sarah MacKenzie.

"If you truly want to offend my mother's sensibilities, you should consider joining me for dinner at the Dragoon Inn. I'm told all of the best gossips and successful politicians dine there."

Would she take the dare? He hoped so; he didn't relish sharing another meal in the sole company of men. He'd had weeks of that aboard ship. "I promise to behave as an officer and a gentleman."

"I will not change my mind about your family, so why should you wish to take a meal with me?"

Because he intended to change her mind about one Elliot. He'd stake his considerable fortune on it. But now he had to call on his mother again and learn the particulars of his brother's fall from grace. Then he would return to his peaceful and quiet rented rooms.

"I asked you to dine with me because I believe you are an infinitely more pleasant companion than either a troop of horsemen too long at sea or the mother I hardly know."

He surprised her, for she opened her mouth, closed it, then stared at the fire. "Very well, but there's a condition."

Addressing stipulations was a way of life in the foreign service. Michael knew he would prevail.

She rose and handed him the sack of candy. The pouch was warm from her touch and damp from her palm. So, he thought, she wasn't as composed as she'd have him believe.

Hoping to leave on a cheerful note, he rose. "I promise to use knife and fork, chew with my mouth closed, and leave my hat and gloves with the doorman."

"What of your good intentions? Where will you leave them?"

"They are a veritable constant in my character." He took her hand, brought it to his lips, and kissed it. "Ask the king. He will vouch for me."

The banter pleased her, for she struggled against a smile and pulled her hand away slowly. She glanced from the ceiling to her upturned palm. "No gemstones fell from the sky."

She referred to the old tale, one of hundreds about the Complement. "You must declare yourself my sweetheart to receive the prized jewels." An outstanding but impossible idea, he had to admit.

Obviously having second thoughts about her boldness, she waved him off. "You're an Elliot. Charm flourishes in the men of your clan."

Yes, and she'd been his brother's choice for a wife.

Stowing his disappointment, Michael bowed from the waist. "Shall I come for you at nine o'clock tomorrow night?"

Serenity fell like a cloak over her features. "Only if I may invite a guest."

Michael didn't question her desire for a chaperon; he'd drag the bishop of Saint Andrews to the table if Sarah MacKenzie shared the meal.

3

Later that day, over a meal of rizzared haddock and hashes, Michael sipped claret and waited for his mother to ask about his meeting with Sarah MacKenzie. Mother's delay in broaching the subject puzzled him, for she'd been insistent earlier. He would tell her as much as his good conscience allowed. Then he intended to find out the details of his brother's incarceration. But for now he was simply interested in watching the woman who had given birth to him; it inspired introspection.

Had she been pleased at her first sight of him? Had she thought him a comely babe and worth the travail? Silliness, he knew, and entirely unmanly, but he was certain he would treasure looking upon his own newly birthed child. If it were proper and his wife consented, he'd even enjoy watching the birthing itself. Welcoming a new life must truly be a miracle. After spending so many years in a country where women were sequestered and excluded even from meals, Michael found himself interested in the general aspects of a Christian female.

Mother's white satin gown and heavily dusted wig contrasted sharply with the Elliot rubies at her throat, her wrists, and her fingers. Lines of age blemished her mouth, pulling her lips into a perpetual frown. Considerably shorter than Sarah MacKenzie, his mother was still a slender woman with pretty hands and well-tended skin.

Buttering a piece of muffin, she complained of everything from the slowness of the post to the small print in the doited *Scots Magazine.* "And those deplorable slums," she cursed. "They've spoiled the lanes for any outings to view the boats in the harbor."

Pinched-mouth, Sarah's epithet, perfectly suited his mother's disdainful manner. Yet she was an attractive woman, or at least elegant and fashionable. She was also woefully rude, for she wasn't in the least interested in her younger son or the events of his life during the last 15 years.

Michael hadn't expected to be bothered by that. He hadn't anticipated being hurt by her indifference. Grown men shouldn't pine for a mother's attention. Or should they? If not, then why did he feel hollow inside when he expected to feel fulfilled?

"I had hoped to add a portrait gallery," she went on, "but with that window tax, none of the brilliant architects will take a commission in Edinburgh. They cannot build a decent mansion here. The Exchequer would have us go back to hill forts with smoke holes and arrow slits for light. Not in London, of course. Can you imagine Chatham taking kindly to being told how many windows he can afford?"

Michael couldn't resist saying, "I do not think Pitt lacks a window allowance."

"Neither would the Elliots if our coal concerns still prospered."

The family estate in Fife, where Michael had been raised, provided the Elliots their wealth. Having only his boyhood knowledge of the business, he chose a cordial reply. "I'm certain Henry does his best, Mama."

"Of course he does." She picked up her wineglass and put it to her lips.

The glass was empty, but she pretended to swallow rather than bring attention to the fact that she'd already drunk all of the claret. She'd done that twice since the hashes had been served.

She rang the servant bell. When the butler appeared and refilled her glass, she ignored it. "The export tax robs us of our profits. Shipping coal to the Baltic has become a charitable enterprise."

Watching her, Michael realized he didn't know or couldn't remember the color of her hair. A son should know that, among other generalities about his mother, such as the name of her closest acquaintance or her choice of books — additional information for his list of important family matters. When he married and had children, he would conduct his family in a more friendly fashion. They would know each other, travel together, share thoughts and opinions. Most of all, they would be loyal to each other.

She sighed and drank from the goblet. "Poor Henry. When I think of him languishing in that cell —" She squeezed her lips tighter and clutched a perfectly manicured hand to her throat. The Elliot rubies twinkled in the candlelight. Were there other jewels? A chest of family gems? Sadly, he recognized how little he knew of the Elliots' legacy.

Searching his memory, he found a vague recollection of this room, with its wainscot walls, crystal chandelier, and carpeted floors, but be could not recall the occasion of his last visit here. Hadn't the ceiling been much higher and the table a vast expanse of lace-covered oak? How old had he been? Probably six or seven; when he'd sat in one of the high-back chairs, his feet had dangled above the floor.

He had felt clumsy then. He felt confused now.

"Are you listening, Michael?"

At his arrival at Glenstone Manor earlier in the day, she had excused herself, but only briefly, from a visit with the vicar. Standing in the unlighted hall, Michael had glimpsed his mother for the first time in fifteen years. The urgency of her tone during their conversation had brought out his heroic intentions and sent him hurrying to Lawnmarket to slay the dragon, Sarah MacKenzie.

On rellection, his eagerness galled him.

He put down his fork. "What precisely was the misfortune that befell dear Henry? You didn't say."

Turning her head away, she breathed through her nose. " 'Twas that scoundrel, the duke of Richmond. He preyed upon your brother's decent nature and lured him into a gaming den."

The condemnation was at odds with what Michael knew about Richmond, and he rotted not having questioned his mother at length before dashing off to confront Sarah MacKenzie. "His grace is reputed to frequent the better gaming clubs, but his honor has never been questioned."

She grew very quiet, then asked, "How would you know? You've been in service in India."

She made his chosen career sound vile. As a second son he'd had few options beyond the family crumbs. What would she say if she knew of the fortune he'd amassed? He'd reserve that information. "Tell me what occurred."

"Richmond cheated at some game — dice most likely — and when Henry refused to pay him fifteen thousand pounds, the wretched duke had dear Henry clamped in irons and carted away. 'Tis appalling."

"Fifteen thousand pounds is an appalling amount to wager at dice."

The butler served the brandied pears, then dusted debris from the table.

When he had exited, she said, "Yes, Michael, I'm certain you would see it as a fortune."

He wanted to laugh. Instead he thought of Sarah. She'd been fierce in her conviction that she would not squander her dowry on a gaming debt. He shared her dislike of wasteful practices and had the feeling they would agree on more than issues of moral principle.

She could even pick apart a law and derive its maxim. *Maxim.* How many women — or men for that matter — even knew the meaning of the word? Not many, he was forced to admit.

Taking his silence for confirmation of her opinion, his mother continued. "I've received a letter from Henry's solicitor. The duke has threatened to take the matter before the House of Lords. He advises that we send Richmond a token payment." Lifting her eyes, she settled a pleasant gaze on Michael. "You must cashier yourself out of the career we bought for you."

Aghast, Michael blurted, "I repaid you long ago." He'd also left the army the day he joined the Complement.

"Repaid us?" Her laughter trilled to the ceiling. "You mean those small sums you sent? Were they not gifts to me? I put the money in the poorbox, Since had no need of more carrying-around money at the time."

Carrying-around money? For six years, he'd dutifully sent home half his pay. He'd been an angry youth, determined to make something of himself. When dangerous missions arose, he stepped forward to earn advancement. The more perilous the assignment, the greater his reward. Now he knew why she had not acknowledged receipt of the money; she had not valued his contribution.

"We even recommended you to lead the Complement."

A lie. He'd earned his original appointment through bravery in a bloody quagmire on the plains of Madras. Command of the Complement was decided only by secret ballot of the members. First officership of the Complement could not be bought, which is why Michael had wanted it.

Tonight another leader would be chosen. Michael was ready to hand over the reins. His mother's summons had provided a perfect opportunity to put the soldiering life behind him. He had not expected her to ask him for money. What he had envisioned from her was so far off the mark, he'd as soon forget his sentimental expectations.

A sarcasm gripped him. "No man could ask for a more notable family than the Elliots." Unless he was a Borgia or a Medici.

"We are fortunate in that," she purred. "Which is why I disapprove of that MacKenzie girl from the start. She has a lot of brass, even for one who is bastard born. She was fortunate to attract Henry's eye."

"I doubt that, Mama. She's lovely."

She gave a casual shrug, but eyed him like a charmer watching a puffed-up cobra. "In a countrified way."

Proclaiming Sarah's elegant beauty to be provincial was like calling the maharajah's palace in Bombay a rustic hunting lodge. The comparison was so absurd, no comment came to mind.

"I'm sure it's an imposition, but could you perhaps find the wherewithal to rid her of that dowry? If your wits fail, then woo her. I'm certain Henry wouldn't mind, unless you turn base and — and — ruin her for the marriage bed."

Woo Sarah for deceitful ends? Did his mother truly expect him to stoop to dishonoring a lady? He'd been on his own too long. For much of his life Michael had forgotten he even had a brother. Three years separated them. They had not been tutored together. Henry had been sent to foster with the duke of Argyll; Michael had been kept at the country estate. The vicar's son had been his tutor. He'd been away from both family and country for so many years, he couldn't summon a single tie to bind him either to the woman who had borne him or to the brother who administered the Elliot estates.

How could Michael be expected to woo, for what amounted to profit, the woman his brother had chosen? It went against all propriety. It also offended him to his soul.

His mother eyed him appraisingly. "You do favor your father's people, and all of them have a way with women."

Michael hadn't known his father. The earl's twice-yearly visits to Fife had been brief and formal. He'd died three years after Michael shipped out to India. Word of the death had come to Michael by formal announcement. The notice, sent through the ordinary post, had reached him months after the funeral.

"Do attend me, Michael. We've no time to lose. You must woo her in Henry's stead."

Henry wooing Sarah, Sarah loathing the Elliots. How had she tangled herself up with them?

"How much will they give you upon resignation? More than we paid, I should hope."

Beyond shock, Michael simply stared at her. She still thought he earned a wage. He grasped a random, paltry sum. "Two thousand pounds."

Her mouth tightened in a perfect picture of Sarah's description. "Give it to me, and I'll take it to London. Perhaps his grace will be pacified by it. We cannot have our family affairs dragged into Parliament."

Knowing he'd break the family crystal if he had to endure another moment of her overbearing company, Michael rose. "I'll take it myself the day after tomorrow."

"I have friends to see in London, and I must look after Henry."

As much as he hated himself for it, Michael tried to reason with her. "Henry has manly needs, Mama. Toiletries and things unmentionable in mixed company."

"Nonsense. I am his mother."

That did it. He crumpled his napkin. "I do not appreciate being accused of speaking nonsense."

She sat motionless, surprised. "Your father never allowed me an opinion."

With good cause, Michael thought, and wondered if she'd been born a shrew.

"Go then, and do not skimp where Henry's comfort is concerned." Judging from the vigor with which she rang the servants' bell, Michael knew her acquiescence was hard won. She spoiled it by saying, "You may take port in the study. There hasn't been money for brandy or for the tobacconist. The housekeeper has prepared you a room, in the family wing, of course."

He assumed this was a great compliment, considering her tone. But as her son, he expected more than civility from her. It wouldn't come today or tomorrow, and in the meantime, he'd keep a distance.

"You're very accommodating, Mother. But I've arranged rooms at the Dragoon Inn."

"Nons—"

"My lady," he interrupted, "I'll be staying elsewhere."

"You said 'rooms.' Have you brought a mistress with you or taken a wife?"

She actually believed he would marry without telling his family? The idea had certainly never occurred to him.

She's a stranger, his bruised pride said.

She's a damned disappointment, his heart replied.

Buck up, the mature soldier insisted. "No, I travel with a manservant." Turnbull would chuckle at being relegated to that.

"Can you afford a valet?"

Michael wanted to roar in frustration.

71

Instead, he told her what he thought she wanted to hear. "I'm thrifty to the core, Mother."

Realizing she'd gone too far, she gave him a conciliatory smile. "You will keep me informed as to your progress with that MacKenzie woman?"

"By all means. Shall I give you a report now?"

"Only if the news is good."

She'd take what she jolly well got. "I told her you sent apologies for calling her an ill-bred, uncivilized ne'er-do-well."

"You wouldn't dare take her side."

No, he wouldn't. He must try to establish loyalty among the Elliots. "She's sorry she said that you were a pinched-mouth crow."

"Oh, she'll pay for that slander. I'll see her pilloried beside Mercat's Cross with other liars and thieves."

"She also indicated she would fight any suit we brought against her."

"She thinks she knows so much. No decent family will send their children to that Sunday school of hers, and I've just begun."

A teacher — it fit Sarah perfectly. "I'm dining with her tomorrow night."

"Remember what I said about ruining her for your brother."

Ignoring his mother's rudeness, Michael bid her good night and escaped to the darkened streets of Edinburgh. The wind chilled him to his bones, but he'd walk before he'd ask his mother for the use of the family carriage.

A sedanchairman called out, but Michael waved him off. He couldn't abide the confinement of those wobbly, upright caskets. His teeth were chattering by the time he found what looked like a familiar landmark, a pair of lampposts with griffins on top.

Hoping the inn was around the next corner, Michael hunched his shoulders and kept going. The wind fluttered his kilt and sent icy bursts of air to his private parts. Tradition be damned; henceforth he would wear trews beneath his plaid.

"Fancy this, a gentleman who lacks the coin for a sedanchair."

Cold forgotten, Michael stopped and searched for the sound of the voice. From the shadows emerged a stooped man, a blanket cloaking his shoulders and dragging the ground. In one hand he held a broom.

Was he truly a streetsweeper or a criminal bent on evil? Michael didn't know. He summoned the voice he reserved for Calcutta's most tenacious beggars. "What do you want?"

Waving an arm expansively in the dim light, the man declared, "A coronet on my head and a chest of gold would make me smile. That and a castle full of bonnie Highland lassies to call my own."

The absurdity did not lessen Michael's apprehension. He was alone on a dimly lighted street in a city he'd visited only a few times years ago. Darting a glance over his shoulder, he looked for accomplices.

The man laughed. "The thin purse of an Elliot ain't worth the bother."

"Neither is losing your teeth," Michael warned, noticing that the man had a full set. "Be on your way."

"I'll go about my business when you leave Lady Sarah out of yours."

The man's intervention was so preposterous, Michael almost laughed. But he couldn't; his jaws were on the verge of cracking with cold. Clamping his jaw tight, he said, "Listen well, whoever you are. I won't be —"

"Cholly." His head came up. "That's my name." Then he stepped back into the shadows, but not before Michael glimpsed his eyes.

Their youthful gleam belied his wretched form, and the hand holding the broom looked strong. For a man of the streets, he had a sober expression and well-tended, straight teeth. Michael brushed off the contradictions. This was not the slum warrens of Calcutta, but Edinburgh, where a man was recognized and judged by the sett of his family plaid. It also felt like the most frigid city in the world.

He stomped his feet and anticipated roasting his backside before a roaring fire. Turning, he retraced his steps.

The broom handle thunked on the damp cobblestones. "Ain't that way," the sweeper called out. "You were headed in the right direction. The Dragoon Inn's just past Pearson's Close. Unless you're afraid of an old man with a broom and a care for a well-bred lass on her own in Auld Reekie."

Michael spun around. "How do you know so much about Sarah MacKenzie?"

The man lurked in the gloomy shadows. "From the lad Notch. His tongue's as loose as an Elliot's morals. We'll all champion the lass. So have a care or keep the Complement at your back."

Again, Michael looked behind him. The street was empty. A blessing, for he couldn't think past his rattling bones and shriveling parts.

"Yes, well." He moved around the streetsweeper and toward the next lamppost. "A pleasant good evening to you, too."

"The tailor in Putnam Close has smallclothes for them that wears the kilts, to keep your noble ballocks toasty warm."

Ignoring the taunt, Michael forged ahead. Relief came when he spied the sign above the arched doors of the Dragoon Inn.

The next evening, Sarah thumbed through her notes to refresh her memory. She must present a convincing appeal to Mayor Fordyce. Laying out the facts without placing blame was the sensible way to converse with a man. Insist that he already knows what he does not, and beg his patience to endure your meager attempt to reflect upon his causes. Make him think the idea was born of his own brilliance. Flatter his fairness and guide him to the brink of an idea. Smile sweetly and sigh with relief at his ability to help a mere woman reason out the difficulties of life.

She could do it; she'd learned her lessons well from Juliet, the duchess of Ross. But the thought of finessing wealthy and powerful men to do their Christian duty soured Sarah's mood. Women shouldn't be made to play the inferior in order to have a say in the workings of good governance.

What would Michael Elliot think about her methods? She really shouldn't care. If she were truthful, she didn't in the least value his opinion. But she was curious. What would he do when he realized she had tricked him? Given the example of his family, he probably wouldn't understand her reasons or sympathize with her cause. Money was all the Elliots cared about.

Rose came into the room. Over a dress of white muslin sprigged with tiny heather blossoms, she wore a lace-trimmed apron. A prim little cap, starched and positioned to perfection, covered her black hair. Draped over her arm was Sarah's favorite gown.

"It's the devil's own misfortune," she fussed, "that handsome soldier turning out to be an Elliot."

Since Sarah had told Rose of the assignation tonight with Michael Elliot, her laments over his identity had been constant and increasingly dramatic. Laying the silk gown out on the bed, Rose tisked. "Laura, that's Lady Jane's maid, says the powder from the wigmaker in Dewar's Close is the finest in Scotland. Shall I send Notch for it tomorrow?"

Sarah had yet to find a powder that didn't send her into a fit of sneezing. People thought her provincial for not wearing wigs, but opinions of the haughty didn't matter to her. Disapproving glances wouldn't keep her at home or force her to abandon her cause.

She folded her notes and tucked them into the pocket of her dressing gown. "He's to bring only a bit of the powder."

Rose walked to the vanity and picked up a pair of silver combs. "No sense wasting another batch. Sit here and I'll make something of your hair."

Sarah blew out the lamp and moved from the writing desk to the stool before the mirror. Rose dragged the brush through Sarah's freshly washed hair until her scalp tingled and she hummed in delight.

"Notch had it from the letter carrier that Lord Henry's brother wore his family tartan to the tailor shop in Putnam Close. Commissioned a fine wardrobe, so the postman said." Rose sighed so forcefully, the flame on the vanity lamp wavered. "A penance from God, making him an Elliot. Does he do a plaid justice?"

Sarah had ceased denying that she found him handsome. "He has very long, straight legs, and he's taller than Lachlan MacKenzie."

Rose nodded so vigorously she shook with the effort. "Ha! Didn't I say it right there on High Street with Notch and the others to hear? But I'll wager his knees are as plump as ripe cabbages."

Sarah choked back laughter. The first time she'd heard the expression, she'd been in Glasgow with her family, attending a harvest ball. Rose had described the tartan-clad earl of Clyde as having knees like ripe cabbages. At three and ten, Sarah and her sisters had giggled like tickled children. Even years later, it was a private jest between them and a reliable source of good cheer.

"Actually, his knees were not my primary concern."

"You're young yet. There." Rose secured the combs. "Better than a runny nose." She twitched her own. "Very unromantic for a woman to sneeze in public."

Sarah examined the twisted figure eight Rose had made of her hair and rather liked it. "Thank you, but I do not expect tonight to be a romantic evening."

Rose clutched the brush to her breast. "Heaven forbid! He's a bletherin' Elliot. But what if some other eligible gentleman is there? Wearing that gown, you'll turn a few heads."

Sarah didn't like the implication, but Rose was smiling, and there was little enough joy to be found in this house. Tonight was important. The dress gave Sarah confidence. She loved the feel of wearing a furlong of silk. "I'm interested only in speaking with Mayor Fordyce."

"If *he* looks askance at you for not

being wigged up like the ladies of fashion, be sure to tell him it's the powder's doing. If that fails, tell him what you told the countess when she disapproved. That handsome rascal of hers ought to hear it, too."

Glancing up, Sarah met her maid's gaze in the mirror. "I'll tell him no such thing. He'll learn for himself that I am sensible. Now get my dress. It's almost nine o'clock."

Rose stayed where she was. "When will you tell him you're not the daughter of the duke of Ross? Or will you? You know what his grace said, and don't think for a moment that he'll stand by and let ill befall you."

Lachlan MacKenzie's promise of protection was better ignored for now. Sarah rose and discarded her robe. "I'm saving the news of my parentage for Lady Emily alone. I want to win over the mayor tonight."

Rose fetched the dress and held it so Sarah could step into the skirt. The cool silk rustled as it floated into place.

Walking in a circle around Sarah, Rose fluffed out the voluminous skirt. "The countess was a boor to send her second son to demand money from you." She shivered with revulsion.

At the mention of the woman's machinations, Sarah cringed inside, and her mood turned sour. Did Michael feel that he was being used, or had she mistaken his manly aloofness for hurt pride? The latter, her instincts said. "I sense that he doesn't like her."

Rose uncorked Sarah's favorite perfume and dabbed the fragrance on her neck and wrists. "That's something else in his favor. Let's just hope his gentlemanly behavior comes from the other side of the family, too. He doesn't bear the tiniest resemblance to Lord Henry. But why is he currying favor with you? I mean —" Rose winced. "I'm sorry."

Sarah took no offense. She had long ago made peace with herself over mistakenly choosing Henry Elliot. Since her meeting with Michael yesterday, she had spent hours mulling over the man and his mission and comparing him to Henry.

"You needn't apologize."

"You like him," said Rose, her voice laced with awe.

"Michael was — uncomfortable, and he admitted to not knowing the countess very well. He's been in India for a long time."

"What's he truly like — aside of being an Elliot?"

"He has a gentleman's way about him — never looked me in the eye when he spoke of my dowry. I think the mission ill suited him. But he's as bold as Agnes when a notion strikes."

"My lady . . ." Rose grew pensive, which made her appear younger than her 40 years.

Their gazes met. "What is it, Rose?"

"I fear you're setting yourself up to be hurt again by the Elliots."

As always, Rose was concerned. Sarah grinned. "Never. I'm going only because he must witness my conversation with Mayor Fordyce."

Shaking the brush at Sarah, Rose tisked. "You're too clever for the likes o' them Elliots — or the tight-fisted betters in this reekin' place."

"I haven't succeeded yet." She transferred the sheaf of papers to her purse. "But if preparation counts, I should present a good argument."

Rose went to the washstand and returned with a damp cloth. "You've ink on your fingers."

Sarah wiped her hands and succumbed to a bit of vulnerability. "I do hope it goes well tonight."

"You'll change that mayor's mind about giving over that customs house. Weren't you the one who convinced his grace to let Agnes go off to China?"

"A position I regret taking."

"Worry not over the hellion. Aside from those foreign fighting skills, she learned a few womanly wiles."

Dear Agnes, she had her own special quarrel with the world. "A disgusting term for intelligence."

"The principle remains, my lady. You shouldn't be made to put up your dowry for a crumbling building. You didn't turn those poor children out. 'Twas merchants and guildsmen sowing their seeds in the tawdry ones who leave their babes to fend for themselves."

Sarah grew melancholy, for Rose had perfectly described the methods of the sheriff of Tain. He'd seduced Sarah's mother and left her to die here in Edinburgh. But Lachlan MacKenzie had taken in Smithson's bastard daughter and raised her as his own. Why had Lachlan likened her fair features to those of his mother, when all along

Sarah's true blood kin lived a mere bowshot away?

A hand touched her shoulder. "Will you write to him? He loves you, and you're fair breaking his big heart."

Sarah knew the feeling well, but how could she face Lachlan MacKenzie now? He'd told her a thousand times that Henry Elliot was not the man for her. He swore that Henry would bore Sarah to tears within a fortnight of the ceremony. But she's ignored his advice and rushed into the betrothal.

If she were honest with herself, she had to admit that it wasn't really Henry she'd wanted. Whether calm or angry herself, Sarah was adept at listening between others' words and sensing their thoughts. She'd often heard her stepmother, Juliet, say that an intelligent woman instinctively knew when it was time to leave. That was why Sarah had chosen Henry. Not because she truly loved him, she'd just given up finding the kind of man she wanted. Henry was the least objectionable. But more, it was time for her to leave the nest and fly on her own. Lachlan and Juliet were busy raising their second family, and although Sarah loved them all deeply, she knew she was in the way. As for Henry, it now appeared he'd wanted her only for her much-needed dowry.

"Write to him tomorrow." The plea in Rose's voice was heartfelt, bringing Sarah back to the present. "Give him a jolly laugh. Tell him how you spent an evening convincing the mayor of Edinburgh to go against the town directors."

Too many obstacles stood in Sarah's path. Once she'd established herself, the going would be easier. She'd find the courage to journey across town and visit her mother's grave. By then she would have forgiven Lachlan for likening her to a MacKenzie.

"Not yet, Rose."

"Time'll come, and he'll be awaiting."

Rose was right. But what remained a mystery to Sarah was what Michael Elliot would say when he found out who owned the customs house. What would she do if he learned the truth before she broached the subject tonight?

4

Michael arrived in a hired carriage promptly at nine o'clock. After helping Sarah and Rose inside, he took the facing seat and began a pleasant conversation about the fine quality of the food at the inn. Warm bricks were stacked on the carriage floor, and thick blankets covered the cushions. The combined effects gave the impression of a comfy nest rather than a traveling coach.

Her host wore a caped woolen cloak over a waistcoat and breeches of oak-brown velvet. A bright yellow neckcloth, wrapped and knotted modestly, added a splash of color to his masculine appearance and complimented his sun-bronzed skin. His finely polished boots reflected the golden light from the carriage lamps.

To Sarah, his modern clothing was a sharp contrast to the other attire, one ceremonial, the other cultural, that she'd seen him wear. Did he feel differently in each garment? While she'd like to know the answer, it was an intimate question that only a sister asked a brother or a wife posed to a husband. Sarah MacKenzie certainly couldn't ask it of Michael Elliot. Such frankness represented one of the many special expectations she had for marriage, another closeness and comfort she would one day share with her mate.

Michael spoke congenially during the short ride through the darkened, narrow streets. All went well until they were handed down from the conveyance. With a hand at Rose's back, Michael nudged her forward as he summoned the doorman.

"This is Mistress Rose, Lady Sarah's companion," Michael said. "You're to make certain she is comfortable and entertained."

"Shall I seat her in the lower salon with Turnbull?"

"That will do. Serve her promptly, and she's to have whatever takes her fancy."

Rose looked as if she'd melt into a puddle of feminine gratitude. "Thank you, my lord." She caught Sarah's gaze, then stared pointedly at his knees. "I'll be surprised if they have cabbages. I ain't seen any ripe ones about."

Laughter bubbled up inside Sarah, and she had to cover her mouth and turn away. Michael hadn't worn a kilt tonight, so Rose couldn't have seen his knees. He'd so completely charmed her, she had forgotten his family name and complimented him anyway.

He did have impeccable manners tonight, and as Sarah recalled, exceptionally nice knees.

"A private jest?" he asked, a curious smile enhancing his manly attributes.

Her back pike-stiff, Rose snickered as she followed the footman into the inn.

"Yes," Sarah confessed, "and far too silly to share with you."

"If you insist." He guided her through the door and helped her remove her cloak.

Looking up at his profile, she had the notion she'd disappointed him by not sharing the jest. It was a tiny withdrawal of sorts; she'd seen it often in Notch.

Notch and Michael Elliot. Whatever had made her match them together? An orphaned lad and a distinguished noble son could have nothing in common.

"Have I dirt on my face?"

She'd consider the comparison later. Now she had a more immediate concern. "Nay, you haven't a speck."

"Would you tell me if I did?"

"Of course. Watching another suffer embarrassment is wicked and thoughtless. I'd never stoop so low."

"Good. Now will you tell me why that swarthy-skinned fellow behind you is bearing down on us like Suleiman leading the Ottoman army into Buda?"

What an interesting analogy, but then he was a military man. She turned. It was the mayor, and Michael Elliot didn't know him. She had gambled and won.

Inspired by her own accurate judgment of Michael's character, she threaded her arm through his. "That's Mayor Fordyce. He's the guest I spoke of."

Michael murmured, "He doesn't look especially pleased."

An energetic, tidy man, Fordyce hurried everywhere. He wore a bottle-green short coat and matching knee breeches. His hose were stark white, same as his ruffled shirt, and his fashionable bagwig had been dusted with pale green powder. The perpetual frown was as much a part of him as his stylish tastes.

Under his breath, Michael said, "Are you certain he wants to dine with us?"

He didn't want to dine with Sarah, but Michael needn't know that. "Our good mayor never looks pleased. That's actually a smile."

"Not in any culture I've encountered."

Sarah chuckled at his effortless repartee and wondered how many exotic places he'd been. She was still battling the giggles when the mayor reached them.

"Thank you for the invitation, Elliot. Delighted to meet you."

"I'm sure," Michael replied, sending Sarah a puzzled glance.

By way of weak explanation for penning the invitation to Fordyce in Michael's name, she said, "Everyone is eager to welcome the Complement."

Fordyce bowed. "Good evening, Lady Sarah. You're lovely, as always. That's a Tremaine gown, is it not?"

The sapphire-blue silk was a design created by the exclusive Viennese modiste. Agnes had sent it to Sarah last summer on their birthday. She was saved a reply when the innkeeper led them to a private salon off the public room.

An extraordinary fire roared in the wall hearth, and the table had been formally set for three. A pair of crossed Lochaber axes embellished one wall; the others bore landscape paintings done in the Dutch grandeur style. Sarah chose the chair facing the door. Michael took the seat nearest the fire, leaving the mayor to view the ancient Highland weapons.

"A refreshment before dinner?" the apron-garbed innkeeper asked.

Michael turned to Sarah and lifted his brows. "My lady? What is your pleasure?"

Continued good luck throughout the evening was her first request. Being allowed to speak directly to the innkeeper and have him answer to her was her second wish. She cursed the man who had begun the ridiculous custom of making women speak to one man through another. "Tell him I'll have the claret, if it's smooth," she said to Michael. "If not, I'll have Johnson's newest ale."

"For a certainty, sir. 'Tis the very same wine the Complement drank last night."

Michael said to Sarah, "You're fortunate there's some left."

"Why is that?"

"Some of my friends took a liking to it last night."

The jovial proprietor slapped his thigh. "Which ain't to say the Complement didn't make a bonny affair of it after you retired, sir. That new fellow you broke in — little of him was seen above the table, except his nose. After that, he lay still from necessity."

"I'm sure he has an aching head for it today. What will you have, Fordyce?"

The mayor held up his empty glass. "I'll venture upon a few more drops of wine."

"A bumper of claret, then," Michael said. "And leave the door open."

Most considerate, Sarah thought — especially so, minutes later, when Count DuMonde and his mistress took a table in the main room directly in Sarah's line of vision. DuMonde sat with his back to Sarah, but she did not need to see his face to know he was smiling fondly at his mistress. Their shared joy was obvious in the lady's eyes.

Sarah felt oddly discomfited. She'd

93

seen that adoring look many times before: her stepmother gazed at Lachlan MacKenzie in that very way; David Smithson mooned over Lottie at every occasion.

"Is something wrong?" Michael asked.

"No, everything is delightful." According to Notch, Lady Winfield was DuMonde's mistress. But that was obvious, now that Sarah had seen them together.

"I was just about to broach the subject of the weather with Mayor Fordyce," Michael said, his brows lifted in entreaty to Sarah.

"It's been cold of late," she said.

"Much more so than in India, I assure you."

They chatted amiably over a feast that began with succulent lamb flavored with thyme and costly cracked pepper. Between courses, Sarah continued to sneak glances at the couple in the next room.

Envy filled her, but not because she wanted to take Lady Winfield's place. Oh, she liked the Frenchman; he was gay and entertaining — too much so to be considered seriously as her lifelong mate. Sarah's jealousy stemmed from her own romantic yearnings, which Du-Monde did not inspire. She coveted the love shining in Lady Winfield's eyes. DuMonde's lover looked like a woman assured of a place in paradise with the man of her choice.

The Frenchman should marry his mistress, Sarah decided, and vowed to tell him so.

"We're boring Lady Sarah," Michael said pointedly. "I doubt she's entertained by the king's business."

She had heard their conversation on the English rule in India; she could listen and observe at the same time. Should she expound upon the subject? Yes. A perfect way to distract him. With her thumbnail, she absently raked bread crumbs into a pile. "English expansion is a prickly subject to a Highland Scot."

Michael set down his wineglass. "Are you a Jacobite?"

"No, not in the traditional way. The Bonnie Prince is too old now to take the throne, even should the populace want him, which they do not. He failed in his duty to continue the Stewart line."

The mayor pushed his plate away. "He sired a daughter by another woman and legitimized her."

A noble move, Sarah had to agree, but easily arranged when one's brother is both a cardinal and the duke of York. "Since Lady Charlotte cannot take the throne from the Hanoverians, the point is moot. What's troubling to me is that we looked to Hanover at all for our monarchs. Wouldn't it have been better if our royal family were born of this land and spoke our language?"

"Interesting." Resting his elbow on the table, Michael propped his chin in his palm. "What language would he speak? Scottish, Welsh, Irish, or English?"

He had a keen mind for issues, a trait she valued. "Touché. But I think once on the throne, he or she should have the courtesy to learn to converse intelligently with his or her subjects."

Mayor Fordyce belched loudly. "Pardon. George the Third speaks the king's English."

"Three generations into Hanoverian rule? A bit tardy to my way of thinking."

"She has a point, Fordyce. It's not too much to expect in return for wealth beyond tallying and a place in the history of the greatest nation on earth."

His area of interest engaged, the

mayor scooted closer to the table. "Raising taxes and spending money are his watchwords. He should look elsewhere than Scotland to fill the royal coffers."

"He has," Michael was quick to say. "Since losing the American colonies, he's determined to have India completely under his thumb."

Sarah jumped in. "But he will not respect the culture of the people he chooses to rule in these isles. The Scots lost their plaids and bagpipes for thirty-six years, the Welsh lost everything, and the Irish lost the right to wear their green."

Michael turned up his palm. "That's how the English or any other ambitious country prevails. Subjugation is the first rule of conquest."

Sarah knew only what she'd read in books and newspapers. "What has our government taken from India?"

"Her trade. Her wealth. Her singularity in the world."

"Do you oppose the king?" Sarah asked.

"No, I support him fully. Objective governance is necessary in India to keep the many religious factions from destroying themselves."

"You speak of religious freedom," Sarah said, "an odd concept for the first officer of the Complement. Your benefactor, Henry the Eighth, made a mockery of our faith. Sir Thomas More stands as martyr to that."

A teasing half-smile signaled his slight retreat. "Perhaps the crown has learned from past mistakes."

Fordyce dropped his fork onto his plate. "Where *did* the server go for more of that wine? All the way to Burgundy?"

Michael winked at her. "We're boring Mayor Fordyce with our talk of kings and chancery. I think he prefers the subject of collecting taxes."

Not since leaving her family had Sarah enjoyed a livelier discussion. But she'd come here to further a cause, not to involve herself in a lengthy exchange of ideas with Michael Elliot. The other man was her foremost quarry for now. "My apologies, Mayor Fordyce."

The innkeeper returned with the wine. Michael took the flagon and refilled the mayor's glass himself.

Fordyce said, "Lady Sarah, didn't you know that Elliot's resigned from the Gomplement? They saluted him till moonset, or so the innkeeper said."

He didn't look the worse for a long night of merry-making.

"That's why they came here — to escort him home," the mayor added.

She didn't for a moment believe retirement was Michael's sole mission. Her dowry was what he wanted. How far would he go to get it? "Truly?" she asked. "Is that why you've returned to Edinburgh at this particular time?"

"Yes, well . . ." With his thumb and forefinger on the stem, he twirled his glass. "I've done my duty to king and country." Turning to Sarah, he added, "No matter on which continent his majesty's interests lie."

"Cleverly phrased," she murmured.

"How delightful that you think so."

She was tempted to rest her hand on his sleeve. Lady Winfield had touched DuMonde just so, and with great success, for the Frenchman appeared completely at her disposal. If Sarah could disarm Michael Elliot, she stood a better chance at winning over the mayor and the owner of the customs house. She had made progress, for they were conversing easily.

The servants cleared the dishes and returned with a plate of figs, cherries, and oranges. DuMonde and Lady Winfield quit the inn. From the adoring gaze in the woman's eyes, Sarah knew where they would go.

"Do you care for fruit?" Michael asked.

She'd eaten more tonight than was proper for a lady in public, but the conversation had stimulated her appetite. She chose a plump fig and cut it into quarters while she prepared her first verbal attack. Both accomplished, she put down her knife and looked at Michael, who popped a cherry into his mouth.

"Are you aware, Michael, of our mayor's concern for the growing number of children who are abandoned on the streets of Edinburgh?"

Around a mouthful of orange, the mayor said, "Any above one is a sorry number."

Michael didn't spare a glance at Fordyce. "An honorable concern."

As the object of his curious gaze, Sarah felt the weight of her responsibility grow, but she would win this fight. "Most of the poor souls are under the age of ten. The church never provides more than twenty-five pairs of shoes in a given year."

The unsuspecting mayor plucked an orange seed from his mouth. "There are other organizations to help. The Ladies' Benevolent Society collects what they can."

She knew the moment Michael sensed she was up to something other than idle chat, for his now-probing gaze darted from her to Fordyce. Suddenly doubtful, she placed her hand on his arm. "Our good mayor's efforts are gallant, but unfortunately they fall short of the mark."

Fordyce grasped her purpose, too, and his expression turned cool. The issue of turning the customs house into an orphanage was a sore matter with the mayor.

Suddenly defensive, he said, "I *am* a compassionate man."

She charged ahead. "An understatement. Your charity knows no bounds."

With finality, he said, "I beg to differ, my lady." He dipped his hands into the water bowl and reached for a napkin. "Complaints from the window tax alone kept me busy the whole of yesterday. I'll be a year straightening it all out. Yes, it is a priority."

So what? her conscience grumbled. "If last year is any indication, ten children will be buried in the Penny Cairns by Christmas next. What will you have done to prevent it?"

"Penny Cairns?" Michael asked, staring at her hand.

The velvet of his sleeve felt soft and warm beneath her fingers, and the inquiry in his eyes gave her pause. Had she gone too far? No. She applied a gentle pressure. "Shallow graves topped with a pennyweight of stone rather than a proper cairn of rock."

"But the ground *is* consecrated?"

Tears thickened her throat at the cruelty visited on the poor. "Not always."

Fordyce put down the unfinished orange. "This is hardly the proper place to discuss the dead or the customs house."

Sarah's passion stirred; retreat was impossible. "Not the proper place? Even if one of the dead is most likely a child who'll never know a third birthday? Don't you see?" She looked from one man to the other. "A small part of the collected tax will buy the customs house."

"Out of the question!" the mayor

snapped. "Seek private subscriptions if you must. The city hasn't the money. The lord provost told you so."

Her preparation saved her. "I have collected other support. I've spoken to the carpenters' guild. It offered to make some of the needed cots. The mercers in Bull Close will give the blankets and linens. Saint Margaret's will donate the school desks we're already using, and the stonemasons have promised new slates."

"You'll be decades getting enough money from common folks."

Yes, thanks to the countess of Glenforth and her cruel vengeance, the titled families no longer included Sarah in their social events. The citizens at large had been Sarah's source. "I never thought to do it alone," she admitted. "But someone must give it a start."

Into the fray, Michael said, "How much is the property worth?"

Sarah rejoiced; he did not know who owned the building, and he was sympathetic to her cause. "As is, three thousand pounds — an outrageous amount. It's tumbledown from top to bottom. The plaster's falling off the walls, and most of the floors are rotting.

The back stairs are passable. The main staircase hasn't a bannister."

"How much will the renovations cost?"

The mayor looked justifiably puzzled.

"Nine thousand pounds," Sarah said. "That includes food for a year. It's not so much money, but just enough to do the job properly. Once the property is donated, I'll even learn to hammer a nail myself if necessary."

"You must understand, Elliot," the mayor rushed to say. " 'Tis a bad idea from the beginning. We ought not think about new furnishings and a staff to keep the place up — even if the building is handed over, which it will not be. Apprenticeships are good enough for the children. Imagine," he scoffed, "orphans having servants and a house of their own."

"Caretakers, my lord," Sarah insisted, "women to clean and prepare the food, someone to tend the children's cuts and bruises, adults to help wash their hair and dry their tears. They're just babes turned into orphans by parents who did not care."

Fordyce's sarcasm knew no end. "What of the laundry and the darning of socks?"

"Laundry?" That injustice cut her to the bone. "Most of the children have only one set of clothing at a time. The apprenticeships you speak of are no more than forced labor."

"The answer is no." Fordyce carefully folded his napkin and addressed Michael. " 'Tis too grand an effort. But even if it was done, there'd never be an end to it. Lady Sarah'd be coming to me every week begging for this or that. Next she'll have us sending those urchins to Edinburgh University." To her, he said, "Get Elliot here to release your dowry. Then you can buy the building."

Stay calm, she told herself. *Stand up for what is right and avoid the subject of the dowry, which the mayor obviously assumes is already in Elliot hands.* "I did not turn those children out to steal and die in the cold."

"Are you accusing me of —" He was flustered. "— of low behavior?"

Rumor had it that in his youth he had paid an occasional visit to the women in Pleasure Close, but reminding him of an old transgression was unfair. Saiah knew she must appeal to his Christian sense of duty. "Of course not, Mayor Fordyce. Your reputation is unblemished. You speak and act for the people of Edinburgh. You are their conscience and their voice. If you aid the orphans, you fulfill your promise to the citizens who elected you to make the streets safer for everyone. But you cannot think you do not have an obligation to the less fortunate, simply because the ballot is denied to them."

He grumbled into his goblet. "I do not make the election laws."

"Yet you entertain foreign dignitaries and oversee their interests, even though they do not participate in our elections or pay our taxes."

At last she'd dented his stern opposition, for he sighed and said, "You've a passion for this orphanage."

That was an easy criticism to defend. "Listen to your contradiction. If we are not passionate in the causes that count, such as assuring dignity for all of our people and regard for the future, we're no better than animals in the forest."

"Mayor Fordyce." Michael's commanding voice dropped like a stone into the conversation. "I'd be willing to buy the property and place it in Lady Sarah's keeping — in the name of the Elliots."

Sarah almost wilted in relief.

The mayor stared, mouth agape. "You cannot buy it."

Michael sent the mayor a remarkable look. "I beg to differ."

Now truly angry, the mayor glowered. "I thought you asked me here tonight to help me dissuade her from acquiring the customs house. I expected you to refuse her outright and put an end to this quest of hers. You cannot buy a property if the Elliots already own half of it."

Sarah watched Michael closely, looking for a glimmer of deceit. He went very still and his eyes stayed fixed on the wine in his glass. "Who owns the other portion?"

"I do," said the mayor.

"Then we'll conclude the transfer when I return from a visit to my brother in London."

"But Lord Henry manages the family properties, and the countess will never let that one fall into Lady Sarah's hands. Unless your mother changes her mind."

"She will. Good night, Mayor Fordyce."

Like a treed fox given an escape, the

mayor moved to leave. "Give our best to Lord Henry. Damn that Richmond. You'd think he'd play fair — a man with his good breeding."

"Yes, well . . ." Michael looked at Sarah, but spoke to Fordyce. "I'll tell him you asked about him."

He could only stare at her, but he was distracted. Was he angry? Was he waiting to upbraid her?

"My congratulations, Lady Sarah." The mayor gave her brief bow. " 'Twas a pleasure."

When they were alone, Sarah immediately felt a greater withdrawal in Michael. She moved the candle aside and said cheerfully, "A pity we cannot choose our family."

He squinted, but not with poor vision. "Pardon my frankness, but had you not agreed to marry my brother, you and I wouldn't be sitting here distrusting each other."

Trusting Elliots had been her least successful venture. "You're angry because the countess withheld information from you."

"The subject of the customs house has not arisen between my mother and me."

"You cannot truly be angry with me because I believe the citizens have a responsibility to Notch and the other unfortunates."

"No, not for that. I'm *unhappy* because you could have told me that my family held an interest in the property. Instead, you chose to embarrass me, a practice you earlier condemned."

Curse his memory. "Pardon me, but a nick to your pride is a small price to pay to save the orphans of Edinburgh. They have no one, Michael. No parents to love them and leave them an inheritance. No one tucks them in at night or soothes them when goblins visit their dreams. They struggle merely to survive." She sniffed back a tear. "I'm sorry for deceiving you, but how could I know that you would be so generous?"

He looked at her then, and his face boded ill. "You might have taken the time to find out. 'Tis true I'm of Clan Elliot, but I am not my brother. I would not have wagered most of your dowry in a dice game with the duke of Richmond."

She believed him, but one high mark for philanthropy was not enough to forgive the sins of the Elliots. "Richmond was happenstance. Eventually Henry would have offended one peer or another. The timing was simply fortuitous for me, since I had not spoken vows to him."

"You miss my meaning. It was *his* fall from grace," Michael insisted. "Not mine, and by association, you blame me. It's the same injustice as someone blaming you because Notch is an orphan. You had nothing to do with it, as I played no part in my brother's activities in London."

She did feel a twinge of guilt, until she remembered their first meeting. "You stormed into my home yesterday and demanded my dowry."

"Without success. As I said, I had just arrived after a very long absence. All of what goes on here is new to me."

An awful possibility occurred to her. "Your family did not write to you of the betrothal?"

When he grew even more distant, she had her answer. But another question arose. "Did you resign from the Complement at the request of Lady Emily?"

"Nay, 'twas my choice."

Relieved, she gave his hand a gentle

squeeze. "Thank you for donating the property. You won't be sorry."

He chuckled without humor. "I'm already sorry."

He did look sad, and she hoped it was a trick of the dim lighting. "You're also a poor liar."

"Yes, well." He slid her a wary glance. Wavering light from the hearth played over his face, and the reflection of the flames glittered in his eyes. "Having admitted that my brother is a wastrel, why did you agree to marry him?"

"I told you why. I thought I loved him."

"Who's the poor liar now, Sarah?"

She felt the pull of his gaze and knew an instant of weakness. She'd always been attracted to bold men, but after becoming better acquainted with them, they changed, and the brazenness that she found so appealing invariably hardened into a determination to dominate her. She liked a forceful man, but only until he took liberties with her personal beliefs and freedoms.

Resisting Michael Elliot was an option she would not take just now, for her toes were curling with an unfamiliar excitement. There was much more about his character that she wanted to explore. She had wrongly spoken ill of him, and he'd been forthright enough to point out her mistake.

"If you will confess what you are thinking," he said, "I will arrange to shoe every orphan in Edinburgh."

Like iron to a magnet, she was drawn to the allure in his smile. "An equitable exchange."

Interest sparkled in his eyes and sharpened his features. "Is tomorrow soon enough?"

Very aggressive. "To know what I am thinking?"

He leaned forward. "To share thoughts."

Catching a whiff of his attractive woodsy scent, she leaned back. "Oh, I know what's on your mind."

"Do you?" He glanced at her hand, still resting on his, and his look was pointed, challenging. "Then we've made a pact. Tell me what's on my mind. But if you are wrong, you must agree to accompany me to the cobbler and select the shoes yourself."

Only cowardice would keep her from setting him straight, and she'd have none of it. "You were *not* thinking about visiting the cobbler and selecting shoes."

"A twist of the bargain." He placed one hand over hers and wrapped the other around her forearm. "Enlighten me then, and I insist that you furnish every detail of my thoughts or admit you were boasting."

"On our second meeting, you expect me to recite what I believe to be your intimate thoughts? And in a public place?" She shook her head. "I'd be mortified."

He sprang to his feet and slammed the door shut. Returning to his chair, he again took her hand. "I promise to catch you if you swoon."

Rather than address the fact that everyone in the inn now knew she was alone with him and assumed he was taking liberties, she decided to show him she was no easy mark. She surveyed the table and the space around her chair. "Catch me? Impossible. I've nowhere to fall."

He moved closer. "What time shall I come for you?"

Brazen didn't begin to describe him, and reckless completely suited her mood. The customs house was hers. She had prevailed.

She caught his gaze. "I haven't lost yet."

"Shall I call for more wine then, and give you time to think it over?"

She laughed and tried to pull her hand away. "Entice me into drinking another glass of wine, and you'll be mortified because you'll have to carry me home."

He chuckled and threaded his fingers through hers. "Very incorrect. I wasn't thinking about seeing you too sotted to walk. The victory is mine."

She was enchanted, but the man was much more potent than the wine. "I wasn't trying to read your mind just then."

"Yes you were, and for spoils you'll have to call for *me* on the morrow."

Prudence demanded a full retreat. "You said you were going to London to see Henry. Please let go of my hand."

He did. "You have a good memory where my brother is concerned."

He probably had no inkling of how deep her enmity toward the Elliots went. But he was new to the battle.

"After you've spoken with Henry, you may regret ever setting eyes on me," she said.

"Wager your bonny blue eyes on that, and you will lose."

Pretending to ignore the compliment, she went on. "Not to mention giving me a building and agreeing to refurbish it. I'm very grateful, though."

"Yes, well . . ." His gaze moved to her mouth. "You've a crumb on your lip. May I?"

He touched the napkin to her mouth, but frowned. Dropping the cloth, he replaced it with his finger. "Ah, this works much better." In a movement so smooth she barely felt it, he curled his fingers around her neck and pulled her toward him. "I know just the remedy. May I kiss you?"

She was unprepared for a polite offer, especially when his eyes demanded that she yield. Options beckoned, but the pull of him was so strong, she ignored them. "Do you think it's wise?"

"Who's thinking?"

We both are, she thought, and their minds traveled the same enticing path.

He chuckled again, low and seductively. "I couldn't have said it better myself, Sarah. I adore the way you think."

He'd read her mind, and the knowledge disarmed her. In that stunned anticipation, he filled her vision, and at the first whisper-soft touch of his lips on hers, her neck went limber, and her eyes drifted shut. His strong hand steadied her, and he kissed her with an inquisitiveness that quickly turned to purpose. She sensed an authority about him, a confidence and an ease that made her want to linger in his arms and discover the greater intimacies he was surely conjuring in his own mind.

He tasted deliciously of sweet cherries, and he smelled of the forest at eventide. Joyous contentment thrummed in her, urging her to throw her arms around his neck and find out precisely where her limits of decorum lay.

They'd be like the lovers she had watched in the next room. Like a man and his mistress. Stunned by the notion, she drew back. "Michael, you must stop."

The hand at her nape tightened, holding her firmly in place. His eyes drifted open. Dreamy passion lingered in his gaze, but beneath it lurked a force of will that both frightened and inspired her.

"Dear Sarah, you're thinking you must protest for propriety's sake. Be truthful, if not to me, to yourself."

"You swore I was a poor liar."

"Then admit that you enjoyed the feel of my lips on yours. Admit that you like me."

Words of agreement perched on her tongue, scrambling to be said. But she could not.

"Coward."

Her pride rallied. "You're a stranger. I will not lose my innocence to you."

"Which innocence would that be? We mature in many different ways."

If he wanted to speak frankly, she would oblige. "I will not fall in love with you."

"But you wished to marry my brother, so you cannot be innocent in matters of the heart. Oh, I've no doubt that you are physically virtuous. You are an honorable woman and will meet your husband's expectations."

She laughed. "*Demented* is too flattering a word to describe your methods."

"You said we were strangers. Remedy that. Ask me something about myself."

Persistent didn't begin to define his character, and his fingers were kneading her neck in the most delicious way. Sarah couldn't resist asking, "Why did you smile when you caught sight of us on the street yesterday?"

"Why I smiled at you is a tedious question."

Flattered to her earlobes, she stifled a maidenly sigh. "Then Notch. What were you thinking when you saw him?"

"I was enormously happy, in spite of his cheeky way. I've never led the Complement into a Scottish town." He shrugged. "I was glad to be home. Now, is there anything else you'd like to know before I kiss you again?"

His honesty further disarmed her, and curiosity took the fore. "Do you feel differently, dressed as you are now, compared to the tartan or the uniform of the Complement?"

The question surprised him, for he paused. At length, he said, "The truth of it is, the helmet is a nuisance and the capes are not to my liking — rather showy for modern times."

"And the kilt?"

A hint of color rose in his cheeks, and he scratched his nose to hide a budding smile. "A private jest."

"But I'm from the Highlands. I know all about men and their kilts."

"Such as . . ."

"Catching it on a bramble bush and dislodging the pleats. A hound pup once pulled down my brother's tartan. It pooled around his ankles. He was still a child and mortified."

"Then I needn't mortify myself." Clearing his throat, he added, "I will say that most of the time I prefer current styles. So, my inquisitive Sarah, if your curiosity is satisfied, I should like to get on with kissing you."

She hovered at the edge of a swoon and rested there, basking in the lightness he brought to her soul. When he moved closer, she blurted, "Isn't there anything you'd like to ask of me?"

"Yes. Will you be so kind as to open your mouth. I have a fierce yearning to taste that tart tongue of yours."

Before she could draw a breath, he turned his head to the side and took her lips in a kiss that stripped her of conscious thought. Her mind spun with dreamy visions of a lazy afternoon in an idyll — a blanket spread beneath an ancient oak, a nearby burn ambling gently to the sea, a man reclining beside her, plaiting posies into her hair and caressing her neck with the tips of his fingers.

Another image rose in her mind. She saw a massive bed with cool white linens. She wore a virginal white sleeping gown and languished on the bed in anticipation of the man who would soon join her there.

She felt his hand slip into the bodice of her gown and cup her breast. At the first gentle drag of his palm over her nipple, she shivered with longing. A responding masculine groan vibrated against her lips, and then his tongue was plunging into her mouth in a beguiling rhythm that turned her insides to porridge. With every touch, each movement, she felt devoured, seduced, and flung toward complete surrender.

Frightened to her soul, she pulled back. "No. Stop. You're Henry's brother."

His lips were damp from their kiss, and the expression in his eyes was pure heaven. "Very cowardly of you, Sarah."

Bother him. She'd brought it on herself. "You cannot change the fact that your family has been ghastly to me."

"Yes, well . . ." With his finger, he traced the curve of her mouth. "I shall miss you while I'm in London."

He had the oddest way of speaking. He began with a softly spoken and very deceptive, "Yes, well," then followed with an unrelated statement that made a lie of his original capitulation or changed the subject entirely.

That verbal trickery was something she had just noticed, and she intended to watch out for it, among other things about Michael Elliot. He had an answer for everything.

Miffed, Sarah said, "What will you tell Henry about me?"

He grinned like a well-fixed dandy in May. "Certainly not what I'm thinking."

Sweet Saint Margaret; he could disarm the devil himself. "Which is?"

Mischief turned his smile boyish, but the look in his eye was all predatory male, and the touch of his hand on her neck grew familiar.

"Tell me."

"Yes, well. I'm thinking that very soon I'll find out . . ." He slowly withdrew his hand.

"You'll find out what?"

He tapped her on the end of her nose. "Whether you can hammer a nail."

He'd done it again. Baffled, she said, "What does hammering nails have to do with kissing me? And don't deny you were thinking about it."

"I wasn't thinking about kissing you." He rose and held her chair. "Like my thoughts, my intentions have gone far beyond mere kisses."

5

Bundled in her sleeping gown and robe, her feet tucked beneath her, Sarah sat on the rug before the hearth in her bedroom. She poured two cups of warm, sweetened milk and handed one to Rose.

Seated across from her, the maid had traded her best dress for a nightrail and a floppy sleeping cap. The latter gave her an elfin quality. Peering up, Rose blew on the steaming milk. "Now will you tell me what the mayor said?"

Sarah dodged another onslaught of guilt over her wanton behavior with Michael Elliot late in the evening. As if the intimate exchange had not occurred, he had chatted amiably in the carriage. When he'd seen her inside her home, he had turned to leave, but stopped.

"Have you a message for Henry?" he had asked.

"Yes. He cannot have my dowry."

"Because it rightfully belongs to the man you marry?"

"Yes, and I'll make a better choice next time."

"My lady?" Rose looked worried. "Are you ill?"

Sarah banished the memory of her last conversation with Michael. "No. I'm fine, Rose."

"I'll wager the mayor was impressed with what you plan to do, wasn't he?"

With little embellishment, Sarah relayed the discussion about the acquisition of the customs house.

"Bless Saint Margaret," Rose exclaimed. As quickly as it had come, her elation vanished. "What if the countess refuses to give over her part?"

That possibility hadn't occurred to Sarah. But Michael had made a promise, and he appeared to be the sort of man to honor his word. "Her younger son is very persuasive." An understatement; since saying good night, Sarah couldn't stop thinking about him, his charitable gesture, his hand fondling her breast. No man had ever touched her there.

She trembled at the memory.

"Are you chilled, my lady?" Rose

124

moved to rise. "I'll toss more coal on the fire. The Odd lads filled up the buckets today."

"No. Sit down."

Rose settled in again. "He has a charm about him," she said. "But didn't Lord Henry, too?"

Sarah had to agree, but Henry's affability lacked excitement. Both brothers had asked permission before kissing her. Only Michael hadn't waited for an answer. "If charm is a family trait, it passes through the *men* of Clan Elliot."

"Ever so true," said Rose. "It's a fine thing he's doing. The orphans will have a safe roof over their heads. Poor mites. They need a helping hand. After talking with Master Turnbull, the general's valet, I cannot say as how I'm surprised that you talked him into it. Turnbull speaks highly of the general, and not because he's in service. We know the difference."

Sarah suspected that Rose thought highly of someone else in the Elliot household. "Tell me about Michael's valet," she said.

"Master Turnbull ain't one to gossip."

Sarah tasted the milk, then added another dollop of honey. "What did you talk about?" Obviously something that pleased Rose.

"The general. That's what the first officer is called."

"They address Michael as general? Like England's Gage and Percy?"

"Not when there's others to hear. It's a secret amongst the Guard — that's what they call themselves." She sniffed in disapproval. "They're fat with the swearing of manly oaths and ceremonies."

Sarah smiled. "You don't consider that gossip?"

Balancing the cup on her knee, Rose pushed the sleeping cap out of her eyes. "I was hoping to wheedle something important out of him. Such as learning if the general's married or betrothed. Never did learn that. Master Turnbull goes quiet, same as Lady Juliet when she's miffed at his grace."

Michael. Married. Sarah hadn't considered that, and were she honest with herself, the possibility that he belonged to another woman troubled her. "But this Turnbull — he speaks freely of the Complement?"

"He has a journal about it. Memoirs." Rose dragged out the French word.

"Must have bindings leafed with gold. That's how he came into the service of the general."

"To write a book or because he was a presser of goldleaf?"

"Neither." Rose leaned forward and in her best tale-telling voice, said, "The book was burnt, you see, in a nefarious and mysterious fire in Calcutta. So Master Turnbull tells it."

Sarah could picture Rose enthralled by a well-traveled manservant. "He sounds quite melodramatic, your Master Turnbull."

Rose's skin flushed to crimson and she stared into her cup. "He's much too sophisticated for a Highland maid."

Sarah felt a burst of righteous anger. "That's a dreadful thing to say. You're as good as anyone in the king's own household. You're pretty, and you've never been one to let a handsome footman turn your head." Sarah recalled a favorite Scottish saying. "Your're a Highlander, Rose, the best o' this island and beyond."

Rose's chin came up. Cocking her arm, she picked up her cup and drank with the grace of any duchess. "I told him I could read his book in Scottish and the king's scrawling language, too, if I took a fancy to. That's when he said it was burnt to cinders, but the knowing of it was in his head."

Rose, too, had felt the isolation, for she seldom expressed so much interest in an outing. Perhaps boredom was why Sarah had allowed the conversation with Michael to drift to the intimate. Bother him and her girlish notions. Dozens of other topics interested her more. Thousands. Such as Rose's evening, which had been uplifting for the maid.

Sarah put down her cup. "It seems to me that Master Turnbull likes to talk about himself."

"Not so much as to manage the conversation. He often inquired about you."

Sarah toyed with the end of her night braid. "I doubt he wheedled any gossip from you."

Rose preened, and with a toss of her head, flipped the cap out of her eyes. "When he asked why we didn't pack up and go back to the Highlands, since you refused to marry Lord Henry, I said you were weary from turning down marriage proposals from half the eligible dukes in Scotland. I said the peers flock to

Rosshaven Castle after you like lint to a velvet footstool."

Sarah chuckled. "You lied to him."

"Only after he said the general kept a harem house of fifty women. Even your father never had fifty women, and he was a rogue of the kind ain't been seen since he mended his ways."

Lachlan MacKenzie's exploits in seduction were legendary. Rumor said he'd broken more hearts than all of his contempoaries combined. *Oh, yes,* Sarah thought, *be she lover or daughter, the female who trusted the Highland rogue was doomed to heartache.*

Resolutely she put Lachlan out of her mind. Images of Michael Elliot crept in.

My intentions have gone far beyond mere kisses.

At the memory of his lusty declaration, she trembled inside. Overconfidence had led to her temporary downfall, but she was sensible Sarah MacKenzie. She had suffered a brief lapse in judgment. Henceforth, she would set the tone of their meetings, and keep their association amiable — certainly no more fondling.

"Don't speak well of the India women, if fifty of them would gladly share the same house and man," Rose grumbled. "Wouldn't Lady Lottie have something to say about that?"

Something unrepeatable and indefensible, Sarah was certain. "What else occurred with Turnbull?"

"Nothing so improper until Notch and William sneaked into the inn." Worry scored her forehead. "It was after the sounding of the curfew drum."

The boys roamed the streets of Edinburgh at will, but not for long. Soon they'd be tucked into soft beds at the orphanage by ten o'clock, instead of dodging the constable and his curfew, thanks to Michael Elliot. Would he teach the boys a lesson in geography or history, if she asked him to? Would he speak to her at all after Henry had his say? That possibility troubled her.

"Ain't you interested in what Notch did?"

To hide her uncertainty, Sarah banked the fire. "Very much so. Did he behave himself?"

"Ha! About as well as Lady Mary did when the earl of Wiltshire told her a woman lacked the mental strength and moral discipline to be a great painter."

Sarah remembered the occasion vividly. "He belittled Mary. He ought to have known better, after spending the entire winter asking for her hand in marriage."

Rose nodded so vigorously, she almost dislodged her sleeping cap. "He was hat-throwing angry 'cause Mary got the upper hand with him."

"She's happy now," Sarah said. "Just as we are. Tell me more about Notch."

"He asked Turnbull if the king was dead."

"How did Turnbull reply?"

"After he stopped looking at the lad like he was a tear in his master's best tartan, he asked Notch who he was and what he was doing in a salon reserved for betters."

Sarah couldn't stifle a groan. "I can imagine what Notch said back."

"Aye, you know him well. The scunner told Turnbull the same thing he tells the sparks in the lane." Whenever the question came up, Notch liked to proclaim that he was a delouser of gentlemen's purses.

"He must stop declaring himself a thief, or the constable will toss him into Tolbooth Prison for a common nuisance. What did Turnbull do?"

"Tucked away his purse and told Notch to take himself off to the nearest moving carriage and throw himself in front of it."

Laughing, Sarah put away the fire iron. "I shudder to think what Notch did."

"You would have been proud of the lad — after I told him to mind his manners and remember your teachings. He turned boyish and politely asked Turnbull his opinion on the rumor that the king had gone to glory. Turnbull settled himself down and said the king was hale and hearty. Then he explained that the Complement was in Edinburgh to fulfill a tradition. They always escort their general home when his service is done. Then they vote amongst themselves to choose a new general."

"I hope Notch thanked Turnbull."

"Not quite. In parting, the lad told Turnbull to inform the general that if he so much as thought to take a liberty with you, he'd wish he'd been born Cornish."

"Notch said that?" Lachlan MacKenzie had said those very words.

"I think it came from Cholly. All of

Notch's fancy notions do. After the lad left, I found out from Turnbull that the general took rooms at the inn."

That shocked Sarah. She expected Michael to stay at Glenstone Manor. It did explain why he'd arrived in a hired carriage rather than the crested Elliot coach and how he knew so much about the fare at the inn. "Did Turnbull say why?"

"Nay, and that's the bloody English in him, for he didn't favor the question in the least. He puffed himself up and said a gentleman of the general's station could stay where he ruddy well pleased. Then I said only a sinner facing the fires of hell would stay with the countess. I was ambling up to his good will, you see, by telling him the truth about her. Sharing my experience, as good staff does with others in service."

"Was he grateful?"

The cup rattled in the saucer. Rose tried to steady it, but almost spilled the milk. Huffing, she put the china down. "The wretch told me I had a foul mouth and said if I was an India woman, they'd cut out my tongue and chop off my nose. Of course I told him he was three parts drunk from Johnson's ale."

Sarah had read of the custom of harem-keeping. But gleaning the information from a book and imagining Michael with a host of willing women at his disposal were two different things. And both unfortunately disturbed her. Again, she put Michael Elliot out of her mind. "You're smiling, Rose."

Rose demurred. "As Lady Agnes is fond of saying, I enjoyed a frolicsome time tonight."

Sarah laughed. Agnes could thwart a suitor's efforts quicker than Lottie could stir up trouble. Rose deserved a respite from the bleak atmosphere in this empty house. Sarah was glad the evening had provided it.

"I never did learn why the general's in boarding rooms."

"Perhaps he prefers it."

"Could be. The Dragoon Inn's a lovely place, even the staff salon. That's where I met Turnbull. After he took his leave, I saw the kitchen, and it's as clean as cook's pantry at Rosshaven. The laundry maid showed me one of the rooms — 'twas empty, of course. I cannot imagine Turnbull under the same roof as those laggards at Glenstone Manor." Rose yawned and shook her head. "The hearthboy at the inn said the general had taken rooms until September. He gave the stableman a crown to look after his horse. A crown above the board! Even his grace don't give a crown for that."

Sarah hadn't considered that Michael might be wealthy; he had demanded her dowry. He had also promised to buy Mayor Fordyce's half of the customs house. Did he possess enough wealth to free Henry? What if they returned together?

Sarah grew anxious. She had not seen Henry or heard directly from him since long before his incarceration. Her conversations had been with Lady Emily. The details of Henry's crime and punishment had come from Notch, who heard them from the streetsweeper. A note from Mary, along with a clipping from the *London Weekly Journal* had confirmed the news of the downfall of the earl of Glenforth.

Rose finished her milk. "Turnbull's father was butler to the earl of Suffolk. That's where he gets his uppity ways. When the earl's third son took up a career in the East India Company, Turnbull went with him. Poor gentleman fell in a battle, and after that Turnbull came into the general's service. Seems an adventurous life, over in India."

"I was thinking of asking Michael to teach the children history, once the orphanage is finished."

"His tutoring cannot come up to yours. Everyone knows the sheriff of Tain could've afforded an Oxford man for his children, but he'd have none but you."

Just thinking about confessing the truth of her parentage exhausted Sarah. She yawned.

"You're toilworn, my lady," Rose said. "I'll just be off to bed. We've a long day ahead of us tomorrow. If you have everything you need, I'll take the dishes down."

Sarah handed her empty cup to Rose.

What would Henry tell Michael? How would the information affect Michael's opinion of her? Would his interest fade to cool regard? That possibility saddened her, for she found him interesting. *And far too exciting,* her sensible nature warned.

She blew out the lamp and climbed into bed, wondering if the enmity toward her ended with Lady Emily. What if Henry felt it, too, and influenced Michael?

But as she closed her eyes and drifted to sleep, she couldn't block out the memory of his hand cupping her breast and his lips moving on hers.

Late the next morning, lunch basket and writing tools in hand, Sarah and Rose set out for the mile-long walk to the customs house. She planned to inspect every room and commit to paper the needed repairs. A count of the broken windows would top her list, with the needed stair runners and floor boards next.

Just as they reached the last bastion of the city's east gate, the meridian hell of St. Giles chimed the hour of midday. Wagons and sedanchairs cluttered the lane, and gusts of wind scattered debris. High Street bore traces of the crowds that had come out earlier in the day to see the departure of the Complement. Had Michael looked for Sarah in the crowd? Had her absence disappointed him? What would he think of her after visiting Henry?

"My lady!" Rose grasped Sarah's arm

and yanked her back.

A coal wagon lumbered past; Sarah had nearly walked into its path.

This preoccupation with the Elliots had to stop. Michael would believe what he chose to believe. Sarah MacKenzie would carry on, with or without his endorsement.

She shifted her box of writing materials and continued on her way to Reekit Close, as the area around the docks was called.

Wedged between a towering tenement and a warehouse used for the storage of kilned lime, the four-story customs house looked like a sturdy letter box dwarfed by burly ruffians. Across Harbor Street and above the lintmaker's establishment were meeting halls for the hammermen's and candlemakers' guilds. Taverns and penny-pie shops dotted the neighborhood, their earthy aromas dulling the odors of commerce and poverty. Decades of grime clung to the arcaded stone facings of the buildings, and the few remaining panes of window glass were gray with neglect.

Most of the orphans had come from the tenements of Edinburgh, and on her first excursion here shortly after meeting Notch, Sarah had tried to match his face and that of the other orphans with the weary prostitutes who frequented the aleshops and loitered in the shadowy alleyways. The process had been depressing and short-lived. Sarah realized the women could scarcely feed and care for themselves, let alone lament the loss of a child they had turned out years before.

Were it not for Lachlan MacKenzie, Sarah might well have been one of the orphans. She seldom explored that fact, for it brought back the pain of their last meeting.

Good fortune would now come to some of the orphans, and Sarah was enormously proud of her own part in it. Formal credit for the orphanage would fall squarely on the lap of the Elliots. That irony irked her. She didn't expect glory for doing her Christian duty. Caring for children was a woman's responsibility, especially for one who'd been raised with love and in luxury. It just wasn't fair that the Elliots would reap the praise when they had stood in opposition for so long.

Until Michael, the Elliot who stirred her blood and inspired her passions.

Her stomach floated.

"Lady Sarah!" Notch skidded to a halt before her. "Come and see the warship, Lady Sarah. You said you ain't never spied one close up."

William said, "Edinburgh ain't seen one since afore Notch pecked his way outta that egg."

"Stow it, you flower-cheeked bumpkin."

William fumed, as he did when Notch teased him about his girlish good looks.

Sarah couldn't very well refuse them, and she was curious about the infamous vessel, *Intrepid*. "Very well," she said. "Let's have a look at the flagship of the king's navy."

With Rose at Sarah's side and the lads in the lead, they covered the short two blocks to the quay. Anchored at least 100 yards away, the apple-bellied man-o'-war dominated the port of Edinburgh. Pennons flew from a dozen places in the rigging, and the deck teemed with smartly uniformed soldiers.

In a great show of strength meant to impress the onlookers, the gun ports had been opened. On the quay, the bagpipers from the Black Watch Regiment played a fine rendition of "Loch Lomond." Patriotism captured the crowds. The women dabbed at teary eyes, and the men struggled to contain their emotions.

"I say she can blow the Froggies out of the water like that." An overly impressed Notch snapped his fingers. "See them sixty-pounders, Pic? They're all cocked and ready to defend us."

A splash of yellow drew Sarah's attention. Michael Elliot stood at the bow of the warship, a spyglass pressed to his eye, the distinctive scarf fluttering in the wind. He wore the caped greatcoat and cockaded hat she also remembered from last night, and his dark hair was clubbed at his nape. Surrounded by the uniformed members of the Complement, he looked like a prosperous businessman or a young noble.

"Look, my lady," Notch yelled. "That's Lord Michael and he's waving to you."

He was also staring at her through that spyglass. Her heart tripped fast, and she wished she'd taken more care with her appearance. But she'd planned to spend the afternoon laboring on behalf of her cause, not preening for an Elliot. "He's not a lord," she said, for lack of anything else.

"Lord or lime-shoveler, that's himself bidding you goodbye."

"Don't act like a lord," William said. "Decent to the core, I says of him."

"I'm certain he thinks of himself in the same way, William." Sarah wanted the words back. His amorous advances aside, Michael couldn't be faulted for poor behavior.

"That's your opinion and Pic's." Notch Squinted up at her. "Got your lady-feathers all ruffled up, did he?"

Notch could be absolutely infuriating, not a small part of his charm. She had no intention of discussing her feelings on the subject of Michael Elliot with him or anyone else. "If you believe that, Notch, you're as wrong as you were about the king's passing on."

Reminding Notch of his recent folly had the desired effect. Now humbled, he said, "The king's a bit of all right. I have it on the best authority."

Rose said, "You overstepped yourself last night with Turnbull."

"Me 'n' Turnbull," Notch allowed, "we're the best o' mates. See? There he is beside the general. I'll wager he's wishing he could spy Mistress Rose in

142

her perky bonnet."

"Get on with you, rogue." Rose gave his shoulder a nudge.

Undeterred, Notch sidled closer to Sarah. "Did you truly talk the mayor into giving over the customs house?"

"Who told you about it?" Sarah asked.

"Cholly heard it from the lamplighter, who heard it from the mayor's butler. Performing charitable deeds brings bad humors on the mayor."

Rose gasped. "Enough of your sauce."

"Is it true?"

At the hope shining in his eyes, Sarah said, "Yes. It's true, and I'd like your help looking it over today."

"Now?"

"Soon."

The boys waved and whistled until the sails caught the wind and the ship moved out of the bay. Sarah stifled a bout of melancholy at Michael's leaving, telling herself she was concerned over the delay in the acquisition of the customs house.

Notch replaced his cap. "We'd best be after inspecting the new digs."

Once at the customs house, he propped his hands on his hips and surveyed the building. "Like I was telling Pic and Cholly this morn," he said, "the lads'll take turns guarding the doors at night."

As if reciting a list, William said, "Protecting our womenfolk, our personal effects, and such food as we have in the pantry."

Sarah spent the afternoon listening to their plans and preferences and vowing to make sure they came true. Thanks to Michael Elliot, the orphans of Edinburgh had a chance. Would he change his mind about helping once he talked to Henry?

She cringed, imagining the lies Henry would tell Michael. On a more sympathetic note, she wondered what opinion Michael would form of his older brother, and what the long-estranged siblings would say to each other.

6

"Good God, little brother." Henry gaped, looking up at Michael. "You're a sizeable limb on the Elliot family tree. If I were prone to fanciful notions, I'd swear you were old Hamish come back to life. Come in, come in."

Ducking beneath the door frame of the cell Henry shared with two other men, Michael drew a shallow breath. From the moment the carriage had crossed London Bridge and turned on to Black Man Street, the stench from gin shops and general debauchery had sickened him. The sight of his older brother after so many years sent Michael's emotions into turmoil.

"Not the most accommodating place, is it, Michael?" Henry waved a hand to indicate the small room with three cots, two crusty lamps, and an untended slop bucket.

Wall pegs hosted an array of fashionable if unkempt clothing. Henry wore a waistcoat and matching knee breeches of dark blue satin over a drab brown shirt. His shoes were missing the buckles, and his legs were bare of hose.

Michael said the only thought that came to mind. "This prison is newly built."

"Aye. Gordon's rioters destroyed it back in 'eighty, but the owners couldn't rebuild it quick enough. There's a profit to be made on the sins of man." Moving two stools near a keg that served as a lamp table, Henry said, "Sit down."

Michael folded his long legs to facilitate sitting on the wobbly stool. "Profit?"

"Costs me a shilling a day for these accommodations. Private quarters can be had for two pounds a week, but . . ."

Michael's expectations fell far short of the reality, which was odd, considering the filth and depravity common in Calcutta. The need to aid his brother came naturally. "I've sold the customs house."

Henry's jovial expression faded to disdain, making him look even more like their mother. "Without consulting me? How much did you get for it? A fair price, I hope."

"Fifteen hundred pounds for the Elliot

half, once the papers are signed."

"Give me the money now, and I'll deal with the formalities later."

To his further disappointment, Michael didn't trust Henry; so he withdrew the document and writing materials from his satchel and put them atop the keg. "Let's just get the formalities behind us now."

Henry's mood turned decidedly cool. He scratched his name on the parchment and flicked it at Michael.

The rudeness of the gesture set Michael's teeth on edge, but he tried to put himself in Henry's place. Were their positions reversed, Michael would be less than agreeable. Still, a business transaction was simply that.

Returning the record of sale to the keg, Michael said, "You'll need to affix your seal, if you want the money."

"How careless of me." Henry fished through a tapestry bag hanging on a peg above him.

As he watched Henry melt the wax and apply the family seal, Michael couldn't ignore the irony of the actions, the place, and the participants. Usually younger sons looked to their elder siblings for money and advice. To lighten the atmosphere, he said, "We'll chuckle about this when we pass the tale on to our children."

"Have you any?"

"No, I haven't wed."

"Neither have I." Henry laughed. "If I needed a preacher every time the old sap started to rise, I'd be in gaol for different reasons."

The other occupants of the room laughed, too.

Michael didn't see the humor.

"I say" — Henry looked to the lounging men — "give us a bit of privacy." Listless and bleary-eyed, the men got to their feet and ambled out the door.

Suddenly uncomfortable, Michael moved his stool so he faced the only exit. For lack of anything else, he said, "Speaking of preachers, congratulations on your betrothal to Lady Sarah MacKenzie. She's lovely."

Tipping back the stool, Henry braced his shoulders against the wall. "You've met her?"

"Yes."

Henry stared down his narrow nose at Michael. "Well, out with it, man. What did she say about me?"

Guilt over wanting her for himself

plagued Michael, but now that he was looking at Henry, he couldn't help thinking that she deserved better than the earl of Glenforth.

"She called you worthless and deceitful."

"For losing fifteen thousand pounds? God, the wench is a country bumpkin."

"She also said she'd rather wed a toothless and blind draft horse than speak wedding vows to you."

Henry scratched his unshaven cheek. "She should have thought about that before she proposed marriage to me."

Michael's mind went blank. Prison noises buzzed in his ears.

"I see you're shocked, little brother."

Regaining his composure, Michael took out his pouch of candy. The pungent smell of ginger masked the odors here, same as it did in India. After helping himself to a piece, he handed the bag to Henry, who had the ill grace to pour out a handful for himself.

"Yes, well . . ." Michael said, "Lady Sarah has changed her mind about marrying you."

"Lot of good it'll do her. She's made her bed, as they say, and I intend to frolic in it with her — when the mood strikes me."

Instinctively, Michael wanted to defend the woman who championed the orphans of Edinburgh. But what of the other Sarah who had proposed marriage to the wastrel Henry Elliot?

Too confused to make an intelligent decision about her true character, Michael changed the subject. "What occurred with the duke of Richmond?"

"The bastard was using hollow dice, but he palmed them before I noticed." He smiled crookedly. "I was slightly in my cups at the time."

"Even if you lack proof, surely there were witnesses to speak on your behalf."

As surly as the carpetmongers in Calcutta's bazaar, Henry snarled, "Richmond bought them all off with money or favors."

"Who were they?"

"I cannot recall."

"Then how do you know he bought them off?"

"Because I am an earl," he declared. "But the word of a Scottish earl doesn't mean much against an English duke." With an elaborate survey of the room, he added, "You can see how far the title got me."

"What will you do?"

Sheer arrogance smoothed out Henry's features. " 'Tis better said what I will *not* do, and that is make a public apology to Richmond. He oversteps himself."

"Isn't that a bit reckless on your part?"

He shifted his weight until the legs of the stool slammed to the stone floor. Springing to his feet, he paced the small, windowless room. "You forget who is the heir to Glenforth."

Michael laughed. "Don't expect me to go down on a knee to you."

Henry grew serious. "What should I expect of you, little brother?"

If that were the only question Henry intended to ask of Michael, they'd be here for some time, so Michael broached the only subject they had in common. "Mother asked me to seduce the dowry from your betrothed — so long as I leave her maidenhead intact."

"A splendid idea." He snapped his fingers. "You can even have her damned virginity; just do not burden me with a bastard to raise."

A perch in the Borgia family tree was

looking better to Michael every minute. "What good will it do if you still refuse to make amends with Richmond?"

"I'll deal with that when the time comes. Money is what I need." He eyed Michael's clothing. "Have you any to spare?"

Why, he didn't know, but Michael had to say, "I could loan you several hundred pounds."

"Loan me? Good God, man. I'm the family heir."

"That makes my money yours?"

"Aye, unless you'd rather I disown you."

Michael could only stare at him.

At length Henry laughed. " 'Twas only a jest, Michael. Are you always so bloody dour?"

Michael chuckled, too, but not because he thought the remark funny. "Must be the Scot in me. Shall I visit Richmond on your behalf? I served in India with men who know him well."

"You could, but he's not to think I put you up to it. Find out how far he intends to take this so-called affront. Then report back to me."

Summoning patience he didn't know he possessed, Michael let the remark pass. For the next hour, they conversed, or rather Michael listened to tales of Henry and his dilemma, Henry's adventures in London, and Henry's ambivalence about the family estates in Fife.

Michael quizzed his brother about Sarah, and Henry was more than forthcoming.

"She's three and twenty and a by-blow of Lachlan MacKenzie. She ought to thank me for even considering her. God, Michael, if you only knew that family. One of the sisters, Mary, lives here in London and fancies herself the next Reynolds.

"I'll readily confess it, little brother, I rue the day I lowered my standards for Sarah MacKenzie. If I could find her father, I'd tell him so."

"Where is the duke of Ross?"

Henry chuckled but the sound held no humor. "Who the hell knows where he is? I'm tempted to have my solicitor send someone to the Highlands to search for him."

"I wish you luck in locating him."

"Oh, I'm resourceful — even in this hellhole."

Suddenly eager to be away, Michael

handed Henry a purse and took his leave.

As he passed through the gates of King's Bench Prison, he again pitched tuppence to the prisoner perched in the begging box. Once in the carriage, he let his thoughts dart from Sarah and her sister to the audience he would seek with the duke of Richmond, and then to the business meetings he must attend at the East India Company. When he'd accomplished all he could in London, he returned to Edinburgh on the first available packet.

Why had Sarah lied about the events surrounding her betrothal to Henry?

That question and dozens of others whirled in Michael's mind as he watched the stableman at the Dragoon Inn harness a pair of horses to the newest of the carriages.

Turnbull stood nearby, deep in conversation with a footman about the advantages of gunpowder over lampblack for the repair of boot leather. The normalcy of their discussion offered Michael a respite from the unraveling tangle of conflicting information he'd collected since his first arrival in Edinburgh and during his visit to London.

According to Turnbull, Lady Sarah was much sought after by Highland nobility, or at least her maid insisted she'd had marriage proposals from all of the great clans. If that were true, why hadn't she married years ago and into one of the families that could only be called Highland royalty?

She certainly possessed her share and more of feminine attributes. Added to that, she was bright and knowledgeable and passionate. He grew warm just thinking about holding her in his arms and kissing her again.

But there was more to Sarah Mac-Kenzie. Mingled with all of her appealing traits were a clever mind and a merciless determination. When it came to getting her way, she left no room for compromise.

"All right 'n' tight, m'lord." The stableman passed the reins to the driver.

Michael climbed into the coach. He'd already solved the puzzle of how Sarah had entered into the betrothal with Henry. What Michael didn't understand was why.

He'd find out, and soon.

Turnbull stacked the packages, items

Michael had brought from London for Sarah, on the floor of the carriage. As the valet stepped inside, he carefully arranged his coat.

Persnickety about his appearance, Turnbull carried himself with dignity, a trait he proudly admitted learning at the knee of his father. In India, Turnbull had been treated like royalty by the general citizenry, and adjusting to life at home was posing as many problems for him as it was for Michael.

The coach lurched into the lane. Michael settled in for the short ride to Lawnmarket.

The wind whistled around the corners of the buildings, and gentlemen and ladies in the lane held tightly to their hats. The stench of coal smoke smelled less abrasive to Michael, proving the oft-made statement that he'd get used to it.

What he couldn't accept just yet was the sound of people speaking Scottish, and he had to concentrate to understand the clickety-clacks in the pronunciation of his native tongue. Growing up in Fife, he'd learned Scottish first. Among Edinburgh's elite, English was the language of choice. When his mother realized he couldn't understand her, she had engaged a tutor and forbade Michael to speak Scottish. That edict was forgotten when her sojourn in Fife ended and she returned to Glenstone Manor.

Her hair had been light brown and very straight, same as Henry's. Michael had made that deduction, among many others, during his visit with Henry.

Anger welled up in Michael at the thought of his brother and the shame he'd visited on Clan Elliot. But times had changed in Scotland, and more so in London, during Michael's long absence.

In a nearby alley, a pair of mongrel dogs fought over the right to mount a passing bitch. A bucket of smelly slops cascaded from a window, and the animals quickly forgot their quarrel.

At the next corner, a carter took a switch to his reluctant ox. Michael smiled, thinking of the high value the Hindus placed on their cattle. Were an Indian stockman to visit cruelty on a Brahman, he'd find himself adrift in the Ganges, a rock tied to his feet.

"Sir?" said Turnbull, staring out the window. "Did I mention that Lady

Sarah's maid had the nerve to thank me for providing her with a frolicsome time? Lot of vinegar in that female. I told her what the Indians do to bold women."

Michael grasped the topic that had been high on Turnbull's list of complaints since their departure for London. "I doubt that endeared you to her."

"She's an upland Scot. Before they learn there is a God to be worshipped, the Highlanders learn there is an Englishman to be hated."

Michael couldn't help saying, "Perhaps you shouldn't have told her you're from Suffolk."

"Didn't have to say it. She's got a hound's nose for English blood."

Michael scratched his cheek to hide a smile. "I believe I recall your swearing that you threatened to cut off her nose."

Working his gloves into a smoother fit over his fingers, Turnbull sighed. "I fear I've been in India too long."

The presumed absolute authority of the English in India would be debated for years to come. Now Michael was glad to put those problems behind him. He had enough troubles of his own here in Edinburgh.

Foremost in his mind was his own behavior when last he'd seen Sarah MacKenzie. From the deck of the *Intrepid* with all of the Complement as witness, he'd acted like a lovesick beau, waving at and longing for a woman who did not bother to acknowledge him.

But when she met him in the hallway of her townhouse a few moments later, the subject that popped into Michael's mind had nothing to do with disappointing farewells or the lies she'd told.

7

"What have you done to yourself?" Michael asked.

She held up a bandaged hand. "A minor injury."

"Ha!" said her maid, as she hung up Michael's hat and coat. "She could have crippled herself."

Sarah smiled at the manservant who had accompanied Michael. "You must be Turnbull. How do you do?"

Still holding his hat, Turnbull bowed. "Quite well, my lady. Thank you. Mistress Rose said the lid on the kitchen coal box was loose. I thought to take a look at it."

Sarah glanced at Michael, but said to Turnbull, "You needn't bother."

All of Michael's uncertainties and questions about her came flooding back to him. But amid the confusion stood one undeniable fact: he was drawn to this intelligent and independent woman. Friendliness and the promise of something more lingered in the air about her.

The unknown drew him, and he smiled. "Repair of the coal box is between you and Turnbull."

"It's no bother, my lady." The valet stood taller and passed his hat and gloves to the maid. "Truth of it is, since coming here, I've little to do. If the box needs mending, what's the harm in taking a peek at it?"

Indecision creased her forehead. Michael now knew her age, but that was one of the few conclusive pieces of information he'd gleaned from Henry. According to Michael's brother, seeking guidance was foreign to her. Michael's perception differed greatly; he thought she was merely hesitant to ask for help.

But since it appeared she had passed the matter to Michael, he said, "Turnbull likes to keep busy. He's used to having an entire household to manage. And he's very handy."

As quick as a seasoned general, she made her decision. "Rose, show Mr. Turnbull to the kitchen, and after he's rescued our coal supply, make certain he eats several of those scones you baked this morning. I doubt they have good Scottish fare in India."

Just as she had placated the mayor, Sarah had soothed the maid, for Rose said, "This way, Master Turnbull. I'll be making tea. And there's a tart gooseberry jam, straight from my mother's kitchen in the Highlands."

In single file, the servants traipsed down the hall, the elfinlike, chatty Rose a perfect counterpart to the tall, studious Turnbull.

"You had a pleasant journey to London?" Sarah asked.

With the exception of his visit to Henry, the trip had been more than pleasant. Michael's investments in the East India Company prospered. Civilian life grew more appealing every day. "Very enlightening." He hefted the package. "I've brought you a gift and a message from your sister, Mary."

"I see." Sarah waved him into the library. "How thoughtful of Mary. Just put it down anywhere."

Michael set Mary's gift on the floor between a chair and lamp table and surveyed the well-stocked library shelves. His hostess stood near a thriving potted palm and surveyed him.

He had expected shyness from Sarah;

she wasn't the kind of woman to succumb to a quick seduction without feeling remorse, especially since she and Michael were newly acquainted. Henry swore that she lacked passion. Michael knew that for a lie. What of the other particulars about Sarah that Henry had supplied? How much was fact? How much was prejudice?

A thoroughly confused Michael decided to go slowly. His opinion of Sarah varied greatly from that of the brother he hardly knew. Weighing both opinions while trying to salvage the honor of Clan Elliot posed a challenge. Michael had spent his life in a foreign land overcoming obstacles; ironically, he was doing that very same thing again, only this time Scotland and England were the alien countries. He intended to make a place for himself among his family, and he would take his time in exploring his ungovernable feelings for Sarah MacKenzie.

"How did you hurt yourself?" he asked.

"With a hammer and poor aim." She wiggled her fingers. "It's truly minor. Rose exaggerates."

During their evening together at the

Dragoon Inn, Michael had expressed an interest in seeing her wield a hammer. He smiled, thinking of how much spunk she possessed. He said, "How did the nail fare?"

"Poorly, I'm afraid. Notch declared that I couldn't hit the old castle with a whole apple. I was relegated to the position of inspector and advice-giver."

"What words of wisdom did you offer?"

"When William wanted to know if my blood was truly blue, I told him no, but assured him that yours was. While not altogether unproductive, it was a frolicsome day." A genuine smile enhanced the tale. "Still, I think you will be pleased with what we've done."

"I'm certain I will."

"How did you come to know my sister?"

He could easily grow accustomed to Sarah's directness. "From my brother. London is all abuzz about her, particularly with the earl of Wiltshire openly wagering that she'll marry him by Christmas. I was curious, so I went to see her. You look nothing alike."

Affection shone in her blue eyes. "Mary is very beautiful and talented."

"As are you."

"Thank you." She looked at her hand. "Though the talent part of your compliment is questionable."

"You're much taller than she, and more quiet. Had I not been told you were related, I would not have guessed it."

"I could say the same about you and Henry."

"Who's the more quiet?"

"Neither of you." She strolled to a cluttered desk near the front windows. "I've prepared an inventory and a preliminary work schedule of the repairs to be done on the customs house."

Michael watched her rummage through stacks of books and papers. Bathed in sunshine and dressed in a gown of pale lavender trimmed with delicate white lace, she looked like a confection fit for a king.

His sweet tooth throbbed to life.

She wanted to discuss renovating an old building; he wanted to take her in his arms and kiss her again. But then he'd have to ask her the dreaded question. No, he wasn't sure he wanted to know the answer just yet.

She thinks too much, Henry had said of her. *Inquire after Sarah MacKenzie's favorite mount, and she'll tell you who bred the very first horse, what the creature was fed, and where it now lies buried.*

Michael kept his voice even and his tone friendly. The dreaded question would wait. "I thought you would want to open your sister's gift." Her sister had spoken proudly of Sarah's intellectual and literary accomplishments.

Sarah glanced at the wrapped package, which was obviously a framed canvas. "What has she painted now? The members of Parliament riding to riches on the back of the common man?"

Her controversial sister was notorious for her satirical depictions of the leaders of England at their immoral worst.

Michael refused to be grouped with hypocrites. "I admit to being curious, but if you are insinuating that I peeked at this painting, you are wrong." If a look could condemn, Sarah had found Michael guilty. He'd have none of that. "I did not invade your privacy. I am not that sort of man. This gift is your property."

"I'm sorry I wrongly accused you."

"Yes, well . . . I forgive you. Aren't you

166

interested in what 'Contrary Mary' has sent you?"

Sarah's elegant jaw clenched. "Is that what they're calling her now?"

He'd seen that same defensive expression in Mary when the topic strayed, as it often did, to Sarah. "You didn't answer my question, but yes, that is how the governing fathers refer to Mary. Depicting the twenty-five Scottish members of the House of Lords as bound and gagged in the back of the room has caused quite a controversy."

She continued to shuffle papers.

"Sarah!"

Sighing, she glanced up. "As you often say, you have been away a very long time. The politics of Scotland and England have hardly changed. Mary's work is a sore reminder to all that the English think themselves better than their neighbors to the north." She returned to the search. "Now where did I put those figures?"

Michael moved closer to the wrapped painting. "Given a choice between that list you cannot seem to find and Mary's gift, which is at hand, I choose this." He tapped the package. "But I will not do the unveiling."

"Here it is." Holding up the papers, she smiled triumphantly. "I'll look at that later."

He'd carted the damned bulky painting all the way from London, and now she was excluding him. Mary had predicted Sarah's reaction to the gift. Michael was anxious to see if she were correct. "Mary also sent a verbal message to you."

Tried patience glimmered in Sarah's eyes, and she sighed again but with great drama. "Michael, I prefer to leave my family out of our . . . association."

The estrangement was of deep concern to her sister, and Michael had given his word. "I prefer to fulfill my promise to Mary."

"Oh, out with it, then."

"She pleads with you to write to your father and patch up your differences. If you do not, within a fortnight, she promises to copy a certain nude of Eve, paint your face on it, and deliver it to the lord protector of Edinburgh."

Sarah turned her attention to the windows, and in profile she looked more beautiful and feminine than any depiction of the mother of mankind. The estrangement obviously troubled her, too.

"You sound as if you and Mary have become the dearest of friends."

She can cloak a scathing insult in the prettiest of words, Henry had warned. *Be careful you do not fall into her verbal traps.*

Mary had said, *She's too smart for that witless, shiftless brother of yours.*

Michael rather liked the idea of being snared by Sarah MacKenzie. He only wished his brother hadn't found her first. "Your sister, Mary, is the second most interesting woman I've met since leaving India."

That put a little color in Sarah's cheeks. "You are not concerned about the work I've done on the orphanage?"

Had he hurt her feelings? Odd, for he hadn't considered that, not when faced with the bigger issue of her separation from the family that loved her deeply and worried about her welfare. He wanted to see the MacKenzies reconciled. He wanted harmony among the Elliots. But foremost on his list of wants was the desire to satisfy his own curiosity about the lovely woman before him. Ah, well, if the conversion of a tumbledown building was his only positive link to her, Michael would take it. "Yes, I'm very interested in the progress you've made, but you haven't asked what Henry thought of the idea."

She grew distant, as if wrapped in a cloak of privacy. "I expect you convinced him to do the charitable thing and release the property."

Charity was not a word Michael readily associated with his brother or any of the men imprisoned in King's Bench Prison. But Michael wasn't prepared either to share his opinion of his brother with Sarah or to defend him. The discussion on the sale of the customs house had been brief. At the prospect of receiving 1,500 pounds, Henry couldn't put quill to ink fast enough. With the proceeds, he'd purchased private quarters in the prison and furnished them with everything from woven rugs to a willing woman.

A slight prevarication presented itself as Michael's best alternative to the full story. "Henry was glad to be rid of the building."

"Good. He needs the money. Did the two of you talk about me?"

A half-lie came to mind. "We have not

seen each other in many years. We spoke of a number of things."

"Well said." She picked at the bandage on her thumb. "I'd prefer that Henry, and his mother, ignore me altogether."

She hadn't included Michael. "Am I to assume that you've found one Elliot whom you do not hate?"

"I do not hate them, Michael," she said plaintively. "They lied and blackened my name because I was bastard born. I am curious about one thing." She walked toward him. "How long must Henry stay in prison?"

"Until Richmond is paid." To Michael's dismay, Henry had accumulated more debts since his incarceration.

Sarah sat down in one of the two overstuffed leather chairs, the papers in her lap. "Will you pay him?"

Michael grew uneasy. "Do you think I can afford it?"

"What an odd question. Your personal wealth, or lack of it, is none of my concern. But were I you, and I had earned the money honestly, I wouldn't waste it on someone else's gaming debt. I was referring to the family coal mines in Fife. I thought you would take money from there."

His mother and Henry called Sarah peasant-minded. To Michael, she was practical and forthright. He had asked Henry about the estate. Henry voiced the same complaint as their mother; profits from the mines were at an all-time low due to the high export tariffs. At least that was the explanation the estate manager had given them, for neither actually took part in the operation of the family business.

Sharing his thoughts on the matter with Sarah felt natural. "I'll look into it. The duty on shipping coal seems unnaturally high."

Her expression turned serene and her tone sugary sweet. "But King George must get his money from somewhere. Even you said as much." She smiled and handed him the papers. "Now will you look into this?"

At a loss for a reply to her clever rejoinder, Michael settled into the other chair. The springlike fragrance she wore blended wonderfully with the smell of fine old leather and aged books. It was a heady mixture, distracting and alluring to a man who wanted her madly.

"You haven't taken offense, have you,

Michael? I was only jesting."

"No, I took no offense." Scanning the well-organized lists and neatly set out work schedules, Michael remembered another of Henry's disparaging stories about her. As a birthday gift for the duke of Ross, Sarah had designed a system to pipe water into her father's favorite hunting lodge. She had even commissioned local craftsmen to do the work and supervised it herself. She'd been five and ten at the time.

Henry had been scandalized by both the tale and her pride in the telling. To Michael it was admirable and very thoughtful.

He couldn't help but smile. "You're very resourceful, Sarah MacKenzie, and thorough." She had included a map of the dock area. "You've even added a small stable at the back, although the horse looks a bit out of shape."

She chuckled. "It's supposed to be a cow. I told you Mary received the lion's share of talent."

Delightfully put, Michael thought. He envied her easy affection for the sibling who'd offended half of Parliament and charmed the other half. "I wonder how Mary put her talent to work on this piece." He tapped the wrapped painting.

"Later." Leaning forward, Sarah clasped her hands. Her injury did appear minor. Even so, Michael vowed it would be the last she suffered at the customs house.

"My lack of talent aside, the children will need a ready supply of milk," she said. "The cow can graze there" — she pointed to a spot on the map — "in the field near Anderson's Foundry. Squire Anderson has also promised to provide new hinges for the doors and grates for the hearths. I think it will be good for the children to share the responsibility of taking care of the cow."

She had been busy. But to Michael's delight, she'd found the time to end her association with a certain Count Du-Monde, if the doorman at the Dragoon Inn were to be believed.

"Don't you think the children will benefit?" she asked.

Michael harkened to the subject. "Yes, but when did you purchase the cow?"

She looked pleasantly puzzled. "I haven't, nor will I. Sir Gilbert Gordon offered to provide us with a healthy cow. William swears he knows how to milk it."

"And if he does not?"

She shrugged. "Then I shall teach him and the others."

An image of the stately Sarah squatting beside a cow made Michael smile.

Her chin went up and her voice purred silky smooth with challenge. "You find that humorous?"

"Yes. I've yet to see a duke's daughter labor in the stables before sunrise."

"Then you do not know the duke of Ross. He does not consider himself or his children above honest work." A fond memory captured her, for her eyes glowed with joy.

"Tell me," he said, eager to know what made her so happy.

"We were raised in the country. Lachlan did not marry until we were six years old. He taught us to ride and to care for our own ponies. We each had responsibilities, and if one of us failed to complete her chores, we all were punished."

That brought to mind yet another oddity surrounding Sarah and her unconventional family. "Is it true that you have three half sisters, and you were all born on the same day to different women?"

"We were born to different women, and we share a birthday for the sake of convenience and for our own protection. Lachlan MacKenzie was a bit of a rogue. He feared that our mothers or their families would try to take us away from him or use us as pawns. He's very possessive."

Michael already liked the duke of Ross. "Do you know your mothers?"

As if she had recited the answer hundreds of times, she stared at the stuccoed ceiling and said, "Only one of us does. Agnes and her mother are congenial to each other. Lottie and Mary do not care to know. They're very stubborn. My mother died giving birth to me."

Michael felt awkward. Henry had said nothing on the subject, reinforcing Michael's conviction that his brother and Sarah were more strangers than a couple. "I'm sorry that she died."

Without emotion, she said, "Do not be."

Dozens of other questions came to mind. "Who was your mother?"

Smiling, she toyed with the bandage on her hand. "Shall I give you the cus-

176

tomary answer? The one we were schooled to say?"

"It obviously humors you, so, please, share it."

"When asked, I and my sisters were taught to reply, 'I am not at liberty to name my mother, except to say that she is not an . . .' Elliot or MacGregor, or whatever the person's family who was inquiring."

The duke of Ross had obviously taken precautions on every front to protect his beloved daughters. Michael wondered about the two women he had yet to meet. "Are Lottie and Agnes as outspoken as you and Mary?"

She shook her head and ruefully murmured, "Mary and I are rank amateurs compared to them."

Michael pictured the four young women setting the court on its heels with their wit and independence. "I'm delighted to know that you are not an Elliot. I would feel guilty about kissing a relative."

Her steady gaze held a reprimand. "That's all behind us, Michael, and now that I've told you something about me, will you please tell me if you are married?"

He sprang to his feet, pulled her up and into his arms. "Had I pledged my troth to another, I would not have kissed you."

Her pretty lips quirked in apology. "I should have known. The upright, upstanding, and stalwart Michael Elliot would never act in an unchivalrous manner."

"You make me sound horribly predictable."

"If you're predictable, the king is a Turk."

Warmth pooled in his loins. "If you're seeking my forgiveness, you're likely to get it."

Suddenly she grew shy. Michael would have none of it. Lifting her chin, he looked deeply into her eyes. Honesty and affection looked back at him. Even had he tried to deny his desire for her, he knew he'd fail. So he heeded his heart and kissed her.

She languished in his arms, and her lips grew pliant against his own. As naturally as taking a breath, he opened his mouth to deepen the kiss. As eager as he, she met his passion and inspired him to greater intimacy. He caressed her arms and her back when he wanted to run his fingers through her hair and kiss her every curve and hollow. Desire turned to lust, and with sad acceptance, he knew he must step away or take her here in the library.

Summoning a monk's will, Michael broke the kiss and stepped back. Surprise shone in her eyes and her lips glistened. "Damn!" he cursed.

Her smile turned knowing. "Disappointed?"

Just when he opened his mouth to dispute her, Rose came into the room, a tea tray in her hands.

"I'm just put it to steep," the maid said, setting the tray on the low table.

"Thank you, Rose." Sarah moved farther away from him. I'll give it a little time. How is Turnbull coming along with the coal box?"

Michael almost groaned in frustration.

Rose almost wiggled with excitement. "Fixed that box in a trice and moved on to sorting out the clutter in the stable. But not before he ate three of my scones."

Sarah's sly glance spurred Michael on. If she could discredit the kiss, who was he to argue? "You have a mount here?" he asked.

"Yes." She glanced at the maid. "Thank you, Rose."

The maid curtsied and hurried out of the room.

"When your hand is healed, I'll take you riding."

"What an interesting way to phrase an invitation," she said, meaning the opposite.

Michael returned to the matter they had been discussing before Rose brought the tea. "Had I a wife, Sarah, I would not have kissed you."

She wore bruised pride like a mantle. "Perhaps you have an intended?"

"No. I haven't one of those, either, and I'm sorry I stopped kissing you. It won't happen again." He gave her an evil chuckle. "Forget any notion that intimacy is *behind us,* because you enjoyed it, too. Does that answer your question?"

She flustered beautifully. "I asked only because I'm seeking volunteers to serve on the governing board of the orphanage. I thought your wife or your betrothed might be interested in helping out."

He wondered if that was the real reason she had asked. He liked to think it wasn't. He hoped she was actually inquiring, for personal reasons, about him. "If I *had* a wife or a betrothed, would you be interested in meeting her?"

She gave him a look that Petruchio would have expected from his shrewish Kate. "A tedious question."

But telling all the same, especially so since she was smiling. Michael took heart and broached what he knew would be a dangerous subject. "Will your father serve on the board?"

"My father cannot possibly assist me with the orphanage. His family lives in Tain."

Michael edged closer to the dreaded question. "Henry said your father disapproved of the betrothal."

"He did. He said the Elliots would bore me. He was correct."

Michael hid his exasperation. "If you were bored when last I saw you, I'm the sultan of Madras."

Her darkening countenance boded ill. "When last you saw me, you were too far away to know what I was feeling.

181

You were standing on the deck of the *Intrepid*."

With all of the Complement and the king's best admiral to see, Michael had watched her and waved like a lovesick lad. Remembering that she hadn't even acknowledged him then, he said, "I was speaking of our evening together at the inn."

She jumped to her feet and tended the perfectly set fire in the hearth. "I would as soon forget that evening. I should not have let you kiss me then, either."

Michael hadn't intended to kiss her then or now, but after several hours in her company, he'd been drawn to her. He still was. Only now he knew that she felt the same. "I believe you *think* neither kiss should have occurred. It doesn't change the fact that you fancy our intimacies, brief though they've been."

"Oh, very well," she said grudgingly. "If you are so prideful that you must hear me speak the words, I will admit that I was temporarily distracted — brief though our kisses were. And I was grateful."

Had she confessed to the dementia she often attributed to his family, Mi-

chael could not have been more entertained. He howled with laughter.

"Stop laughing at me!"

He continued to chuckle.

She faced him squarely. "Think what
you will, Michael Elliot, but I *was* and
am grateful. Had it not been for the
kindness of Lachlan MacKenzie, *I* could
have been an orphan on the streets of
Edinburgh."

Michael felt as if he'd been slapped,
but beneath the shock her admission
wrought the truth sunk in. "You were
born here in Edinburgh?"

"Yes. At the Hospice of Saint Co-
lumba, but I do not want your pity. I
just thought you ought to know why I
am committed to helping Notch and the
others, aside from the fact that it is my
— our — Christian duty."

Sarah, an orphan in Edinburgh. The
unfairness of it tugged at his heart. It
took every bit of strength to keep from
rushing to her and pulling her into his
arms again. Instead, he thought of the
positive aspects of her childhood. "I'm
glad your father is a decent man, but I
am not surprised."

"You do not even know my father."

At her condescending tone, Michael's

temper flared. "I'm disappointed, however, that his daughter is a coward."

Sarah fumed, but she was more angry at herself than at Michael Elliot. Eventually her attraction to him would fade. Until then, she would carry on and soothe his bruised pride. "I'm only thinking of the problems that a court-ship between us will bring."

All subtlety gone, he lowered his voice. "Five minutes ago, I was more than courting you. And you were more than agreeable."

"Yes, but never again. Now that you've spoken to Henry, you know the exercise is futile." Would he never reveal what Henry had said about her?

"Yes, well . . ." He glanced at the papers. "The visit proved enlightening. I know my brother better now."

Oh, that infuriating habit of his. The devil take him and what he'd learned about her from Henry. Sarah had her own life now, such as it was. Between working at the orphanage and battling her own attraction to Michael Elliot, she couldn't manage an intelligent thought.

She snatched up a bit of rhetoric. "What will you do now that you have left the Complement?"

"I haven't decided, but I rather like the idea of serving on the governing board of the orphanage. If, that is, you accept men in the position?"

That cool manner of his and quick wit would be her downfall. "Of course I'll consider you for the position. Men should be treated as equals."

This time his laughter pleased her. She returned to the chair. "With that cheerful thought in mind, I wondered if you would consider visiting my Sunday school and teaching the children history or geography. You're well traveled, and I believe they respect you. They're still learning to read, but I think you'll find them a worthy audience."

With a slight tilt of his elegant head, he conceded. "I will, if you'll make me a promise."

Past experience told her what he would ask. "No more kissing."

He gave her a grin that could melt a nun's resolve. "Give me your word that you will not again condemn me for the crimes of my mother or my brother."

Why did he have to be an Elliot? Her mood turned blue. "They want money from me for a betrothal made under false pretenses. Henry claimed he was

185

an honorable man. He lied."

He leaned back in the chair and stretched out his long legs. "That is not my concern."

She believed him. Michael Elliot held himself above the pettiness of his mother and older brother. He didn't crow the opinions or malign the less fortunate. He also looked like a mighty Highland chieftain, perfectly at home in a tailored gray frock coat and trousers.

She shouldn't want him at all. He was Henry's brother. But he hardly knew Henry. "Will you agree to drop the subject of my dowry?"

"Yes." He folded his arms over his chest. "Until your father offers it to me."

Her heart tripped like a harvest drum. She had to change the subject. Knowing the attempt was weak, she said, "Henry's found another way to buy himself out?"

Michael reached for the teapot and filled their cups. "He will get out the same way he got in, I think."

Surely Michael wasn't so naive as that. "He'll be old and gray before he wins enough money from his fellow prisoners. They're all debtors and felons in King's Bench. The only money to be had there is printed on foolscap."

"Henry spends only his nights in prison. Every morning he is released — to facilitate acquiring the money to pay back the debt. Richmond recommended it."

Sarah stared at the steam rising from her cup and wondered if Henry would succeed. "A sensible plan, if it works."

"We can only hope it does. Will you also agree to put the past crimes of the Elliots behind you?"

The request was reasonable and could benefit Sarah. She wanted to make a life for herself here in Edinburgh. She had spoken to Count DuMonde, who gracefully agreed to cease his afternoon visits. According to Notch, the gossips were busy with news of the orphanage and speculation about her evening out with Michael Elliot. At least the former spoke positively of her good character. The latter was her own cross to bear.

"I agree." She held out her bandaged right hand to seal the bargain. "Will you teach the class on Sunday?"

His fingers closed gently around hers. "Only if you are there."

Intimacy crept into the moment, and Sarah searched for a light reply. "Of course. I'm a very good student."

His gaze fell to her injured hand, which he examined with great care. "Are you attentive, Sarah?"

"A veritable constant in my character."

His grin told her he recalled saying those very words to her. "No pranks and no giggling?"

With such an appealing teacher? She wanted to chuckle, but knew he'd take advantage of a humorous moment. "I left those bad habits in my stepmother's classroom. Do you care for milk and sugar?"

"Only sugar." His gaze seared her. "I have a fierce sweet tooth."

He made the simplest of statements sound provocative — that, or her imagination was at fault. Then she remembered the ginger candy he'd offered her on his first visit. "Where, I wonder, have I heard that before?"

He lifted his brows. "Surely from a gentleman with impeccable manners, honest intentions, and the most unquestionable good taste in all important things. Added to that, I am an excellent judge of character."

He was speaking of her, and the

knowledge made her dizzy. Leaning toward him offered a remedy for the dizziness, she knew from past experiences. But she must mount a defense against his seduction, and thoughts of his brother no longer worked.

"You haven't sweetened your tea," she said.

His hand moved past her wrist to the tender skin of her forearm. "No, I haven't."

The air grew close between them. She scrambled to control the conversation. "Speaking of your honest intentions, are you prepared to visit the cobbler tomorrow? You did agree to furnish shoes for all of the orphans."

"I agreed to pay for the shoes *after* you admitted what was in your heart."

"Are you welshing?"

"Aren't you?"

"We both are. Tomorrow afternoon is convenient for me to accompany you to the cobbler."

If appearances counted, Michael Elliot looked prosperous. But so did the rest of his family. He took rooms at an inn and was generous to those who served him. She remembered Rose's tale of his giving a crown to the stableman for the care of his horse. "You've made arrangements to pay the cobbler?"

"The members of the Complement are responsible. They all wanted to help."

"Then you are not a wealthy man?"

"At this moment, I feel wealthier than a king."

She found the strength to pull her hand away. "That's no answer. You made a very generous offer to aid the orphans. At the time, you couldn't have known the Complement would agree."

"Oh, but I could. As I said, I'm an excellent judge of character. And in reply to your very personal question about my finances — if I were comfortably fixed, wouldn't I buy my brother's freedom?"

He made her sound nosy, but money was at the core of her entanglement with the Elliots. "I do not know you well enough to venture an opinion. Would you buy Henry's freedom?"

"Ah, now I understand. You are worried that Henry may soon be released and you will have to face him."

Owning up to her worst mistake didn't frighten Sarah; she welcomed the opportunity to look Henry Elliot in the eye and tell him exactly what she thought of him. "Will he soon be released?"

"I do not know. There is much more to the charges against him than a gaming debt. He truly insulted the duke of Richmond, who has threatened to bring the matter to Parliament."

In spite of her trembling hand, she picked up her teacup. "I'm not surprised."

With an infuriatingly steady grip, he also sipped from his cup. "Just how well did you know Henry before the betrothal was formalized?"

The tea grew bitter on her tongue. "Obviously not long enough." She put down the cup and moved to the lamp table. "Do you still want me to open that package?"

"A clumsy effort, Sarah, but —"

"But you're a gentleman to the tips of your fine imported boots."

"For the moment, yes," he warned. "I'm waiting for your reply."

"Did you ask Henry if he had intimate knowledge of me before the betrothal?"

"I will stake my reputation on the fact that you are a virgin."

Gasping, she bristled with umbrage. "That's not what I meant."

He chuckled without humor, and his

expression spoke of greater intimacies.

Unable to bear his gaze, she turned away. "The betrothal was a mistake. Isn't that enough?"

A cup clattered against a saucer, and she heard him rise. "Sarah, look at me."

He stood so close she could feel his warmth and power. "No."

Strong hands grasped her upper arms, and he turned her around. Determination blazed in his eyes. "You did not tremble when my brother held you."

She dragged in a breath, and as she exhaled, his neckcloth fluttered. "No. I did not."

"You're trembling now."

Oh, God. He was going to kiss her again, and she couldn't summon the words to dissuade him.

His hand touched her chin, and with gentle pressure, he tipped her head back. He smelled of masculine illusions conjured by a woman in love. *No*, her heart cried. She couldn't love Michael Elliot.

"Run, Sarah," he whispered. "If you are fearful of your feelings."

"Swear that you do not have at least one reservation yourself."

"I cannot, but neither will I lie to

myself. I prefer to face my quandaries."

"And conquer them."

"No. I'd rather overcome them. Only enemies must be vanquished, and you, Sarah MacKenzie, are the very farthest thing from an enemy."

She touched his chest. "You do fear something, but you keep it locked away, here in your heart."

She lifted her brows, inviting him to reveal his weakness.

Not for all the world's riches would Michael bare his soul to her. "Now, my inquisitive one, you may open Mary's gift."

"You're overbearing."

"You're just miffed because I asked you to admit your feelings for me."

With unsteady hands, she untied the string and unwrapped the painting. "Oh, Mary. How could you?"

At her mournful sigh, Michael peered over her shoulder.

In the classic style of her mentor, Joshua Reynolds, Mary had depicted Sarah and a man who could only be the duke of Ross. Sarah's dress was perfectly detailed, down to the embroidered thistles at the hem and around the daring neckline. Lachlan wore the

193

flashy tartan of the MacKenzies and an elaborate chieftain's sporran.

Behind them in the painting, a fire blazed in a massive stone hearth, and the room abounded with small details. The toys of her younger siblings littered the floor, and the remains of a meal cluttered a table. It was as if Sarah and her father had been captured in a moment of time.

Above the mantle was a framed picture of a woman wearing a MacKenzie tartan sash. Judging from the old-fashioned dress and ducal coronet, she must be the duke's mother.

Mary's skill far surpassed accurate details. Her ability to capture the love and joy shared between father and daughter went beyond that of the great masters.

Sarah's knuckles were white from gripping the frame, and tears dotted the bodice of her lavender gown.

"Is that your grandmother?" he asked.

She cried harder.

He took the painting from her and let it fall to the carpet. "Why does it trouble you so, Sarah? It's obvious he loves you. I know you're stubborn, but you cannot deny his affection. Surely you long to make amends with your family."

Michael wrapped her in his arms and rubbed her back.

She curled kittenlike against his chest. "You don't understand."

"I'd like to." He discovered that she didn't wear stays, but Sarah MacKenzie needed no artifice. She needed a friend. Michael gladly took up the role.

In a cheerful voice, he said, "Did the duke crow, 'Didn't I say so?' when you changed your mind about marrying Henry?"

"You sound as if you know him."

"I'm beginning to. Then he commanded you to come home."

She sniffed. "He knows better than to command me."

Michael fished out his handkerchief and gave it to her. "Of course he knows better. Or do you truly stay in Edinburgh to escape the best intentions of half of the Highland's eligible dukes?"

A change came over her; the weakness fell away like a discarded shawl. "Rose said that to Turnbull."

The coil of her hair formed a golden eddy at the crown of her head. "You are Rose's favorite topic of conversation."

"She exaggerated about the peers

coming to Tain."

"Thank goodness. I fair poorly when compared to dukes."

"Even if he were a prince or a clerk's apprentice, I do not want a husband."

"Not Claude DuMonde?"

Now completely alert, she wiped her eyes and sniffed with finality. "How did you know about him?"

Michael thought of another Highlander he'd seen of late. "From the doorman at the inn. He heard it from that streetsweeper, who will take up his broom to defend your honor."

"That's Cholly." She retrieved the painting from the floor and rested its face against the wall. "He knows all of the gossip before it's spread. I had Notch tell him he could also pick out new shoes."

"I doubt Cholly rises that early, since he prowls the streets at night."

She glanced toward the front door and cupped her hand to her ear. "Can you not hear the slide of his broom? That's him sweeping the stoop, even as we speak."

The cocky laborer could sweep the rooftops for all Michael cared. Now that he'd helped Sarah master her sorrow, he phrased the question he'd been avoiding. "This Cholly fellow is welcome to come to the Cordiner's Hall tomorrow. At the moment, I would like to return to a bit of unfinished business between us."

She looked wary and with good cause.

"I did ask Henry about the reasons for your speedy betrothal. Which brings me to the dreaded question . . ."

"Which is?"

"Why did you propose marriage to him?"

8

That question and the ensuing quarrel still rankled the next day as Sarah stood in the stables and groomed her horse. Michael couldn't possibly know the truth, could he? He'd been speculating, fishing for confirmation of what he thought was the truth.

But how much of his actions were governed by loyalty? He often admitted that he was a stranger here and new to the problems facing the Elliots. What of his feelings for Sarah? One moment she thought his affections for her were heartfelt. The next moment she named him a knave doing poor service for his older brother.

Most of the time she felt confused. Yet sadness pervaded her uncertainty, because Michael Elliot possessed fine qualities. He'd been quick to take her side against Mayor Fordyce. He'd been quicker to offer immediate aid, in the form of shoes, to the orphans. But those kindnesses did not excuse his joining forces with Lord Henry and Lady Emily against Sarah — not unless he wanted her dowry for himself.

Why did you propose marriage to Henry?

Sarah had spent the night and morning remembering the doubt in Michael's voice and seeing the anticipation in his eyes. He couldn't know the reasons behind her promise to the Elliots; even a desperate Henry would not have revealed the details.

Sarah's dilemma grew, and she must harden her heart to him.

"I'll have me a horse someday." Notch sat astride her sidesaddle, which Turnbull had moved to the block the day before.

Sarah had come to the stable to escape troubling thoughts of Michael Elliot. She grasped the diversion Notch offered.

"What kind of horse will you have?" she asked him.

He screwed up his face in disgust and rubbed his thigh. "Not a gelding."

Rose poked her head out of the next stall where she'd been polishing the new window glass Turnbull had installed. "Watch your tongue in the presence of a lady. We'll have no vulgarities here."

Notch eyed her assessingly. He'd long since stopped back-talking Rose, but he still considered a bold retort now and then; the practice of standing up for himself was too ingrained.

In acknowledgment of his good manners, the maid smiled at him. "You'll be smart enough by that time to know that a mare's the best, because she'll make little horses for you."

He pondered that.

Sarah raked a brush through her horse's mane, the movement slightly awkward because of the bandage on her hand.

The lad said, "Having little horses is the same as paying her own way, ain't that it?"

"See, Lady Sarah?" Rose chirped. "Didn't I say Notch was a bright lad? He'll be strolling down High Street one of these days, a passel of governors currying after his favors."

Bursting with pride, he arched his back and jammed his left foot into the dangling stirrup. "She'll be a sorrel," he declared. "With a white sun 'twixt her ears and . . ."

Sarah said, "A mouth as soft as summer butter?"

"For a certainty, my lady." He flapped his legs and jerked on invisible reins. Without the cap and oversized coat, he looked small and endearingly young.

He was also wearing new clothing.

"That's a nice shirt, Notch," she said.

He touched the almost-new fabric of his sleeve. "A contribution from the mayor himself. I gave Pic my others. There's still a bit o' wear in 'em."

Notch refused to refer to the items that came his way as charity. He accepted all of the "contributions," then doled out garments, food, and precious pennies to the other children. One day soon they'd escape the darkened alleys and smelly mews. Once in the orphanage, Notch would spend his days in the classroom and his spare time — as he was now — simply being a boy. Precious moments like these would be the standard in his life rather than the exception.

He made clicking sounds and cooed praises to his imaginary steed. "Lady Sarah?" he said. "Cholly says the general's taking lunch today with that button-mouthed ol' countess." Sneaking a glance at Rose, he waited to see if she would reprimand him. When she did not, he added, "Carried a satchel of papers with him."

"I'm certain they had business matters to discuss." It was better said that they had a lack of financial prospects to ponder.

"Will he be keeping his promise to contribute shoes to the cause?"

"Yes," Sarah said without pause. Michael Elliot was unhappy with her, but he would not make the orphans suffer. For the sake of the cause, she would put aside their quarrel today. She had agreed to call for him this afternoon, and she would — but in an unexpected and, she hoped, convincing fashion.

"Mistress Rose?" Another subject captured Notch, and his voice broke. "Does that countess know how to read?"

The maid peered at a spot on the already sparkling glass. "She don't read anything to sweeten her bitter humors."

Notch laughed and Sarah did too. But curiosity filled her. Lady Emily had been suspiciously quiet since Michael stepped foot on Scottish soil — not that Sarah frequented the same homes or merchants as the countess. Sarah enjoyed going to market with Rose, and she'd yet to see Lady Emily in the bookstore or the stationer's shop where Sarah purchased quills and ink.

They did not attend the same church; Sarah preferred the uplifting atmosphere at Saint Margaret's Chapel to the dour crowd at Saint Stephen's. Did Michael plan to attend services with his mother?

Like an awesome specter, a vision of Michael Elliot loomed in her mind.

Why did you propose marriage to Henry?

On his lips the question sounded like an accusation, which it was, if she believed his daring behavior and blatant promises of seduction. But if she were forced to defend herself to Michael, he should do the same. Were his reasons for wanting her honest ones? Nothing about their association was untainted. The Elliots wanted — needed — her dowry. Michael could not know the truth about the betrothal, on that she'd stake her very salvation. What troubled her most was her own ambivalence on the regrettable subject of her promise to wed Henry.

Notch cackled with glee. "Cholly says

you marched the general out the front door yesterday and bade him take his scandal-ridden self elsewhere. Did you truly blister his ears and send him off with his tail 'tween his legs?"

Remembering the ugly scene, Sarah winced. "We disagreed on an important and private matter. I hope the street-sweeper can be trusted not to spread the tale to anyone else."

Watching her, Notched looked puzzled. "Cholly laughed beyond measure at the telling of it, but he don't mingle with the gentry."

Rose marched out of the stall. "Just to be sure, I'll be having a talk with that Cholly."

Notch sprang from the saddle. "Oh, nay, Mistress Rose. Cholly don't have nothing to do with women. He swears they're no better'n the plague. You get closer'n a broom's length of him, and he'll run the other way."

Drawing herself up, Rose huffed in disgust. "He oversteps himself."

A common occurrence among the men of Edinburgh, Sarah thought. She was still boiling mad at Michael Elliot, but she couldn't help wondering how he fared in the meeting with his mother.

And stay away, Michael Elliot!

Oh, he'd darken Sarah MacKenzie's door again, but next time he'd be more circumspect in his questioning of her. He wouldn't be deceived by a pretty face and alluring manner, for beneath her ladylike exterior and charitable disposition lurked a veritable virago.

You're a conniving, deceitful Elliot.

He'd yelled back that he wasn't his brother.

You're worse.

Just as she slammed the door in Michael's face, an anxious Turnbull had come running out of the alleyway.

Women weren't supposed to guard their privacy or overvalue their own opinions. Michael thought she excelled at both.

She's a thinker, Henry had said of Sarah. *Give her to the count of ten to ponder an answer, and you'll rue ever posing the question.*

Michael blew out his breath in frustration.

"It's rather boring to me, too," his mother said, misinterpreting his sigh.

Michael didn't bother to correct her; he was too confused about his feelings for Sarah MacKenzie.

Standing in a hallway in Glenstone Manor, he stared at the tartan-clad image of the fifth earl of Glenforth. If he ignored the dated clothing and beard, Michael could have been staring at a looking glass, so similar were his features to those of his famous ancestor. If the broadsword in Hamish Elliot's massive hands were an indication of his prowess, Michael's great-grandfather had been a formidable soldier. He'd also been both a ruthless businessman and a notorious womanizer.

"A Dutchman painted that," Lady Emily offered. "The Elliots had fled to Europe with Charles I. Garish, those Dutch, and heavy with a brush. Henry chose a good English painter for his." With her handkerchief she swiped at the canvas bearing Henry's regal likeness. The gesture was useless; the surface of the painting and the frame were as clean as the rest of the mansion. Even the occasional shield and well-worn battle-ax were polished.

Michael knew little about his ancestors. That knowledge and the Elliot legacy at large had been passed on to Henry. Their grandmother had lived at the estate in Fife, where Michael had been raised, and some of her possessions remained there. But she'd died years before Michael had been born.

The old caretaker had sworn the dowager countess couldn't abide Glenstone Manor after Michael's mother came into the family. The caretaker's wife believed Lady Emily had packed off her mother-in-law to the country. For the moment, Michael sympathized with his grandmother, but his mother had requested this meeting, and he still harbored hope that they could find common ground on which to build a measure of civility.

After all, she was his mother. She had likes and dislikes, pleasures and sorrows. Only by getting to know her would he cease to see her as a stranger.

He chose a benign subject. "Have you seen the great old tapestries in Rouen? I imagine those would be to your liking."

"Yes. Henry took me there the year after he returned from his grand tour. I did find those ancient weavings cheerful and pleasing. Henry, of course, prefers manlier works in stone and marble. He dragged me all over Europe and would have only the best accommodations for us."

Michael didn't miss the pride and affection in her tone. Her spirits always brightened when she spoke of his brother and the past. For that closeness, Michael felt a stab of jealousy. But Henry had spent his life under the same roof as their mother. Michael must now make his own way with her. She could do her part in bridging the gap by asking him questions; as yet, she was disinclined to do so.

Again, he took the lead in the conversation. "The sultan's palace in Bombay is filled with Moroccan mosaics. They cover the floors and soar to the ceilings."

"Heathens."

She couldn't be as ignorant as that, and she certainly wasn't a zealot.

Michael felt bound to defend the country he'd called home for so many years. "Their artistry is timeless and not always of a religious nature. Chesterfield bought an entire wall from an old palace near Bombay and shipped it home to Bath, piece by piece. They say he acquired it for a paltry sum."

"Did he now? I wonder you didn't send one to us."

She could have asked him why he hadn't brought home a band of Bedouins, so surprised was Michael. "I did not know your preference on such matters."

More reasonably, she said, "You never inquired after the needs of this family."

"Yes, well . . ." He turned and started down the hall toward the morning room. "I can see why you wanted a portrait gallery."

The family heirlooms were scattered about the hallways, rooms, and the stairway landings. The disarray mirrored perfectly his own feelings for his kin.

"I suppose we could manage with only a few windows, but anything less than a dozen will shout the news that our straits are dire. The embarrassment will be devastating."

Her selfishness troubled Michael. Rumor would be the only evidence that the Elliot purse had grown short; she dressed in the latest styles. Today she wore a morning gown of pale green silk with outrageously wide panniers trimmed in golden tassels and bows. Her towering powdered wig played host to a real bird's nest complete with a feathered occupant. The creature looked so real, he expected to see sparrow droppings splatter her bare shoulders at any moment.

Michael chastised himself for the unkind thought. He'd never establish a foundation for affection between them if he continued to judge and malign her for circumstances beyond her control. Henry managed — or mismanaged — the family assets. She was a powerless mother, dependent on the sons of her clan. Assurance was what she needed. "I'm certain our circumstances will improve."

She sighed painfully. "Oh, when will Henry be free to come home and make sense of it all?"

Michael felt her anguish and rose to the occasion. "I plan to go to Fife and see what can be done about the coal concerns. I have some experience with commerce." He'd actually commanded thousands of workers building roads and shoring up dikes before the monsoon season, but he worried that his mother might view his volunteering that information as bragging.

She looked up at him, but her gaze flitted away. "Wouldn't your time be better spent with that reprehensible

MacKenzie girl? Twenty thousand pounds of ready cash is what we need. She and her father did promise it. If Henry is to be held accountable for a wager he innocently made with a corrupt duke, His Grace of Ross should be made to own up to an honorable agreement made with decent people."

Her convoluted rationale baffled Michael, and his first impulse was to defend Sarah, but then he remembered her angry words.

Trouble yoursef no more, Michael, on the matter of my betrothal to your brother. I'd rather give myself to the church than wed Henry Elliot.

"Are you listening, Michael?"

At the reprimand in his mother's voice, Michael returned to the present. "You'll get the dowry money only if Henry marries her." Even as he voiced it, Michael discarded the notion. In spite of their angry parting, he still wanted Sarah for himself.

He would face her father and demand the dowry only when he had the right, as Sarah's husband, to do so.

His mother grew vindictive. "We'll get the money. You just wait and see."

"Mother," he said patiently. "Do not

expect Lady Sarah to rush to London soon to speak her vows over a gaming debt."

She glared up at him. "I ask you, Michael. Whose fault is that? Henry wooed her once. Surely you can champion his causes. You *are* his brother, and although you haven't his wherewithal, surely you can make an effort."

He felt like a servant charged with a duty for which he was unprepared. Or was he oversensitive? He didn't know. Stretching the truth seemed wise. "I'm actually a stranger to both Henry and Lady Sarah." He almost added, "and to you," but just the thought made his mission appear impossible.

"Yes, you have been away from civilization for a very long time. Young women today have improper ideas about the formality of making a match. I counseled Henry against offering for her in the first place."

She had an odd way of putting it, considering the size of Sarah's dowry. "What precisely did Henry *offer* for her?"

"Our good name and legitimate heirs. He even agreed to those silly stipulations of hers."

Oh, Sarah, he thought, *for a woman with such noble ideas, you've a way of stirring up the devil's own wrath.* "What stipulations?"

"Lot of ridiculousness." Lady Emily paused to scrape a piece of wax from one of a pair of standing candelabrum. "Separate properties for any daughters she bears. Promises to educate all of the children — even the girls."

What would Mother say if she knew that Michael had agreed to share his knowledge of world history with the children in Sarah's orphanage? The occasion loomed like a patch of calm on a stormy sea.

She huffed in disgust. "A morning in that woman's company, and 'tis plain to see why women have no business in the schoolroom, let alone standing at the head of it."

Mother's shallowness chipped away Michael's good intentions. "Even if Sarah passes on her knowledge to the unfortunates of Edinburgh? Surely you can see the benefit in educating the orphans."

"Apprenticeships have always sufficed for those urchins. Good, honest work to keep them off the streets and out of our purses."

A point to consider, Michael had to agree. In addition to reading and writing, the children needed to learn a trade. "Why haven't the local craftsmen taken the children in?"

"I'm sure I wouldn't know — except to say that *she* has probably driven off the best merchants with her offensive demands and hoity ways. She expects Henry to give her allowances for her charity work." Lady Emily shivered with revulsion. "Allowances for books and money for passage home to the Highlands every New Year's Eve. She even required a holiday in the fall in London."

"A holiday?"

"She has a sister there — and almost everywhere else. Her father is as base as a mongrel dog." Her mouth snapped shut like a trap. "The rogue, they called him," she said through gritted teeth. "But I was willing to overlook all of that because Henry wanted the girl."

This version differed greatly from Henry's. The only opinion of the affair they shared was disapproval of Sarah MacKenzie. "My brother actually con-

214

fessed to you that he loved Sarah Mac-Kenzie?"

"Love? What a silly notion, Michael. Marriages are made for practical reasons. Although Henry did not take my advice, he knows the value of my experience." She choked up with tears. "I should like to go to London and comfort him. But we haven't the money."

She needed the comfort, not Henry. Michael couldn't help offering solace. She was his mother. "I'll see what I can do."

Her mood turned gay, and she smiled. "I'm relieved to hear that. We thought you'd forsaken us."

Did she really think that? Odd, since the Elliots hadn't bothered with him. How could a lad, fostered out early to an estate miles away, be expected to acquire an affinity for those who turned him out? He'd done what he could from Fife and India to foster his own loyalty to the Elliots. As a boy, he'd written to his father every Saturday, as duty dictated. But without reciprocation, the exercise was doomed to failure. And more, the lack of interest in him by his father increased Michael's belief that as a second son he was expendable. Only in India had he prospered and become his own man.

"It's ironic, Mother. You thought I'd forsaken you, and I felt you'd abandoned me."

Missing the point, she said, "I'm not condemning you, limited as your prospects must be, but it is about time you contributed to the family coffers."

In an absurd way, she was justified in her belief. Not counting honorable service to the crown, what had he ever done for the family except send a little money home? Part of the blame for his estrangement rested squarely on his shoulders, he realized. Telling her of his successful investments would ease the way between them.

The voice of reason, the voice in his mind that had kept him alive in battle and enabled him to succeed in commerce, spoke loudly to Michael. It demanded to know if purchased approval and acquired loyalty were valuable. He wasn't sure, but hoping to change the situation, he took the initiative. "I'll have Turnbull make the arrangements."

"Where did you get the money?"

For lack of anything else, he said,

"Where do you think?"

Her look turned knowing. "The faro table at Trotter's!" She threw back her head, sending a shower of wig powder onto the carpet. "You and Henry are more alike than I thought. You both were gifted with good luck by my family. The Fletchers have a knack for a profitable wager."

Losing fifteen thousand pounds of someone else's money and insulting an influential peer in the process could hardly be termed a profitable wager. An error in her logic, but Michael saw no reason to point out that he and his brother were as different as rock and glass. Instead, he smiled benevolently and tossed one of her own insults back in her face. "I can see to your passage and other necessities. Will two hundred pounds be enough *carrying-around money?*"

She did not miss the sarcasm, for her lips tightened. "Now that that's settled, I have a surprise for you. Henceforth you will style yourself Viscount Saint Andrews. There's no property or money with it. The title belonged to your grandmother's father, but I think you should have it, Lord Michael."

He'd been addressed as "sir," or "general," or simply, "Elliot," for so long, Michael wasn't sure how he felt about the title. "I don't know what to say."

"You needn't go on about it, but I think you owe me an explanation for your actions regarding the customs house. You had no right to buy that building and then give it away. I'm appalled."

She spoke as if his money were hers. Outrage threatened to rob him of composure, and he had to struggle to maintain a civil demeanor. How dare she speak to him as if he were an ungrateful son living on her patronage? "Did the mayor tell you I plan to call it Elliot's Haven for the Poor?"

"I care not if you put pearly gates at the front of it. You should have spoken with me first. I forbid you to put our name on a charitable institution, especially when we have no money. Henry is imprisoned. Every shilling should be pledged to remedying that sad state of affairs. He is the heir and deserves all of our attention."

"Yes, well . . ." She could forego her trip to London, too, but he knew she would not make that sacrifice. "What did Fordyce say?"

"Not all of it can be credited. He had the absurd notion that you were smitten with Sarah MacKenzie and she with you." She laughed without humor. "Imagine that nonsense."

The rein on Michael's temper grew taut. "What was your reply to the absurd notion that Sarah MacKenzie found me attractive?"

"Now, Michael," she fairly cooed. "You mustn't be miffed at me over gossip I didn't start. Fordyce doesn't see through that Elliot charm of yours. I know you were only pretending. Remember, I married your father, and you are more like him than you know. I'm not surprised that that Highland lass finds your dark good looks appealing. Before fair Henry, the Elliot men were known for wooing women."

"Better that, Mother, than having a reputation for poor judgment and poorer manners at a gaming table."

Her neck flushed bright red, but it was the only outward sign of her displeasure. As quickly as it had come, her irritation fled. "I have an idea, and I cannot imagine why I did not think of it before."

Foreboding settled over Michael. "What idea would that be, Mother?"

"You must find out who owns that townhouse she occupies. Have him cancel her lease. When she learns of the eviction, you can set her up in a residence in Henry's name. Nothing extravagant, though. She *is* a by-blow."

Bewildered, Michael could think of nothing to say.

"If word gets out that you were involved, just deny it. The stain on your reputation will be nothing more than a smudge."

For years Michael had led an honorable life. By example, he'd taught the young recruits under his command to do the same. "Stain or smudge, the answer is no."

"I know it's a sacrifice, but this family would do no less for you."

Michael's head began to pound. "Refresh my memory, Mother. What has this family done for me?"

As innocent as a spring lamb, she blinked. "We bought you that career, and as soon as this wretched business is behind us, I intend to find you an acceptable wife with a decent dowry."

That prospect filled him with dread.

"Yes, well . . ." He searched for a way to change the subject, but how could he when he truly wanted to rail at his mother for her selfishness? Worse, how could he form the words to protest when he wanted Sarah for his own?

Lamely, he said, "If you will excuse me, I'll speak with Turnbull. When would you like to go to London?"

Flapping her silk handkerchief at any sign of dust, she flitted about the sitting room. "Tomorrow, if there's a ship with proper accommodations. I cannot abide a long coach ride or one of those leaky packets with rooms the size of wardrobes and no decent quarters for servants."

"How many servants will you be taking?"

"Just Betsy and a footman, since we are near destitute. We'll need lodgings and money for bribes while we are there. Are you certain you can afford it?"

Accounting for himself was as awkward to Michael as taking orders from her, but if he did not offer an explanation, she might grow suspicious about his finances. Most of his wealth was always invested in cargoes, but if he needed money he could acquire it. He did not live extravagantly. He did not gamble, and he again grew bitter thinking about Henry wagering fifteen thousand pounds of Sarah's dowry. Most asuredly, Michael Elliot did not take money from women. If a man could not meet his obligations, he had no business acquiring them.

"You're not having second thoughts about my journey to London, are you, Michael?"

He considered going with her and confronting Henry in her presence. But he'd given his word to Sarah, and he must look into the coal concern in Fife. "No, Mother. I'll send Turnbull around with the details and the money." He headed for the door.

"I thought you were taking lunch with me?"

Michael had lost his appetite for more than food. "Have the cook pack up my share, and you can take it with you on the trip."

"What a remarkable idea. The food on even the best of those ships is ghastly. Do find out about the owner of that townhouse of hers."

Hurt and disheartened, Michael

cursed himself for a silly, sentimental fool. With effort, he shelved his bruised feelings, bid his mother goodbye, and made his way to the Dragoon Inn. He considered going to church, but in his heart he knew even a blessing from the pope couldn't ease the grief that tainted his soul. He'd been born into a den of vipers who could not find their own way out. Duty demanded that he make an effort to redeem the Elliots. He owed it to Hamish Elliot and the grandmother who had tatted lace in a country house in Fife.

His brief experience with his mother and Henry told Michael the practice was futile, but he had to try. One day he'd bring children into the family, and he couldn't bear to think of them paying the price for sins committed by their selfish grandmother and weak uncle.

Relief came with the knowledge that Sarah had agreed to fetch Michael today and a good deed awaited. After his mother's vile company, he planned to sit back in Sarah's carriage and bask in her goodness.

At the corner of Pearson's Close and High Street he spied a familiar figure. Over the swishing of the broom, the streetsweeper said, "The Highland lassie fair scorched you with her hot temper."

Michael ignored the man. The last time he'd seen him, the laborer had been leaning on the lamppost near Sarah's and witnessing her angry tirade. That Michael had deserved her wrath only added to his discomfort. Recalling the moment, he knew he'd been wrong to accuse her, but Henry had sworn that Sarah had approached him with a proposal of marriage.

Unfortunately, Michael had believed him. Or had he merely been seeking a confirmation of his fondest wish — that she hadn't been in love with Henry?

No answer came, and he supposed it was guilt over his own growing affection for Sarah. Whatever the reason, Michael should not have voiced the accusation. He should have known better than to give her an excuse to drive him from her life.

Get out, you bletherin' Elliot!

"Even if you shoe every orphan in Christendom, she's too good for the likes o' the Elliots."

To a man accustomed to commanding

224

others, the insult felt like salt on an open wound. Michael whirled and faced the interfering Cholly. Again, he was struck by the strength and bearing of the man. Gazing into sharp blue eyes that did not fit the soot-stained face, Michael said, "Listen well, you ragged gossipmonger. Slander my name again — or Lady Sarah's — and I'll sweep up the streets with you."

"Then you should call back the Complement. You'll need their help."

A distance of 10 feet separated them, but Michael could feel the man's force of will. "You'd best guard your loose tongue, you doddering old fool."

With a Scottish curse, the street-sweeper tossed off his blanket cape, drew himself up, and brandished the broom as if it were a staff. "Let's make a brawl of it."

Michael reassessed the man. Oh, he could take the older fellow down, but it wouldn't be the one-sided fight he'd assumed. They stood before the tobacconist shop, where a crowd had begun to gather.

"Watch him, lads," the streetsweeper addressed the onlookers. "If this Elliot ponders too long, the poltroon in him will prevail. Cowardice is the way of his clan."

That did it. The anger that had been building in Michael since yesterday burst into full fury. By God, he wanted a fight. Yanking off his hat and cloak and tossing them to a man nearby, he began rolling up his sleeves, all the while glaring into the face of a man who glared back.

A voice in the crowd yelled, "Two o' my quid says Elliot'll be the last one standin'."

"If you *had* two quid, I'd be takin' it," came another voice. "Cholly knows what he's about."

"Take the bugger, my lord."

When they were within arm's length, Cholly swung the broom. Michael caught it in midair. Wrenching it from Cholly's hands proved no easy feat, but Michael's anger raged out of control. He twisted, seeking the better leverage point. Grunting, the streetsweeper did the same. Only the clash of power kept them upright. Quickness had always given Michael the advantage, and he used it to catch his heel in the bend of his opponent's knee. One kick and he'd have the man on his back.

"Here comes Lady Sarah!"

Both men froze. Cholly's fierce gaze flitted to the sound of an approaching horse. Equally apprehensive, Michael looked there, too.

The pause aided the streetsweeper. He pushed Michael back and sneered. "What'll she think about catching you in a common street brawl, Elliot?"

She'd condemn him for a bully, an assessment he could not fault, Michael admitted. But the disastrous events of late had obliterated his good intentions. He looked back just as Cholly disappeared into an alleyway, his broom forgotten in the lane.

"Here's your hat and cloak, my lord," said the man beside him, "although I cannot say you was the victor."

Michael began righting his clothing, but his mind bounced between what Sarah would say and why he'd underestimated a simple streetsweeper.

9

Sarah led her horse into the parting crowd that filled Pearson's Close. In her left hand she clutched the leading reins to another mount. Michael stood head and shoulders above the onlookers. Behind him, the streetsweeper hurried away through the throng, his blanket cape flapping as he left the scene. She had heard the shouts of encouragement from the spectators but no explanation as to what had brought two such different men to blows.

Michael looked up, and his expression was reminiscent of a boy caught raiding the biscuit box.

Inordinately pleased, Sarah said, "I hope I haven't interrupted an important fight?"

"No." He took great care adjusting his cockaded hat. "Only a minor disagreement."

Guffaws sounded from the now-thinning crowd.

She took in his stiff countenance and tightly clenched jaw. "Then I hope I never see you truly angry."

"An excellent way of thinking." He glanced at the old mare. "What have you there?"

At his cockiness, she moved closer and tossed him the reins. "I promised to collect you today for our visit to the cobbler. Since I haven't a carriage, I acquired a fitting mount for you."

The startled expression on his face was worth the trouble she'd encountered in finding the plodding draft horse.

Without the prospect of a brawl to occupy them, the spectators shared unkind remarks about the big brown horse.

"That will be all, gentlemen," Michael announced. "You may take your leave."

They grumbled good-naturedly, but obeyed him all the same. He did not dwell on the accomplishment; Michael Elliot appeared at ease ordering others about.

Walking around the hired mount, he shook his head and laughed without humor. "Your judgment in horses is exceeded only by your taste in prospective husbands."

Except for the keepers of nearby shops, the lane was now empty of onlookers. "If you don't like the mare, you may ride my gelding."

His gaze slid to her knee, which was hooked across the sidesaddle and draped with the folds of her riding skirt. His mood turned stormy.

Sarah waited, silently urging him to rail at her. He'd meddled in her life and toyed with her affections. She wanted a confrontation with him. Relieving him of his pride in Pearson's Close seemed a good place to start.

A moment later, he began to laugh in earnest. His shoulders heaved with the effort, and the exotic feather in his hat danced on air.

She bristled. "What's so funny?"

He dabbed tears from his eyes. "My life of late."

Seeing that her carefully planned scheme was falling short of the mark, that Michael Elliot wasn't at all humiliated, Sarah took a different tack. "Do not expect me to feel sorry for you. You brought it on yourself."

He laughed harder.

"I demand that you stop that this instant!"

Sniffling, his eyes squeezed shut, he continued to chuckle.

Her mount sidestepped. She drew rein and stroked the animal's neck to steady him. "What is wrong with you? Have you gone daft?"

"Quite possibly." He looked skyward, but pointed to the mare. "Where did you find that tragic beast?"

Somewhat mollified, Sarah strove to appear innocent. "You are unhappy with the mount?"

A baleful stare lent elegance to his powerful frame. He drew on his gloves and scratched the horse's ears. "This beast was ancient in George the Second's time."

Satisfaction poured over her until he said, "I'll walk this poor creature to the stables at the inn and fetch my horse. You go along to the cobbler."

The contemptible blighter was dismissing her! "I think you should mount it."

"I think you've had your fun, Sarah."

Not yet ready to end the matter, she guided her horse closer to him. "In future, I think it would be best if you cease addressing me informally."

The undertaker's conveyance sped by them. Over the noise, Michael said, "I'm to call you Lady Sarah?"

Something in his voice warned her that she tread close to dangerous territory, but she could not back down. "Have you an objection to the use of good manners?"

"Not in the least." His tone grew ominous. "But know this, my prank-playing Sarah. I'll gladly address you as a lady when you begin acting like one."

"You wretched Elliot."

He expelled a breath and surveyed the shops on the facing side of the cobblestone street. "You've said that before."

"I'll keep saying it."

"What's this? My overly schooled *Sarah* has run out of inventive insults?"

Not for a very long time. Not when he intruded into her life and thwarted her best intentions. Not when he set her pulse to racing and inspired maidenly dreams. "Fitting words to describe your family have not yet been coined. And I am not *your* Sarah."

"Yes, well . . ." A warning glimmered in his eyes. "Go along, *Sarah*. The cobbler and your band of unfortunates await."

Feeling wretched, Sarah watched him lead the ancient horse away. "You haven't a dot of the good sport in you," she called after him.

He turned and cupped a hand to his ear. "What did you say?"

"I said —" She stopped, hearing the shrillness in her own voice.

Looking as innocent as a lad at prayers, he shook his head. "You'll have to yell louder, Sarah."

She had been shouting, but he'd goaded her into it. Judging from the curious faces peering at her through the shop windows, the townspeople had heard her as well. Regret washed over her.

When he spoke kindly to the beast, she felt worse.

Wheeling her horse around, she joined the stream of carts, sedanchairs, and the ever-present coal wagons in High Street. By the time she reached the Cordiner's Hall in Con's Close, a score of orphans had congregated out front.

Notch broke away from the others. "Lady Sarah!" He ripped off his cap and

233

jammed it under his arm. All excited lad, his eyes grew as big and as bright as brass buttons. "Did you hear about the fight 'tween the general and Cholly? The cheesemonger in High Street said 'twas all bluster and little brawling until you arrived."

Michael and Cholly — their enmity still baffled her. "What were they fighting about?"

"The aleman at the Blue Seal Tavern — that's Reamer Clark — he saw it all, start to end, from no more'n arm's length away. He says Cholly was having the general on over the wicked tongue-lashing you gave him. The general had Cholly on for a foosty gossipmonger and swore to sweep up the streets with him — every lane from Reekit Close to the old castle."

An ambitious threat, she had to admit, and surely colored by a lad's imagination. "So they were only trading insults."

"Not for long. The general charged Cholly, who skippered out of reach. Reamer had it that Cholly moved like a fancy dancing master."

She wondered if Michael would regret setting a bad example for the children.

She'd find out soon, if he were true to his word. The Cordiner's Hall was only a short distance from the Dragoon Inn. If he did not dally, he'd arrive here before the rumors cooled.

"What did you see, my lady?"

"No bruises on either one of them." Come to think of it, she'd seen Cholly only in retreat.

Notch's expression fell. "All the same, I wish I'd been there. Wagers were favoring the general. No decent Scot takes an insult to his clan and keeps goin' on his merry way."

"What exactly did Cholly say?"

"He swore the Elliots were toad-swiving —" He gulped at using the vulgar word. "Uh, he named the Elliots toad-kissing Lowlanders. That's how he sees the Elliots."

An astute opinion, she thought. "It's over and done, Notch."

"Pity that. I could've turned a profit on Cholly."

"You think an old streetsweeper could have bested Michael Elliot? He's a trained soldier."

"Beggin' your pardon, Lady Sarah. Survivin' on the street is trainin' of itself. And Cholly ain't that old."

He certainly looked ancient to Sarah; his back was always bowed and his head perpetually down. But other than his satisfactory tending of the street and his association with Notch and the others, Sarah knew little about Cholly.

"Will the general still come?"

"Of course. Having a row has only detained him."

"Good." Notch jerked his head toward the group of orphans across the street. "They'll be disappointed, don't he come."

The other children milled on the walkway and peered through the windows of the mercantile that flanked Cordiner's Hall. With smudged faces and soiled clothing, the young girls looked like dolls carelessly dropped in the dirt. Every cloak was torn or poorly patched. Breeches were too short; skirts dragged damp and tattered in the lane. Some of the older children had no hats or caps to block the wind; most had runny noses and chafed ears.

The injustice stirred Sarah's ire, and she pledged to call on every tailor from Grassmarket to Farley Close to secure a proper suit of clothes for each of the orphans. For now, shoes would have to do.

She gazed fondly at Notch. "Are all of your friends here?"

He kicked at a pebble. The sole of his shoe flapped loudly. "All but Left Odd. For twelve shillings, we apprenticed him out to the flesher in Niddry's Wynd. 'Twas his idea to go."

More often than not, *apprenticeship* was a polite term for slave labor. Based on the theory that Left Odd would earn a marketable trade, the orphans had scraped together the money to buy the lad a position. They had pooled their savings before in similar ventures, often with disastrous results.

But Sarah had met the poultry flesher. Mr. Geddes quoted the scriptures and hired a carriage for his small family every Sunday afternoon. Just to reassure herself about Left Odd's welfare, Sarah vowed to make the acquaintance of the flesher's wife. "I hope your friend fares well there."

Notch thrust his hands into the patch pockets on his bulky coat. "Left Odd ain't one for highjinks, you know. He'll come away from that fleshery with a journeyman's token." In a quiet, vulnerable voice, he added, "He promised to bring home a dressed-out pheasant for each of us."

Even the promise of a delicacy failed to stir excitement in Notch over the apprenticeship of his friend. She knew that he'd seen too much human misery, experienced too many failures in the effort to rise above poverty and starvation.

"Where did you eat last night?" she asked.

"Cholly got us work picking linings at the trunkmaker. The cook at Moffat's Lodging House had extra drippings. She sold 'em to us for tuppence."

Selling kitchen scraps was a common practice and one of the perquisites fortunate servants enjoyed. That employment was far above squatting in old trunks and ripping out the worn cloth linings. "Surely the food was cold by the time you arrived home" — wherever home was.

"Nay, she had good cinders, too. We built a toasty fire in the mews. Pic acquired a bucket o' milk."

He spoke of the meal as a triumph. For a group of children under twelve, it surely was. At their age, Sarah's greatest dilemma had been deciding which book to read next.

Sarah added the grocers to her list of folks to visit on the orphans' behalf. "You could have come to me for help."

He shrugged, but fierce pride lay beneath the surface of his nonchalance. "We was out of want's reach."

"Still —"

"Leave it be, Lady Sarah. If we lodged up with you, the toffs and that foosty ol' countess'll start up their wicked rumors quicker than you can recite the kings of Scotland."

At his gallantry, tears stung her eyes. The self-proclaimed betters in Edinburgh could learn a lesson in humanity from this decent lad. "Things will be better soon."

He gave her a rare smile. "Aye, we'll be happily circumstanced in Reekit Close."

"Yes, you will."

His mood further brightened, giving her a peek at the playful lad beneath his tough surface. "Is it true that you hired a nag and brought it to the general to ride?"

"The general's coming!" shouted Sally.

Michael rode the fine crimson bay, the

horse she'd admired on his arrival in Edinburgh. Garbed in city clothing, he bore little resemblance to the first officer of the Complement, until she looked into his eyes. There she recognized the determination and arrogance of a man born to lead and bound to exact revenge.

Sarah stiffened her resolve.

Beside him trotted a stable lad dressed in the sedate blue livery of the Dragoon Inn. A workman pushing a scavenger's barrow moved into the lane. The bay sidestepped, then started to rear up, but Michael easily contained the animal.

Notch donned his cap, murmured, "By your leave, my lady." Then he raced toward Michael.

After exchanging greetings with the stable lad, Notch called out, "Welcome, general."

Without sparing Sarah a glance, Michael dismounted and tossed the reins to the liveried lad. Then he conversed at length with Notch, who pointed to the still-milling children.

"But first, General," Notch said, " 'bout that fight you 'n' Cholly had. Did he truly call you a coward after you said he was a decrepit old scunner?"

Michael rested a hand on the boy's shoulder and guided him toward Sarah. "We'll discuss it later. How nice to see you again, *Lady* Sarah."

Good manners dictated that she ignore his sarcasm. "Very nice indeed, sir."

"You had a pleasant morning?"

Good intentions fled. "It was rather boring."

"How can that be, my lady?" asked Notch. "Cholly said you traipsed all over Grassmarket lookin' for the poorest mount to be had."

"We must commend her on the search, Notch," said Michael. "But I believe the MacKenzies are renown for their prowess at selecting any number of *things.*"

The thinly veiled insult spurred Sarah to say, "One of the many outstanding attributes of my clan."

The determination in his eyes turned to lusty promise. "I anticipate discovering them all."

Notch craned his neck to glance up at Michael. "You miffed at her over that jest with the mare?"

"Not miffed."

Knowing Michael meant worse, Sarah looked him boldly in the eyes and smiled.

Misunderstanding, Notch blew out his breath in relief. "Good. Squire Mac-Crumb says he'd take 'er, even if she didn't have all her teeth."

"A man of discerning tastes, this Squire MacCrumb."

"Not that. We cannot abide the thought of him comin' 'round her ladyship. But he's a generous one with his contributions."

Having heard enough, Sarah folded her hands. "Speaking of generous, will you help me? There isn't a mounting block in this lane."

"I will." Notch dashed forward and fell down on all fours beside her mount. "For a penny."

"Notch is earnin' a penny," Pic exclaimed.

The news chirped through the throng of children, and they stared expectantly at Sarah.

Michael stood over the boy. "I'll help her, lad."

Knowing a penny would feed all of the children tonight and understanding that Notch wanted to earn the sum,

242

Sarah sent Michael a pointed look. "I'm certain Notch can do the job. Could you just steady me?"

An instant later, enlightenment gleamed in Michael's eye, and he held out his arm. The muscles felt like steel beneath her fingertips. She gave him all of her weight, which he bore without effort. As she stepped down, she barely tapped Notch's back with her foot.

Michael's expression turned pensive as he watched Notch spring to his feet and dust off his hands.

"Thank you." Sarah gave him a penny.

He tucked it away. "We're ready for the fittin' of those shoes, general."

Still watching Sarah, Michael nodded. "Gather the troops, lad."

Notch dashed across the street, whistling as he went. "Citizens at large! All those here for gettin' brogue-shod, let yourselves be heard."

Squeals and hoots and a deluge of scurrying children were his reply. They surrounded him until Michael marched to his side and drew him away from the others.

He towered over Notch and spoke sharply, but Sarah couldn't make out the words. The lad listened intently, his gaze darting from his friends to the still-closed doors of the hall. Inside, a trio of cobblers awaited. Above the shops was the large meeting room where the Cordiner's Guild gathered to manage their trade.

With a final word of what could only be encouragement, Michael gripped Notch's shoulder. The lad gave a brisk nod, pivoted on his heel, and approached his young friends. Holding up his arms, he whistled loudly. "Quit your squawking and make a line here, starting with Pic and Peg." He pointed to the empty space before him.

Michael went inside the building and returned a moment later with an elderly cobbler. The older girl, Peg, was escorted inside first.

Feeling left out, Sarah asked the stable lad to watch her horse. Gathering the cumbersome train of her riding skirt, she joined Michael inside the establishment.

The heavy smells of oil and leather hung in the close air. In the rear of the shop, apprentices with tacks pressed between their lips wielded hammers and mallets as they plied the trade. Huddled near a lamp, a snaggle-tooth boy threaded a needle to stitch bows onto a pair of silk slippers.

"Peg wants the sturdy boots," Michael said by way of explanation. "But I think the buttoned ones suit her better."

He hadn't considered what Peg's life was like on the street. To him, Peg was a quiet 12-year-old in cast-off clothing. His generosity couldn't be faulted.

"Tell him, Lady Sarah," the girl pleaded. "Them shoes ain't for gatherin' thatch from Bruntsfield."

Sarah picked up one of each of the shoes and compared them. "I agree the buttons are stylish." She handed that one to the cobbler. "But Peg has a need for boots." Catching Michael's gaze, she lifted her brows. "Perhaps we'll choose the button-ups next time for Peg."

He understood. "Then boots it is for Peg."

Sarah took up the post of observer, commenting only when Michael solicited her opinion. He looked at home in his philanthropy, and she wanted to ask him to share his feelings on the day. But how could she and still keep him at a distance? Eventually, the quandary drove her outside.

When Right Odd's time came, he lifted

Sally from his shoulders. Just as he set her feet on the paving stones, she wailed and tried to scramble up his arms. Her tiny fingers clutched him in a death grip, and her cherubic features were pinched with displeasure. The pink shawl Sarah had knitted for the girl only two months ago was already tattered and soiled. The special bond she shared with the burly Odd brothers was born of something stronger than blood. Sarah had asked Notch about it, but he brushed off her query. Loyalty kept him mum on the subject, and she understood. Until Sarah had learned the truth of her birthright, kept secrets had been a rarity among her and her half sisters.

The cobbler's wife emerged from the shop, a stick of candy in her hand. She held it before the fretful girl.

As if burned, Sally jerked and turned her head away.

Right Odd groaned. "She don't take to strangers offerin' up sweets to her. Gently, Sally." He jostled her on his hip. "None's to lay a hand on you."

Sarah cringed inside at the possible reasons for such behavior in the adorable child.

"Give 'er to me," Notch said, holding out his arms. "C'mon Sally, it's just ol' Notch to look after you. Will you bide a wee with me so Odd can get shod with his fine new brogues?"

Her cries turned to hiccups, and she peered cautiously at him.

He further cajoled her with, "We'll be frolickin' in the greensward with our new shoes, won't we now?"

Fat tears rolled down her cheeks, leaving a trail of clean, pink skin.

Waving the riding crop, he said, "The general give me this special tool to keep all the mates in line. But look there." His face contorted in a comic grin, and he waved the crop toward the waiting children. "It's a bunch of scattered Turks they're acting! I'll need someone stout of heart to help me with the lot of 'em. Will you lend a hand, Sally girl?"

She giggled and grabbed for him.

He scooped her up, and with a grunt, perched her on his shoulders. "I knew you be after rescuin' ol' Notch."

She snatched the crop, and squealing with laughter, whacked him on the head.

"Oh-ho, brigands! She's a fearsome taskmaster, our Sally is." With a firm grip on her thighs, he skipped the length of the line, whinnying like a kicked horse all the way. Right Odd hurried inside the hall.

The other children waved at Sally; one eager lad of about nine tried to take the crop. Sally clutched it to her skinny chest and shook her head violently.

Her movement tipped Notch's balance. "Hey, leave off, Patrick," he yelled, bracing his legs. "Let Sally have 'er fun."

Looking like the princess of the ragamuffins, Sally urged Notch on. As they moved down the line of orphans, she dubbed each of them with her magic wand.

Michael came outside and called Notch's name. Taking giant steps and hefting Sally with each one, the lad moved to the door.

"You're next," Michael said. "Then we'll start with the little ones."

"But what about Sally? It's just me and the Odds she'll let handle her. I'll wait."

"You'll go now. We're at the cobbler's disposal." Michael plucked the girl from Notch, but winced at her near-deafening cries. "Look!" he said, holding her at arm's length. "It's a pink horse."

Legs dangling, she stopped in mid-scream and jerked around. "Where?"

"There." He shifted her to his hip and pointed to a dappled gray.

" 'S white," she said, as peevish as could be.

"You know, I think you have me there, Sally. What color is my horse?"

"Red."

They discussed the color and size of every horse passing in the lane, of two dogs tussling over a bone, and even a somberly dressed porter whom Sally dubbed a black beetle.

Right Odd came out wearing black shoes with sturdy wooden buckles. Michael yielded the girl, then approached Sarah in what closely resembled a manly swagger.

"Not altogether a poor effort," he said, "even for a conniving, deceitful Elliot."

He fancied himself good with children, and she had to admit that he was. "I'm sorry for calling you names, but I haven't seen you tripping over your boots to acknowledge me for putting aside our quarrel."

He walked in a circle around her, searching. "Where have you put it?"

He could lend patience to Job. "Do

stop, Michael."

"I will, when gulls bay at the moon." Halting before her, he grew serious. "You address me as Michael, but I cannot address you as Sarah."

"Have you a title other than general?"

"Yes. Viscount Saint Andrews."

Sarah reconsidered her opinion of him and added modesty to his growing list of good character traits. "Truly?"

He looked bewildered. "Nay, I'm actually a room-setter in Cowgate North."

She couldn't help but laugh. "Why keep it to yourself until now?"

"You did not ask."

Feeling as if she'd received a well-deserved setdown, Sarah gave him her best curtsy. "A thousand pardons, Lord Michael."

"Actually, it's recently bestowed."

She remembered that he'd shared luncheon today with Lady Emily and knew the source of his newly bestowed position in society. The conclusion troubled her. Had he thrown in his lot with his mother? Sarah hoped not, for the countess of Glenforth tainted everyone she touched.

As always, Sarah was concerned

about his feelings on the matter. "Are you pleased?"

He shrugged, but she thought he rather liked the idea. "Will you take a seat in Parliament?" His brother hadn't bothered with public service.

"My preference would be to stand for one in the Commons."

He'd chosen the difficult path, facing election among the voting citizens. He also comforted frightened little girls and robbed unsuspecting women of their good judgment. "Will you enjoy the long stay in London during the sessions?"

He looked at her askance. "I haven't won yet."

But he would. She'd stake both of her dowries on that. "Were I given a ballot, I'd cast my vote for you."

"My lady!" The aproned cobbler leaned out the door. "We need your help with the wee ones."

Reluctantly, Sarah left Michael on the walkway. Effortlessly, he always drew her into conversation, and whether the topic proved congenial or controversial, she delighted in the exchanges.

Later, when the youngest lad had been fitted in his new shoes, she was still anticipating the next lively exchange she'd share with Michael.

On that encouraging thought, she walked outside and saw the mare, alone in the street, a sidesaddle strapped onto the animal's concaved back. Sarah's gelding and Michael and all of the other orphans were gone.

Between gales of laughter, the tanner gave her a message from Michael: if she wanted her horse back, she was to follow the crowd to the customs house.

"You infuriating wretch."

Michael ducked just in time. Her gloves whizzed over his head. "Not a boor?" He held up his hands to ward her off. "I thought all Elliots were boors."

"They are, especially when they behave like common thieves."

Standing on the stoop of the partially renovated customs house, Michael coughed to hide a smile. "Will you excuse us, Notch?"

Neither the lad nor his cohorts moved.

Sarah tapped the quirt against her thigh. "Yes, please. I intend to show the high king of the pranksters what harvest his tricks have reaped."

"If you strike me with that crop, I'll

turn you over my knee."

"You'll have to crawl out of your Elliot cave first and drop your club."

Eyes agog, Notch looked from one to the other. "You ain't for beatin' Lady Sarah, are you, general?"

In the absence of the duke of Ross, someone had to take this woman in hand. Michael relished the job. "A lamentable event, Notch, I'm forced to admit."

Grasping Sarah's arm, Michael led her into what would become the library. "Close your mind to her screams, lad, and cover the ears of the younger ones."

The moment the door closed, Sarah's senses sharpened. The musty smell of damp plaster and mildewed wood grew pungent, and the hammering noises from the floors above echoed on the ceiling. Dust sifted to the cluttered floor. Anticipation thrummed through her.

Stepping over rags and broken glass, Michael moved toward her. "I'm surprised that you cry foul when all I did was give you a taste of your own bitters."

He was correct, but she wasn't about to admit it. "You're a heartless Elliot troll, and stop glaring at me. You look just like your grandfather."

"Ah, the Elliot tragedy again. I'd forgotten that you've been a guest at Glenstone Manor."

"A visit I regret."

"Tell me this. Were you suffering from another romantic disappointment when you met Henry?"

She stepped around a dented pail. "Bruised pride did not drive me into your brother's arms."

He plopped down on a keg of nails. "Henry says you kissed him only once. All of the other times he admits to wooing you."

All of the other times? He made her sound forward, and her time with Henry a courtship. Her first impulse was to challenge him, but the subject of Henry always brought trouble between them. Michael's gift of this building and their shared concern for the orphans should form the boundaries of her association with the dangerous and charming younger Elliot son.

She surveyed the windows on the east side of the room. "Do you think shutters or sashes will do for this room?"

"Both, if you intend to protect the

books from rot and fading." He unbuttoned his coat and folded his arms over his chest. "Why were you so eager to wed?"

"Obviously I am not." She moved on to the new shelves in the near wall. "You'll be glad to know that the bookbinder in James Court has contributed four boxes of books for this room."

"Another change of heart? One might call you fickle, Sarah MacKenzie."

"One might take himself off to the fires of hell."

"Or one might find an ally, if she were truthful. How did the betrothal come about?"

She wasn't afraid to tell him, but before she explained herself, he'd have to bare his soul to her. "You want to know what transpired between me and Henry?"

"Every dance, every passionate embrace, every sigh."

None of that had happened. "Will you in exchange tell me your deepest fear?"

His gaze wavered.

She had him on the run, but the chase was short-lived, for he said, "Do you deny proposing to Henry?"

"Unfair." She kicked the pail and sent

255

it clattering across the floor. "You must go first or content yourself with your brother's version of the story."

Cunning settled into his demeanor. "You wouldn't like to hear my suspicions?"

She gazed out the windows. "Keep them to yourself. Ah, there's Rose and Turnbull. Shall we join them outside?"

Michael took her arm and whispered, "You're stubborn, Sarah MacKenzie."

And he was acting on old news. "Astute men are delightful. Stop frowning, or I'll start calling you Hamish Elliot. Wasn't he renown for wearing animal skins and clubbing his prey?" She shook off his arm and yanked open the door.

Easily catching her, he drew her back into the room and slammed the door hard. Plaster rained from the ceiling. "And I suppose the MacKenzies snuggled into loincloths of sheared beaver and sipped their tea from pearly shells?"

His anger was a palpable force; Sarah put a distance between them. "You're predictable."

"You can remedy that by telling me

which Sarah MacKenzie I'm addressing."

She picked her way through piles of sawdust. "I don't know what you mean."

"Then stand still and I'll enlighten you. The Sarah I saw at Cordiner's Hall was a woman brimming with love and hope for a band of ragtag children. She's the one who melts in my arms and kisses me with the sincerity of a lost soul in sight of paradise."

His words poured over her, and her composure faltered.

"But another Sarah lurks behind those bonny blue eyes. Oh, she's equally lovely and as brilliant as an Oxford scholar. She can volley clever ripostes with the skill of the most seasoned wit at court." His gaze slid to her shoulder. "That Sarah breaths fire at the mention of my family's name."

The flame of her anger dwindled. "Then do not mention their name."

"*Their* name? Impossible, for I, too, am cut of the cloth of Clan Elliot. Ponder this, if you will. Suppose I were the enemy of the duke of Ross, and you loved me. Could you disavow your MacKenzie heritage?"

Her attention wavered at the word *love*. But the answer came easily for two reasons. She gave him the one most relevant to the situation. "Yes."

His gaze sharpened. "To which part of the question do you reply, Sarah?"

Quick to ferret out a double meaning, Michael Elliot became a predator, a man prowling after his woman.

Feeling feminine to her toes, Sarah darted away. "To the most important part. And I thought you were going to call me Lady Sarah."

The look in his eyes turned absolutely sinful. "I've changed my mind. I do not wish for you to behave as a lady."

Striving to appear aloof, Sarah presented him her profile. "Oh? How should I behave?"

"With complete abandon."

Her face grew hot, and her heart pounded.

"Without inhibition."

She gulped back apprehension.

"Lacking a speck of scruples."

Anticipation buzzed in her ears.

"I'd have you naked in my bed, Sarah, and acting the wanton."

"No." The word lodged in her throat.

"Yes, well . . ." He turned her around

and pulled her into his arms. When his mouth was a whisper away, he stopped. The invitation in his eyes held her captive.

"You watched me holding Sally today. The look in your eyes made me want to kiss you. Do you recall what you were thinking then?"

Every facet of his rugged good looks moved sharply into focus. On a breathless sigh, the truth spilled from her lips. "Yes."

"Good."

With the gentleness and confidence she'd come to know, he drew her to him and pressed his mouth to hers. She felt engulfed by his powerful form, sheltered and enlivened at once. Manliness, which he possessed in abundance, called up the wanton he thought her to be. His hands explored, his mouth devoured, and as the last thread of her resistance stretched tightly between them, she could not summon a single argument to deny the blossoming love in her heart.

When he drew back, his face revealed an intensity of feeling and purpose that frightened her to her soul. Wishing other clever words were at her disposal, she chose a cowardly retreat. "What were we talking about?"

"As I recall, we were discussing the extent of your wantonness."

The earthy comment triggered the stalwart in her, and she faced him squarely. "I haven't any of that, and you were speaking of hating the MacKenzies and speculating about loving me."

In a lazy perusal, he studied her face and flushed neck. "Only to confuse you."

"Why?"

"Because my dear womanly scholar, when you are befuddled, you forsake your promise to hate me."

Her strength of will roared to life. She knotted her fists. "I have good cause."

"You named the Elliots cave dwellers."

"I do not deny it."

"I heard you, but where is all of that reason and experience you've spent years delving into books to find? Where is the brave Sarah MacKenzie who trots out her brilliance and wit and wears them like badges of honor?"

"I meant the comment in the feudalistic sense. You speak of my misfortune as if it were a sport."

"Sport? *Sport!*" He flung his arms into the air. "It's a damned bloody war you wage."

His anger ignited her own. "It's my damned bloody freedom at stake. I must defend myself."

He flung open the door. "Then I hope you and your freedom live happily ever after."

"Where are you going?"

"To Fife. After bickering with you, I feel like mining coal with my bare hands."

Caught off guard by the heartfelt admission, she followed him into the hall. "When will you return?"

"When you promise to sing hosannahs to my name."

He was shouting, but she knew his anger had waned, for his shoulders were not so rigid and his stiff gait had settled into a familiar swagger.

"You'll be an old man by that time," she shot back.

Without breaking stride, he continued down the hall. On a fake chuckle, he said, "Then I pray you find it in your heart to welcome a doddering graybeard."

Much as she hated herself for it, she

knew she'd miss him. "Then you *are* coming back?"

He turned, his body framed by sunlight and his features thrown into shadow. "Aye. And when I do, I expect you to arrange a meeting between me and your father."

The authority in his voice drew her like flame to oil. "Why?"

"A tiresome question, Sarah, and one I've already addressed. I'll demand the dowry — for myself. *One* of the Elliots must make peace with *one* of the Mac-Kenzies."

Stillness settled over her, and she had difficulty speaking. "Shouldn't you first make peace with me?"

His devilish chuckle echoed in the narrow passageway. "Oh, we'll come to more than that, you and me, if we don't break each other's spirits — or necks — in the process."

"I will not write to my father."

"Then I'll try to find him," Michael said, far too amiably. "And as a reward for the delay, I'll receive a very interesting painting of you."

The nude of Eve. Mary's ultimatum. "If my sister is so wicked, I insist that you bring that painting to me."

"I'll be certain to do that." He doffed his cockaded hat and swept a bow. "Someday." Pivoting sharply, he walked into the sunshine, mounted her gelding, and rode away.

10

After a fortnight in Fife, Michael entered Edinburgh with a passel of problems and a dearth of solutions. As the carriage passed through Queensgate, the busy sounds and ugly smells of the city welcomed him. When a procession of matching sedanchairs halted progress in High Street, he admitted that he'd missed this place. He'd missed the smartly attired gentry walking five paces ahead of practically dressed servants. He missed the church bells pealing the time of day. He missed the bickering between surly shop owners and slow carters.

And he missed Sarah. Thoughts of her greeted his mornings and bid farewell to his days.

A pair of overburdened coal wagons lumbered onto the crossroads. Michael viewed the cargo in a wholly different light. The sojourn in Fife had been more than a survey of the family holdings; it had been a return to the past. In the span of a day, the language of his youth had become as clear as English to his ears.

Only the problems had been foreign. The early decline he'd seen as a lad had settled into a steady plunge toward destruction. Ancient moving machines wasted more coal than they harvested. Rusted barrows worked as sieves in hauling the coal to the surface. Leaky buckets brought scant water to higher ground. Colliers forced to stand to their ankles in frigid water had little heart for the job at hand.

Unhappy miners made for unhappier miners' wives. A bankrupt clergy dispensed sparse blessings for so many who were poor. But there were no orphans among the mining community, and no Sarah MacKenzie. Their last meeting flashed vividly in his mind, and the harmony of their laughter lingered with him.

To his surprise the next time he gazed at her face, her eyes glowed with banked passion, and she languished in the Garden of Eden.

In the newly renovated library of the

customs house, Sarah slid the ladder to the center of the wall of bookshelves. The new mechanism squealed.

"I'll tell the carpenter," Rose said, holding out a stack of leatherbound texts.

Sarah took the last of the 24 volumes of John Rushford's *Old Parliament History* and placed them beside Lord Edward Napier's *Introduction to Basic Science.*

A mix-match of tables and chairs were spaced evenly down the center of the high-ceilinged room. The old world globe occupied a spot by the windows, which stood open to take advantage of the fine spring day. A new globe, naming all of the oceans as well as the continent of New Holland with its infamous Botany Bay, held a place of honor in the upstairs schoolroom. The duchess of Ross had sent the new globe and enough money to buy braziers for every room.

Sarah had sent her stepmother a note of thanks for the gifts, but appreciation was not what Juliet MacKenzie wanted. She had entreated Sarah to send a word of forgiveness to Lachlan MacKenzie.

Sarah could not. Not yet.

"Lady Sarah!" Sally's head and shoulders popped into the window opening. "The general's come home." The girl held up two fingers. "He's got five peoples with him."

"Three people," a male voice below her said.

"Three peoples." She made fists of her tiny hands with only her index fingers showing. "Three peoples coming with the general."

Henry? Sarah ground her teeth. She'd face him eventually, but she first had to come to terms with her feelings for his brother. Just the thought of seeing Michael again put a skip in her step and a smile in her heart.

"Whom has he brought?"

Boyishly dirty hands gripped the sill and Right Odd hoisted Sally higher. When his forehead and nose moved into view, he said, "They're strangers. Country folks, by the look of 'em. And Turnbull."

"Wonder who the other two are?" Rose picked up the empty book box. "Shall I go see?"

"We'll both go. I'm sure Lord Michael has some questions."

Sally and the Odd brother disap-

267

peared from view.

Rose rolled her eyes. "When he sees what you've done 'round here, it'll be more than questions. He'll be praising you till Hogmanay next."

They had made great progress. The boys' dormitory had cots enough for all, with fresh mattresses and old but clean linen. Every room had a lamp and flint-box, and the barrel of oil in the cellar was hardly tapped.

Peg's heavy footfalls sounded in the hall. She called out, "They're steppin' out o' the carriage, my lady."

After dusting off her hands and fluffing out the skirt of her dress, Sarah hurried outside.

Michael spoke to the driver. Turnbull stood beside a man who was handing a woman down from the carriage.

"Lady Sarah," Michael said as he approached. "Please welcome John and Helen Lindsay. They're old friends from Fife."

Past 40, but slender and fit, the couple stood shoulder to shoulder. Both were dressed in well-tailored garments, her dress of blue wool, his suit of parson's brown. Her thick straight hair had turned snowy white too early, giving the appearance that she was the eldest of the couple, but that was deceptive. Her husband was her senior in every way, and she looked very proud to be his wife. She carried an armload of heather.

"How nice to meet you, Lady Sarah. These are for you. The first of the year." She slid her husband a wary glance. " 'Twas kept in a pail of water all the way."

John Lindsay frowned.

Michael said, "John believed it troublesome."

"Thank you." Sarah took the fragrant bundle and buried her nose in it. She thought of home and the Highlands and the family that wasn't really hers. Biting back melancholy, she looked at Michael. His easy manner made her say the first thing that popped into her mind. "Did you think it troublesome?"

"Not in the least. As I told John, to put a smile on a woman's face is worth the bother."

His smile was far too engaging. "Bother?" she said.

" 'Twas no bother," Helen insisted. "And if any man here has a speck remaining of his mother's good teachings, there'll be no more said of bothersome women."

John's attention moved from the high window sills to the cleanly swept paving stones, but his mouth twitched with the urge to laugh.

Michael did laugh. "Come along, friends, and see your new home."

Their home? That was news to Sarah. Catching Michael's gaze, she said, "The Lindsays are orphans?"

Turnbull guffawed. John chuckled. Helen sneezed to cover her mirth. An unsmiling Michael yanked off his gloves and tossed them to Turnbull, who caught them against his chest. Rubbing his bare hands together, he moved close to Sarah and said, "Embarrassing moments will be repaid in kind."

Completely disarmed of a meaningful comment, Sarah spun around and marched straight into Rose, who jumped back.

The air teemed with the fragrance of crushed heather. The smell inspired Sarah to silently vow to keep up her guard.

She handed the flowers to Rose, then changed her mind. "No. Wait. I'll put them in water. Michael will introduce you to the Lindsays."

As Michael watched her leave, he thought he might burst with pleasure. She brought out the meanest swain in him. She also inspired him to gallantry, which he suspected he needed just now. One thought was foremost in his mind: she had missed him and it befuddled her to clumsiness.

Hallelujah!

"Hell and botched bannocks!" Sarah cursed. Her grip tightened on the shears, and with purpose, she clipped the ends of the heather stalks.

Like a quick cat after a slow mouse, Michael Elliot pounced on her every word. But if he planned to extend his overbearing nature one step more, she'd make him sorry for it.

With a patient hand that belied her roiling emotions, she arranged part of the heather in a footed crystal vase.

Rose came into the room. "I showed them to the large apartments upstairs. The one that sits opposite the mews."

"Why did he bring them here?"

"They wanted to come to Auld Reekie. Their son's a chairmaker to the carpenter's guild. The daughter-in-law is expecting their first grandchild. Helen's sure it'll be a lass."

"You became acquainted quickly," Sarah said.

"Helen's country folk and as nice as any Scot back home in Tain. Lord Michael went on like they were coming here to live."

Sarah had been so involved in trading quips with Michael Elliot, she'd lost the opportunity to ask him why the Lindsays were here. But broaching the subject in their presence would have been rude.

"They are staying," Sarah admitted.

"Why?"

"I do not know, but I intend to find out."

Sarah found Michael alone in the library, examining the new bookshelves.

"A well-conceived room, Sarah."

"Thank you."

"You changed the bookbinder's mind."

"What?"

"You said he had promised only a few boxes of books. There's more books here than that."

"There's more than one bookbinder in Edinburgh. How do you know the Lindsays?"

"I was raised in Fife, which is where

they're from."

"Who are they exactly?"

"John is a wheelwright by trade, but in the town of Pittenweem they say he's a better father. Helen mothers even the goslings. They'll look after the orphans."

Sarah had planned to do that; the orphanage was her dream. But Michael held the purse strings, and from the finality in his voice, he'd made up his mind to limit Sarah's involvement.

She must convince him otherwise. "You'll still need me to teach the classes and . . . and dozens of other things." Fear and urgency set her to examining her fingernails.

He rested his hip on the edge of a table and watched. "The Lindsays will live here with the orphans, who need a woman to clean and prepare their food. She'll tend the children's cuts and bruises. The Lindsays will help wash their hair and dry their tears."

Sarah had spoken those words to Mayor Fordyce over dinner at the Dragoon Inn. Michael had remembered her speech. She felt complimented to her shoe buttons.

"Helen will turn their nightmares to

sweet dreams, and you will fill their minds with knowledge and defend them to the death."

"Aye, with all my strength."

"Because you could have been one of them, or because you are one of them. Which is it?"

Today his charm was in short supply. "What's that supposed to mean?"

He patted the table surface beside him in invitation for her to sit down. "You come from a family that makes a farce of Hanoverian loyalty, yet you do not write to them and they do not visit you."

She strolled across the room and made a show of taking the seat farthest from him. "They have their own concerns."

"I think you wanted to wed Henry so you could live in Edinburgh."

"Are we back to that?"

"You feel a part of Auld Reekie because you were born here."

In some aspects, most particularly her association with the orphanage, Sarah did feel a sense of belonging in Edinburgh. But she hadn't yet felt comfortable enough in the city to visit her mother's grave.

But the fact that he tried to second-guess her moved Sarah to stubbornness. "That's an absurd reason. I could have come here on my own."

"But you did not know that at the time. I suspect you are braver now than you were in your father's house, and much braver since your arrival here."

Whether he was correct or not, Sarah was here to stay. "I've managed in Edinburgh."

"Precisely my point, and it thrills you overmuch. You did not expect to live here as an unmarried woman."

Thrilled her overmuch? How dare he? "I assure you, vanity had nothing to do with it."

"Agreed. Rather you are proud of your accomplishments. It's as plain as is the summer sky. Now tell me why this building has a *slate* roof."

Moving the conversation suited her just fine. "I had no choice. For fear of another great fire, the dean of guilds has made masonry roofs a requirement. 'Twas costly."

Michael didn't miss her attempt to switch topics. He anticipated the merry conversation to come.

"Don't you care how much it cost?"

Pushing to his feet, he began to inch

closer to her. "Did you squander money?"

"Never have I wasted a shilling."

"Did you find the best price for the best work?"

She glanced at the door.

He examined the standing lamp.

Evidently satisfied that he would keep a distance, she settled again in the chair. "I asked three craftsman to make offers unbeknownst to one another."

He had known what her answer would be, but he wanted to see that pride again. Moving closer, he passed the fireplace. A sieve for turning tree pulp to paper rested beside the hearth to dry. He stopped to spin the new world globe. "Which one did you hire?"

"The one in the middle."

"Well done." With his index finger, he touched India. "What occurred while I was away?"

"We had some trouble with the flesher who apprenticed Left Odd. I spoke to the magistrate, who fined Mr. Geddes — the flesher — and brought the lad back."

He paused at a side table that held a box of cork writing sticks and a candle for burning them. "He was cruel to the lad?"

"Aye." The need to find an exit forgotten, she shifted in the chair. "Geddes provided no cot for Odd, and gave him the spoiled food to eat."

Four short steps brought Michael to the table where she sat. "How is he now?"

"Unharmed, save his taste for fowl."

"Fleshing poultry no longer suits him?"

"I doubt it ever did. He's actually a blessing to his brother. They share the task of raising Sally."

Michael remembered his own trying time with the girl at Cordiner's Hall. "A task and then some."

Sarah stood, glanced at the door, and realized her escape was blocked.

Michael took out the pouch of his favorite candy and offered it to her. As she approached, he said, "Is that why Notch and the others were living on the streets? Because apprentices are often mistreated?"

"Yes." With her fingertips, she delved into the bag. "Charges must be brought against the craftsmen who take advantage of apprenticeships. They'll continue to mistreat the children if they are not made to answer for it."

Michael noticed that her injured thumb had healed without a scar. "I'll visit the guildmasters and insist that they govern their own."

"I had planned to do that." She popped the candy into her mouth and licked the excess sugar from her fingertips.

At her innocently provocative gesture, Michael's mouth began to water. "They cannot all become wheelwrights under John Lindsay's tutelage."

"I doubt Sally has the hands for it." Sarcasm flavored her words.

Mockery fueled his. "Someone had hands for finding those thistles you ate for breakfast."

Her head snapped up, and contrariness flickered in her eyes. "You're overbearing."

He took another sweet from the bag. "You're just underprepared for a man who befuddles you."

Sarah fumed. In the absence of a middle ground, her every answer was either right or wrong with no room for error, especially on personal topics, which formed the core of his interest. He'd cut off her most convenient escape route, but she would not bring attention to it. She recognized his ploy. Now she must combat it. "I am not befuddled. How are the coal mines?"

"Most of them sit idle because of the export tax and other things."

She took the easy reprieve. "What will you do?"

"To make the mines solvent, a tidy sum must be invested in new equipment and the building of larger transport ships."

"You'd still have to pay the tax, which is inordinately high."

"But moving the coal will become more efficient. Added to that, the holds of the ships will accommodate more coal at a greater profit, and fewer men will be required to move it."

His problem-solving abilities boded well for the orphans he had agreed to tutor. Later, she would remind him of his promise to teach a class in world history. Now she was interested in expressing her own opinion. "Parliament should make better laws. The rich should shoulder more of the burdens."

"One battle at a time, Sarah. Do not think the coalmasters are above exploiting their own labor."

"Some are of the opinion that a good and laborious collier can earn eighteen shillings a week."

"How do you know that?"

Thoughts of escaping the room fled; Sarah had the upper hand. "I took supper at Trotter's once, and the gentlemen in the next salon spoke loudly on the subject all evening."

He toyed with the pouch of candy, but his mind was elsewhere. "When did you dine there?"

At his too-casual tone, she grew careful. "In happier times."

"Before you met the Elliots."

"After I should have known better."

"Henry took you there prior to the betrothal."

"Yes."

"And you spent the evening listening to the conversation of others?"

"Yes. Your brother's ability to discourse on more important matters leaves much to be desired."

"Then why did you agree to wed him?"

Checkmate, he could have said, so quickly did her anger flare. Discussing Henry was not on her agenda for today; financial matters concerning the orphanage demanded all of her attention.

He was surprised when she asked, "What will you do about the mines and where will you look for the financing?"

"I haven't decided."

He also wasn't willing to reveal the source for financing the modernization of the Elliot estate. Like most men, he probably thought her incapable of grasping the subject.

Hoping for the best, she said, "I may have underestimated what the orphanage will need. The roof was an unexpected expense, and the grocers' contribution was a sorry one."

"Helen admired the greensward across the way. She talked of planting a garden there."

"So did I, but the owner also admires his property. Only a crop of tobacco will meet his price, and land farther afield from the customs house is impractical."

"We'll find a spot. Did you write to your father?"

She stood and gave him her best "move aside" glare, but the look in his eyes said he knew the answer.

Mortification gripped her. Mary had followed through on her promise. "Where is the painting?"

"In a private place."

Sarah, naked for him to see. No, not Sarah, just her face on the body of an unclothed woman. Still, the implication staggered her sense of morality. "You cannot consider it yours."

His gaze turned hungry. "Oh, but I can. Mary sent it expressly to me — at no small expense to herself. A guard, in the person of the earl of Wiltshire, accompanied it. He returned to London as soon as I arrived to take possession of the gift."

"Has he seen it? Has anyone else seen it?"

"I'm not so modern as to allow that, Sarah MacKenzie."

She did feel provincial, but she was also curious. Believing that he had no desire to display it before others, Sarah relaxed. "Does it look like me?"

"The freckles are puzzling, consider-ing where they are."

"No," was all she could manage.

"No?" He said coyly. "Would that be 'no,' you don't have freckles, or 'no,' Mary wouldn't be so wicked?"

She felt as if she were facing an un-repentant orphan. Speaking slowly and concisely, she asked, "Did she paint freckles on me?"

"Yes."

"I'll kill her."

"I'm sure you will, especially after you see the scar."

Sarah pounded the table top. "Mary also gave me a scar?"

"A rather intriguing one." He stepped close and touched her temple. "The mark begins here." His index finger drifted down her cheek and jaw to the sensitive skin above her collar bone. "It continues . . ."

She slapped her hand over his to halt its lustful journey. "To where? Where does it end?"

Mock mortification lent him a rakish air. "Only a husband would say the words to a wife."

"The devil with tender sensibilities," she spat. "To where does the scar extend?"

He shook his head slowly and in reproach. "The tail of the mark is shamelessly placed, and I wouldn't dare name specific body parts to a maiden."

Vengeful anger filled her. "I'll shout every one of her secrets from atop the bastions of Tain."

"Not from London Bridge? Her detractors are there."

But the ghastly portrait was here in

Edinburgh. "You will give me the painting."

"Only after I've ascertained if the replacement in my bed is authentic."

She'd get the painting, even if she had to don a robber's clothing and steal into the Dragoon Inn. "Do you sleep with a painting?"

"Only when I'm deprived of the original."

"Only an Elliot would make such a vulgar statement."

"Yes, well . . ." His lips pursed in an overdone and unconvincing apology. "As long as you stand me apart for another's doing, you see me through narrow eyes. At that insulting treatment, even a villain will cry foul. I'm no villain, Sarah."

His weak based logic begged for a challenge, and she was happy to offer it. "In addition to the wickedness of Mary MacKenzie, we stand at odds on a matter of great import to me."

"Whether or not my family should have your dowry."

"Aye."

"Yet you have not asked my opinion."

"Your opinion?" She laughed. "You obviously believe it belongs to them."

"No. I think it belongs to your husband."

Her independent nature rebelled. "It belongs to me! Lachlan MacKenzie knew that I would not waste the money. That is why he entrusted it to me."

Michael was not convinced; she could see the disagreement in his eyes. Sarah braced herself for the argument to come.

"Your father wisely doubted both my brother's ability to husband you and your faculties to see that he was a poor choice."

Had Lachlan? Probably, she had to admit. But that did not exonerate Michael for demanding Sarah's dowry at their first meeting. "If you oppose your family, then why concern yourself with a woman they obviously despise?"

His remarkably pointed look made her blush.

"Well done, Sarah MacKenzie," he said with too much drama. "I feared your powers of observation had taken a holiday. I can see they have not."

Clever missed the mark; Michael Elliot could twist a death threat into innuendo. But he had made the mistake of disparaging the MacKenzies.

Sarah fell back on the argument she'd prepared. "Take your approval and give it to the French. You couldn't see a dung wagon even if it were beneath your Elliot nose."

Her plan worked, and he looked wonderfully befuddled for it.

At length, he said, "Why does it occur to me that our quarrel has little to do with Henry Elliot or your dowry?"

"Because you are a man, and as such you think your beliefs are sacrament. Your kind looks for enemies, and you strike battles in the name of bruised pride."

"At least men do not make war over an invitation misplaced. Nor do we condemn *our kind* overlong for a sharp word spoken when tempers are high."

Twisting a conversation fell short of the mark; he'd braided that reply, and all of her responses favored his convictions. "You make women sound shallow of mind."

"Most are, for they have never been privy to the greater issues."

"Matters like war and capture and weapons of destruction?"

His honor righteously engaged, he

grew aggressive. "Might prevails in this world."

"A world you men have governed poorly and over squabbles."

"Squabbles?" He was so distraught, he began walking in an ever-closing circle. "Oh, I'd say the loss of the American colonies was more than a squabble."

So, he thought to win with one of his "greater issues." Sarah jumped into the fray. "Not at the start."

"It was about the breaking of the law."

"A law with its genesis in a squabble."

"Laws must be made."

"Made fairly."

He frowned and shook his head, as if to clear it. "Do you believe we should have let the colonies go?"

"I believe we should have let them *grow*."

"Grow? What logic is that?"

She almost said "simple logic," but knew what he'd make of that. "They are our seeds. If we tend them they will make nothing new of themselves. They will be as us in another time and place and our squabbles will become their quarrels."

"They will squabble among themselves, just as the Highland Scots do."

He knew the remark was unfair, but before he could speak, she said, "Perhaps. But perhaps not. What if we treated them with respect? If the smallest part of what I've read is true about the strength and ability of colonial females, my gender will bring another voice to the squabbles of colonial men."

"I pray my American brethren are up to the task."

"Mock me while you can, Michael Elliot. Your gender is in decline."

He laughed, but affection fueled his mirth. "I think I should surrender now."

She pounced on his retreat. "Agreed, and for spoils, I'll demand the money to buy a team of horses and a wagon for the orphanage."

"Why?"

"A wheelwright, which you claim John Lindsay is, and his apprentices need a wagon."

"The wagon is not a necessary tool to make the wheel."

The finality in his voice sparked her ire. The arrogant swine. How dare he come here, boast of having that obscene painting, and not even try to kiss her? He'd touched her with easy familiarity when describing that scar on the portrait, but his seduction had stopped with a touch. What lovers' game did he play now?

Having no answer, she took the long path to the door and silently wagered her new quills that he'd demand to know where she was going.

"Where are you going?"

She smiled broadly, rewarding herself because he couldn't see her face. "To watch the laundry dry."

"Sarah."

The entreaty in his voice was also expected. Now he would play the apologetic swain; then he would try to kiss her.

She opened the door.

"Sarah!"

Just as she predicted, his commanding nature took the fore. He was just like other men she'd allowed to court her. Once they'd exhausted their cache of sweet words, they resorted to domination.

Braced for a boring demonstration of male power, Sarah sighed. If he demanded that she explain herself, she'd throw something at him.

Turning to face him, she said, "You bellowed, Lord Michael?"

"Where do you think you're going?"

The flintbox hit Michael squarely in the chest, but he hardly noticed. The fire in Sarah MacKenzie's eyes held him captive. This Highland lass had spirit to spare, and his hands itched to harness her excitement and keep it for his own.

If we tend them, they will make nothing new of themselves.

Watching her stand proudly and fearlessly before him, Michael grasped the meaning behind her statement. Love for humankind was another of the many heartfelt virtues of Sarah MacKenzie. He wanted to know them all. But first, he must give her room to move about, and most importantly, he must respect her. So that ruled out any attempt to do what he really wanted to do: kiss her senseless and feel her surrender in his arms.

Overruling his base desires, he elected truthfulness. "I've angered you." But it wasn't her wrath that he feared. Disappointing her troubled him more. "Will you please tell me why?"

"No." Her gaze slid to the fallen flintbox. "Not today."

In a rustling of petticoats and pride,

she left the room.

Give her to the count of ten to ponder an answer, and you'll rue ever asking the question.

Michael understood another of Henry's assessments of Sarah. But in this instance, one man's displeasure was another's joy.

He picked up the flintbox and examined the heavy scrollwork, but his thoughts stayed fixed on her. She hadn't said "never" in response to his question; she'd said "not today," indicating that she would in the future reveal her feelings and explain what he'd said that riled her so.

A future. It sounded sweet to him. A life spent with Sarah MacKenzie promised extraordinary excitement. He imagined her passing on that courage and intelligence to the daughters she would give him. He pondered that happy dream until the silver box grew warm in his hands.

"Lord Michael?"

She appeared in the doorway and her smile boded disaster.

"Yes?"

"A footman just brought a message for you from the countess of Glenforth."

Her smile turned spiteful. "She's re-turned from London and commands you to dine with her tonight."

Tender thoughts of a happy life with Sarah MacKenzie fled, replaced by dread over the evening to come. Unless Sarah had colored the message.

"I doubt she truly commanded me."

"Rose took the message straight from your mother's footman, who left similar instructions with the doorman at the Dragoon Inn."

"Who told you the footman had been to the inn?"

"Notch, who heard it from your friend Cholly, who was conversing with the doorman at the time. Cholly questioned your mother's servant. The lad said the countess was fairly chirping with good humor."

"What will you do tonight?"

She gave him another of her superior smiles. "Womanly things, of course."

11

Hours later, dressed in the drab and prickly clothing of a scrubmaid, Sarah moved cautiously up the back stairs of the Dragoon Inn. A wall lantern in a rusted sconce provided faint light, but for safety's sake, she extinguished it.

Darkness settled around her, and fear rippled in her breast.

The opened door above led to the well-lit second story and Michael's room. As she made her way there, the stairs squeaked loudly, grating on her already frayed nerves.

Why hadn't she worn slippers?

On that thought, sick laughter threatened to burst from her. She had schemed to play the thief tonight. She'd borrowed clothing and planned the crime. She'd gone so far as to allow the children to conspire with her, and all she could think about at this crucial juncture was her poor choice of footwear.

Conjure up the rewards, Notch had advised her. *Dwell too long on the trouble to be had, and you'll find yourself in it.* Rather than easing her, his remembered advice brought a new wave of guilt.

Then she envisioned Mary's painting and took heart.

Achieving the last step, she spied Notch, who made an admirable attempt at looking busy polishing the oaken bannister with his knitted cap. He even whistled a popular tune about the trials of a heartbroken titled lady and her charming but penniless common beau.

Seeing Sarah, Notch winked.

A door opened and slammed shut. The lad froze and shot her a warning glance. Footsteps sounded, but from her vantage point, Sarah couldn't see who trod the hallway above. When Notch turned toward the sound of the footfalls, Sarah paused, one boot braced on the next step, both hands shaking in terror.

Desperation had driven her here. Mary's obscene painting was the cause. Had Michael done the proper thing and yielded the painting, Sarah wouldn't have been forced to thievery on the eve of her birthday. She'd be safe at home, her conscience clear, her thoughts dedicated to how she would celebrate tomorrow. She prayed it did not find her in Tolbooth Prison.

Scars and freckles — Sarah falsely depicted for the world to see. She cringed at the thought.

A loud belch from beyond the door set her knees to knocking. She felt like a winded fox trying to elude a pack of fresh hounds.

Michael had left the inn at eight o'clock, an hour ago. By now, he would be taking the first course of his meal with the countess.

The plan to go immediately into his room had been foiled by a slow Turnbull. Not until moments ago had the valet descended the stairs for his evening meal and customary game of whist with the inn's baker. William was stationed on the landing of the front steps to keep watch in case Michael returned unexpectedly. Under the guise of learning to make a stew, Peg had stationed herself in the kitchen.

A drunken guest staggered into view, his waistcoat buttoned crookedly and his wig askew. Sarah dashed behind the open door and flattened herself against the wall. Through her narrow line of vision, between the door and the jamb, she watched the man weave his way to the main steps where Notch stood.

The smell of fresh wax and old plaster assaulted her nose.

Glancing at Notch, the man came to a wobbly stop. "What's yer business here, rogue?" he demanded, his speech slurred from too much ale. "You look like a lad o' the streets."

Sarah's heart pounded. From the landing of the front steps, she heard young William curse.

Would Notch challenge the man?

Please, no, she silently begged.

"Pitchin' in to help, m'lord," Notch said, rubbing more furiously at his task.

"You look like a cutpurse to me."

"Oh, no, m'lord. I'm too proud to beg and too dumb to steal. An' have a care on those steps. The railing's as old as Robert the Bruce."

Satisfied, the drunken fellow started down the steps. With a quick wave of his hand, Notch urged Sarah to hurry.

Tied beneath the borrowed wool dress

was a pocket apron filled with the tools she'd need to prize the canvas from the frame. She'd seen Mary assemble hundreds of canvases; destroying one should be easy. She'd also brought flint, steel, and kindling.

Pressing the bulky pockets to her thighs, she hurried from the stairwell and followed Notch to the door of Michael's rented room.

"Be quick, my lady," Notch whispered, opening the door for her. "Two knocks, an' someone's comin'. One knock, an' it's the general himself."

So scared she could barely breath, Sarah said, "If he comes, you're to hide yourself. I won't have you getting in trouble over me."

"As if you ain't faced a devil or two for us."

"I mean it, Notch."

"You stand here grousing much longer, and you'll be caught for certain. I ask you again, my lady. Won't you let me lift whatever it is you're wantin' from in there?"

He and Pic hadn't questioned her reasons for this excursion into theft. "No."

"Then be quick and quiet about it." He pushed her inside. "An' don't break anything or the maids'll suffer for it."

Feeling more alone than ever before, Sarah slipped inside Michael's room.

Having finished the fish course, Michael put down his knife and fork and wiped his mouth. "Now will you tell me what has made you so happy?"

His mother twittered like a maiden at court, setting the diamonds in her earbobs to twinkling and bringing a smile to the face of the footman who stood behind her.

"Not until after the beef," she playfully chastised Michael. "Good tidings before the beef can bring on bad humors. No such occurrence will spoil our evening."

Resigned to the wait, Michael nodded to the butler to take his plate and refill his wineglass. As the servant poured, Michael tried to anticipate the favorable news his mother had to share. Without doubt it involved Henry, for her first-born son was her foremost concern. But tonight she was the merry mother he'd always imagined her to be. Michael intended to enjoy it.

"You force me to guessing games, Mother. I predict Henry has won enough at the gaming tables to set himself free."

She fairly cooed with delight. "No, but that may not be necessary."

If not at cards or dice, from where had Henry received a windfall?

Even though the servant remained close by, Lady Emily rang the bell to summon him. When he appeared beside her, she told him to serve the beef.

Michael rejoiced; the sooner the meal was concluded, the sooner he'd learn the source of his mother's happiness. She had yet to ask him a single question about himself or what had occurred during her absence. Most odd, she had not once mentioned money, or rather, the lack of it, which usually formed the basis of her conversation.

But all in all, he had to admit that the evening was a definite improvement over their past meetings.

When the plate of beef collops was set before him, he speared one of the shilling-sized morsels and found it tender and juicy. Leeks and carrots swam in the thick brown sauce. Michael thought it the best meal he'd eaten since leaving India, where curried mutton and rice dominated every menu, even among the English.

The lacquered case clock in the corner chimed the time — half past eight. The mechanical noise brought to mind Sarah's comment about the quiet dinner she'd spent with Henry at Trotter's Club.

Jealousy stabbed him. On the heels of the fierce envy came the inevitable and troubling question: why had she agreed to the betrothal? Although she skillfully avoided the question, Michael suspected he'd been correct in assuming she wanted to move to Edinburgh, and a marriage to Henry provided the means.

Many aspects of Sarah MacKenzie left Michael mired in confusion. Comfort came with the knowledge that he had plenty of time to gain the answers. She cared for him, of that he had no doubt, and had they met under ordinary circumstances, their courtship would have taken a different, smoother path. *Enough of dreams*, his practical nature commanded. Managing the present and coming to understand the woman across from him must be his primary concern.

Silence, save the wielding of knife and fork, pervaded the room.

Were all of the meals at Glenstone Manor eaten in this fashion? Probably so, for his mother was not inclined to converse, a custom she had obviously passed on to the family's heir. The quiet unsettled Michael. What better time and place, he wondered, to foster familial camaraderie than at the simple ritual of breaking bread? It was almost a crime against human nature to ignore the opportunity at hand.

He tasted the onions and carrots and found them perfectly cooked. The buttered scones were crusty, the bitter orange marmalade a welcome delight he remembered from childhood. But the need to communicate overwhelmed him. "My compliments to your chef, Mother."

She nodded and lifted her eyebrows in agreement. Around a mouthful, she murmured, "Henry brought him over from Paris five years ago. The lord provost and the dean of guilds couldn't wait to get themselves to France and follow Henry's lead."

Her preference for her older son was expected. Henry spoke for the family.

Henry provided for her. Michael couldn't help imagining how dissimilar this evening would be had Henry contracted with someone other than Sarah MacKenzie. But since he could find no logic in the betrothal, he satisfied himself with the knowledge that a wedding between Henry and Sarah would never come to pass.

Michael wanted her for honest reasons, and if he ever set eyes on the elusive duke of Ross, he intended to tell him that and much more.

The annoying silence grew.

Yet Michael hadn't come here for lively conversation. For that, he would seek out Sarah. He filled the void by recalling her impassioned discourse this afternoon on the failings of man. Henry named her a thinker, and Michael completely agreed.

He tried to picture Henry and Sarah together, but another wave of jealousy colored the image. He saw Henry, standing at the head of the table, sharpened knives in hand, carving a holiday goose. He saw Sarah, sitting at the opposite end of the table, holding forth on the plight of the orphans in Reekit Close.

In Michael's imaginings, Henry tried to close his ears to her unsolicited sermon on Christian duty. He wasn't up to the task. The knife ripped through the bird, not in neat head-of-the-family–quality slices, but in ragged hunks unfit for the servant's table in a noble-man's house.

Sarah announced that she was putting up Notch for Cambridge.

Henry growled.

Sarah intended to have a presentation ball for the maiden orphan, Peg.

His patience as ragged as the meat before him, Henry plunged both of the blades into the already mangled car-cass, and ran screaming from the room, the house, and his vows to Sarah.

"What humors you?" his mother asked.

Yanking himself away from the illu-sion, Michael scratched his nose to mask his mirth. "I was thinking of something John Lindsay said."

"Who is John Lindsay? A friend from India?"

Sweet good fortune. She at last broached a topic germane to Michael's life. "John's a wheelwright from Fife. I visited there while you were in London."

"The estate is in good order?" she asked. "The servants haven't turned laggardly, have they?"

Michael sat taller in his chair. "No. The house itself is well kept. The Lindsays came with me to Edinburgh. They'll live at the orphanage and help out with the children."

She frowned, but past meetings considered, her displeasure was comparatively small. "I want nothing to do with that place. And I must warn you, if you put the Elliot name on the building, I'll send a workman to remove any trace of it."

On second thought, Michael would name the place Sarah's House. Yes, that was fitting. The idea had been hers; she should receive the recognition. He'd rather not have his mother involved in the project; he faced too many other obstacles in his quest for Sarah's heart. What would she say when he told her about the name? He wouldn't. After a visit to the stonemason, he'd surprie her instead.

"Michael, I do hope you went to Saint Andrews and paid the family's respects."

He certainly hadn't surveyed the estates that had come with his title; there were none. But his mother wasn't to blame; the estate hadn't come from the Fletchers.

Michael dusted crumbs from his hands. "I saw the mines while I was there. It'll take a tidy sum, but once the improvements have been made, we can be assured that the coal concerns will turn a profit for at least a decade. New equipment —"

"Go to London and discuss it with Henry. He'll be the one to make any decisions. In all events, we shouldn't decide business matters at table. We're not a merchant family, you know."

He felt like a lad, given a set-down for a drastic blunder such as breaking wind in mixed company or eating with his hands. He would not let the insult pass. Not tonight. "What purpose does it serve to disparage the merchant class, Mother? I'll wager their accounts are solvent, whereas the Elliots' are not."

"Ours will be, too," she said, breezing over his reply. "I must return to London in a week or so." She pushed her empty plate away. "Perhaps you would care to accompany me?"

The offer to travel with her pleased

him, but he wasn't about to leave Sarah again so soon. He was still unsettled that his mother didn't appreciate his efforts on behalf of the family.

"Thank you, but I cannot. Another time perhaps. Did Henry send you home to Edinburgh?"

"Righteousness, no. Henry enjoyed my visits. I hadn't the money to stay longer. And I have arrangements to make."

"Arrangements for what?"

"For the concert I'm sponsoring in July."

"A concert. How interesting."

She rang the bell. When the butler stepped forward, she held out her glass for more wine. "You may serve the dessert now."

"None for me." Michael strummed his fingers on the arm of his chair.

"No? Well, Henry has the veriest sweet tooth. I brought him a box of marzipan, from that confectioner in Binderstock Row, and he was so thrilled you would have thought I'd bought him a dukedom." She laughed with glee. "He could go on about nothing else for days. I insisted that he have a new suit of clothes. Yes, we indeed got along very well."

It was almost as if she were trying to convince Michael. Odd, since she'd never given him reason to doubt the closeness of her relationship with the family heir. At least Michael knew where she'd spent the money he'd given her.

She had yet to ask about Sarah Mac-Kenzie, which surprised him. "Then Henry is prospering at the gaming tables?"

Humor fled and her lips formed a thin line. "Luck has forsaken him, I fear."

An eerie feeling came over Michael. "But you said you had good news. Have you located the duke of Ross?"

"Who can find him?" In exasperation, she flipped her wrist, sending the fork sailing over her shoulder. The footman snatched it up and handed her another.

Examining the tines, she continued, "Henry's solicitor sent a man first to Tain and then to Kinbairn Castle, the duke's estate in the western Highlands. His grace is nowhere about."

"Perhaps he was simply unavailable to the solicitor's man?"

"No, the man asked all of the important people, even the duke's adversaries. Lord Lachlan hasn't been seen in either place in months. He probably has a mistress somewhere, although he certainly keeps her a secret."

"How long will Henry continue to look for him?"

She gave Michael a smug smile that he did not understand. "As long as it takes, I'm sure. Henry has the matter in hand. We're not to trouble ourselves over the poor manners of the Mac-Kenzies."

Michael let the insult pass. For now, he was curious about the source of his mother's generous mood. "Am I finally to hear your good news, Mother?"

"Certainly." She paused while the butler set a dish of toasted custard before her. Spoon in hand, she finished with, "It concerns you, Michael."

She couldn't possibly have followed through on her promise to find him a wife. Could she?

The food in his stomach instantly turned to rocks.

"Stop frowning, Michael. It's wonderful news. I met the most interesting young woman in London."

Fighting a groan, he prayed his suspicions were wrong. "How fortunate for you, Mother. Who is she?"

"Do you know, I cannot recall her name. Lady Anne? No, that's not it. Hers was Scottish." She flapped her hand. "Not that her name is that important to what has happened. She saved my purse from a thief."

Michael relaxed a little. "A noblewoman accosted a street thief on your behalf and you cannot remember her name?"

"Of course she didn't fetch it herself, and I'm dreadful with names. I'm sure her footman did the recovering. She simply had the good grace to return my purse to me. Oh, Michael, I despair that you've been away from home too long. How will you ever make it in society?"

The clock chimed the hour of nine. Time crept to a snail's pace. Would she never get to the point so he could get back to the Dragoon Inn and admire that portrait of Sarah?

"You must have a long talk with Henry, and don't be shy about asking him how to behave. Pride goest not before a fall in the House of Elliot."

"Did my father say that?"

"No. I did. It's one of the many aspects of culture I brought to this family. I cannot abide poor manners and disorder. Your father knew that and behaved accordingly."

By taking a residence elsewhere, Michael suspected. On that thought, he reminded himself of his vow to treat his mother kindly, especially since he now doubted she had gone shopping for a wife for him.

She dropped her spoon into the empty custard dish. The butler snatched it up and refilled both of their wineglasses.

"Have you managed to set that MacKenzie woman up in a residence?"

If she knew how much he wanted Sarah MacKenzie, she'd banish him from Glenforth Manor and strip him of his newly bestowed title. But the loss was minor when compared to a life spent without Sarah MacKenzie.

Hiding the delight the subject brought to him, Michael kept his tone casual. "No, not unless you count the orphanage."

"You needn't trouble yourself with her any longer, unless you insist in involving yourself in that charity cause."

Had Henry changed his mind about marrying Sarah at any cost? *Pray yes,*

Michael thought, for she was determined to break the betrothal, and Michael was just as determined to have her for his own. "Why have you lost interest in Sarah MacKenzie?"

"I care nothing for her at all. It's only that Henry's solicitor has assured us that the contract prevails in our behalf where the dowry is concerned."

Wretched misfortune, as Sarah would say. Worse, the news threatened the progress Michael had made with her. His best hope lay in binding her to him before his family wreaked more havoc. But how? He couldn't rely on friendship; that would take too long. Passion was his best bet, but could he, in good conscience, seduce her? When faced with the prospect of losing her, the answer came easy.

"I'm certain we'll be able to collect the money."

Not without the duke of Ross, Michael thought. "Is that what has you so excited?"

She beamed and flipped her napkin onto the table as if pitching coins to the poor. "Certainly not. It was providence, actually. By way of the young lady who retrieved my purse, I was introduced to none other than Vicktor Edelweiss Lucerne."

From her reticule she produced a printed broadside from a Paris opera house. The text extolled the talents of the young man from Vienna.

"Keep it," she said. "I have others. We'll have hundreds made like it, in English, of course."

Michael tucked the paper into his waistcoat. He had never heard of the man, but from the expression on his mother's face, this Lucerne was a fellow of some import. "You are pleased at having made his aquaintance?"

She wilted in exasperation, "Oh, Michael. You are too out of the main. You must catch up on what's important. Vicktor Lucerne is the foremost composer in all of Europe. His friend was impressed when I mentioned Henry. Lady whatever-her-name-is assured me that Lucerne will gladly come to Edinburgh, for a modest sum, and give a concert. It's to be in July. We shall sell admissions, make pots of money, and in the doing, curry the favor of the king. I expect he will attend."

King George come to Scotland? An impossibility. For years, George III had

312

publicly voiced his disinterest in Scotland, save the money the Scots put in his treasury. His ambivalence toward his northern subjects was common knowledge, even a world away in India.

Reminding her of it, however, was unseemly just now. Instead, Michael broached her favorite topic. "How will the king's attendance aid Henry?"

Patiently, she said, "If the king favors us, he cannot side with Richmond. All that talk of stripping Henry of our lands and title will fade like yesterday's gossip."

Stripping Henry of the title could hardly be reduced to gossip; an act of Parliament was serious business. "Mother, if Henry would but take the time to apologize to Richmond, he wouldn't have to worry about censure. The duke will not carry a grudge. I can assure you of that."

"Henry will not beg the pardon of that gamester, duke or no. I expected more loyalty from you. The man cheated your brother."

Beyond the reprimand to Michael, her words were dangerous in any company. "Richmond made it plain that he would accept nothing less than an apology from Henry."

"I know all of that, but the king is an admirer of Lucerne, who will not perform in London. He visits only because Lady so-and-so has a sister who lives there — in one of the better neighborhoods, I'm sure. Come to think of it, she's quite handsome. She wore a necklace of the most unusual pink jade. She bought it herself in the Orient, where she'd also acquired her maid. Henry's not to know about the concert until I see the king. Poor Henry's had one disappointment after another. A surprise will surely cheer him."

Fearful that she would resort to matchmaking, Michael said, "The lady with the pink necklace and Oriental servant is obviously content with this Lucerne."

At her blank expression, Michael knew he'd guessed wrongly. "What will you do?"

"Upon my return there, I'll gain an audience with his majesty and deliver a personal invitation for the entire royal family to attend our musicale. After he accepts, I'll petition him to intervene with Richmond on Henry's behalf."

"What if he refuses?"

"Nonsense, Michael. He will not pass up the chance to see Lucerne."

Her disdain smothered Michael's hope of a pleasant evening He pushed back his chair. "Thank you for a delightful meal, Mother, and if there's nothing else at this time, I'll simply wish you good luck in getting the king to Edinburgh and take my leave of you."

She moved to rise, and the butler hurried to assist her. "Oh Michael," she almost purred, "I'll require more money this time. I cannot attend the king in anything less than the current style. Do you think you can manage?"

Ready to make good his escape, Michael got to his feet and escorted her from the room. "My luck at whist of late is rather good," he lied. "I've a fistful of markers."

"More than five hundred pounds?" she artlessly asked.

Smiling to keep from cursing, he called for his hat and cloak. "Just about that, Mother."

"Will you bring it 'round tomorrow?"

All Michael could do was nod for the footman to open the door.

"Oh, Michael," she called him back.

"There is one more thing. Not that it matters in the least to me, but Henry asked that I bring it up with you."

A sense of foreboding descended on Michael. "What would that be?"

"He is curious as to why you haven't disclosed your assets, as the law requires of soldiers returning from India."

Damn Pitt the Younger and his obnoxious India Act. Michael bit his lip to keep from shouting at her that his assets were his own affair. She'd been pleasant for the most part of the evening; now she'd reverted to the conniving, prying woman. He was tempted to buy himself out of one or two ventures and give her the money to free Henry. But that would be tantamount to buying her affection and going against his principies. He would do neither.

But he was caught in a trap of his own setting.

"Don't look so aggrieved, Michael. Henry only asked a question."

He chose the safest reply. "I cannot imagine what good that will do, save embarrassing the family more. Better we should let it out that I have amassed a considerable fortune."

He'd snagged her interest, for she

gave him a rare motherly smile. "Have you?"

Her words clanged against his nerves like a temple drum. "On an officer's pay?" He forced a laugh. "You speak as if I'd achieved command in his majesty's army, rather than serving the company's forces."

A frown revealed her confusion.

Michael rejoiced and bid her good night. As he traced the familiar path to the Dragoon Inn, he couldn't stave off the rage her question had wrought.

The problem of his majesty's unfairness stemmed from the complications of having two separate armies in India, each under different leadership. Advancement was slow in the Indian army, the forces under the control of the East India Company. Michael had prospered there, but that was before the arrival of large numbers of the crown's forces. The latter enjoyed full pay, even after retirement, and their assignments were less hazardous.

Pitt's disastrous act, passed last year, did not apply to Michael, for he'd cashiered himself out to join the Complement.

Why had Henry broached the subject?

Michael was still pondering the question when he started up the stairs at the inn and almost tripped over William Picardy.

12

Thump.

At the sound of the knock on the door, Sarah stilled her hands on the half-rolled canvas. She glanced at the empty frame and the concealing drape beside it on the floor.

One knock — Michael had returned.

Her feet moved, but her mind went blank with fear. Rolling the canvas into a manageable shape, she raced for the door and threw it open. Notch stood nearby, his gaze fixed on Michael, who was walking up the stairs, a chatting William on his heels.

Michael hadn't reached the landing, so he still faced away from her. A few more steps and he would grasp the newel post and turn — toward Sarah.

Notch gripped her arm and gave her a push. Her skirt caught in the door, yanking her to a halt. She stifled a whine of anguish.

Frozen in terror, she counted the loud

tramping of his boots. Or was it the thumping of her heart? Time slowed to a crawl.

Notch fumbled with the latch. Michael kept walking.

"Ladies' petticoats!" the lad hissed, then said, "Go."

Sarah dashed for the exit. Notch closed the door.

"You there!" Michael called out.

Her toes tangled, and she almost tripped.

"Bother the wench, general," Notch said. "She ain't nothin' but a laundry maid. Off with you, girl. Have a nice evening, did you, general? The clockmaker swore we'd have rain, but I see you haven't a speck on your fine cloak."

"You're awfully congenial tonight, Notch. If I heard you correctly, you were discussing ladies' petticoats with a laundry maid. An interesting subject."

The resonance in his voice floated around Sarah. Her mouth went dry. She eased her foot forward, sliding slowly to gain the smallest distance from him without drawing attention to her flight.

"Petticoats? Ha! You heard it right,

but you got it wrong, general. Ladies' petticoats is my new swear-by. Ain't it so, Pic? I swear by ladies' petticoats at least a score o' times a day."

William stuttered an agreement.

Casting his voice toward Sarah, Notch said, "Get on with you, girl."

Staring straight ahead and praying for divine intervention, she inched closer to the door.

"I'm afraid I'll have to ask her to stay, Notch." The apology in his voice rang hollow. "I'd like to speak to Lady Sarah alone."

She squeezed her eyes shut. A groan escaped her lips.

"Hear her moanin'? That's nothin' but a laundry maid sick to her spine from eatin' turned-bad bannocks. Off with you, girl."

"What's that in your hand, *girl*," Michael demanded.

Sarah peered down. The narrower skirt of the servant's dress did not completely conceal the rolled-up canvas, which was quaking in her unsteady hand.

William fretted. "The ruse is botched."

"Haud yer wheesht!" Notch hissed.

An obedient William grew silent.

"Gentlemen, you are dismissed." Each

word of Michael's command dripped authority.

Now serious too, Notch cleared his throat. "We couldn't be after condonin' leavin' you with her unchaperoned, general. 'Twouldn't be proper."

Sarah started moving again. If she could just get through that door.

"Sarah? Will you leave your accomplices to answer for your 'botched ruse'?"

"She ain't done nothin'." Notch spoke harshly. "Hurry out that door, my lady. We'll hold him off here till you're back at home, safe and sound."

"Yes, Sarah. By all means, act the coward."

The toad. She hoped Michael Elliot fell into a ripe bog and stayed there till All Hallow's Eve.

"Sarah?"

Resigned, she blew out her breath and turned around.

Feet planted, his hands on his hips, Notch bravely faced Michael, whose attention was fully focused on Sarah.

William dawdled at the head of the steps.

Her heart went out to these fearless

children. Her eyes locked onto Michael Elliot.

"Notch," she said. "I'm afraid Lord Michael has a point."

Glancing over his shoulder, Notch winced in agony. "Sorry, my lady, but he almost run Pic over with his long strides. The lad hadn't time to give me his signal."

"You both did your best. Thank you."

"How could you tell 'twas her?" William asked.

Michael's consuming gaze mapped Sarah's form. "I'd know her in a monsoon."

"What's a monsoon?" Staring at the end of his nose, William puckered his lips around the foreign word.

Disregarding the satisfaction gleaming in Michael's eyes, Sarah said, "A monsoon is a seasonal event, characterized by extended torrents of rain, common in India."

Notch looked from Sarah to Michael. "Meaning you'd know her anywhere, sir?"

"In the darkest cave on the bleakest night."

The lad was quick to catch the meaning; his young-old eyes took in the adults and the situation. Sarah was certain he would not desert her, but did Michael know that?

"You've a quarter-hour before the curfew drum sounds." Michael pointed to the front stairs. "Just enough time to get to the customs house before the magistrate catches you."

Sarah must find a way to tell Michael that Notch would seek help on her behalf. But how could she without jeopardizing her position?

Finesse was her only option.

Catching Michael's attention, she slid a meaningful glance at Notch. "Notch is a very bright lad."

Michael studied her. "Very bright," he said much too confidently. "Notch has *seen* many things in his young life." He glanced pointedly at the canvas. "I doubt he understands them all, and exposing him to adult matters could prove harmful. To a lad of his age, *seeing* is believing."

Silent rage stiffened her back. "I understand completely."

"Well done, Sarah." He pulled off his gloves and touched Notch's shoulder. "I wouldn't be at all surprised if Notch here dashes down those stairs and summons the magistrate."

"Don't think I won't," the lad boasted. "Lady Sarah's suffered her share and more o' trouble 'cause o' the Elliots."

Michael's reaction was immediate. His eyes narrowed at being grouped with his family. In spite of her situation, Sarah knew she couldn't allow Notch to judge Michael guilty for the crimes of his kin. She'd learned the folly of that early in her association with him.

"I brought this trouble on myself, Notch," she admitted. Mary should shoulder the lion's share of the blame, but she wasn't here to answer for her part.

Notch stared at his feet. "You cannot be gettin' out of it by yourself, my lady. The magistrate'll take your side when you tell him the truth."

"The truth," Michael drawled.

"Aye, general. Lady Sarah wanted to surprise you with a new frame for your favorite paintin'. That's it she's got in her hand."

"How thoughtful of you, Sarah dear," Michael began in his courting swain's voice. "I've also heard the magistrate is a great admirer of biblical art. Have you heard that, too?"

Biblical art. Eve in Eden. Sarah's

scruples fled. He did not deserve fair treatment from her. In his sly way, he was all but promising to parade the nude before any and every man who came to her aid.

She quaked in shame. "Leave the authorities out of it, Notch," she said. "No need to trouble them at this hour."

The lad nodded in acquiescence. "I'll just get Cholly, then."

"By all means," Michael declared, laughing. "Summon the streetsweeper. Call up the muckrakers. Invite the carters. Move aside the furniture and open a bloody museum. We'll call it 'The Great Cultural Experience for the Common Man.' "

She fumed at his overdone attempt at intimidation. He couldn't possibly carry out the threat. But he'd wreak havoc with his threatening.

Notch headed for the stairs.

Michael stopped laughing and held out his hand to her. The challenge in his eyes was undeniable. "Tell the lad you're perfectly safe with me."

Only a fool would believe that. Yet she must convince Notch that it was true.

"Notch!" She laid her palm in Michael's. "Come back." Her voice warbled, and she cleared her throat. "William, you come, too."

Notch stopped. William climbed onto the bannister to wait.

Averting her eyes, Sarah fought the trembling that promised to shatter her composure. She could not quail before Michael Elliot. She'd been caught. Bully for him. The canvas was in her possession. She hadn't had the heart to pitch the painting onto the banked fire in his room moments ago. But she would if he refused to let her keep it.

"Notch, William, you mustn't worry over my safety or seek help for me from any quarter."

"You're just sayin' that 'cause he's got you scared as a goose on the eve o' Christmas."

Michael's brows rose. The wretch was enjoying himself.

Responsibility for the evening's work was hers. She'd gotten the lads into this mess; she'd get them out. But Michael was making the situation worse, and for that poor behavior he would pay a price. But in the process she'd prove to him that Sarah MacKenzie was no goose awaiting the ax.

Moving the canvas behind her back,

she gave Notch her kindest smile. "I know you are concerned about me. You are a true champion and a truer friend."

He stood taller. "Gentlemen don't take ladies behind closed doors, not if they're quality to the core."

"Do too," said William. "That fancy wee-wee spark with his mah cherries takes Lady Winfield upstairs every night."

Laughter danced at the corners of Michael's mouth.

Sarah longed to cast off her manners and slap him. Instead, she sought a different sort of revenge. "Notch, will you be satisfied if Lord Michael gives you his oath that he will comport himself as a gentleman?"

Notch said, "He'll have to swear on his honor."

"Or his gentleman's box," William put in.

Turning to Michael, she said, "Perhaps you'd care to make that pledge now."

Humor drained from his expression.

Sarah rejoiced in the small victory. "Let's see. It must be a sincere oath. Something to the effect that you will not seek retribution against me for anything that has occurred here to-night."

"What's retribution?" William queried.

"A season in Tolbooth," Notch supplied with authority.

"We'd better be after fetching Cholly." William slid down the bannister, stopping at the turn of the landing.

Turnbull appeared at the bottom of the stairs. "We're drawing a crowd," Michael announced, casually shifting his weight to one leg. "What will you do, Sarah?"

Despise him for the rest of her life, she silently swore. To her dismay, she murmured, "Have Turnbull get them out of here."

"Turnbull," Michael said. "See the lads home and have a chat with the Lindsays."

"A lengthy chat, my lord?"

"Just so. I'm sure you have much to discuss."

Turnbull smiled affably. "Indeed we do."

Michael added something in a language she did not understand. Turnbull's eyes widened in shock, but he quickly regained his composure.

"What about his oath?" Notch said.

"He didn't swear on nothing," William grumbled.

Sarah relaxed. "I seem to recall hearing it said that chivalry was a way of life for you, Michael."

Grudgingly, he turned to Notch. "I swear on my honor that I will forgive Lady Sarah her botched ruse."

Sarah thought his cunning knew no bounds. "You'll also add the part about not seeking retribution."

In a voice meant only for Sarah, Michael murmured, "You're pushing your luck. Tell your friends good night."

She did as he said.

Turnbull motioned for the boys to follow him.

Sarah hurried into Michael's room.

Was it a lifetime ago that she'd crouched on the floor here and pried nails from the painting? Now she examined the room in earnest. For rented quarters, the rooms were spacious and well furnished. A door to the left led to the bedroom, but she could see only the edge of the blue velvet coverlet.

In both rooms, the walls were roughly plastered and the ceiling beams recently polished. Matching high-backed chairs framed the square hearth. An array of brass and wooden boxes flanked the mantel clock. The timepiece was one of Nathaniel Hodges's more ornate designs.

The absence of a display of family miniatures on the mantel or any of the small tables strewn about the room struck her as odd. But if she had relatives like his, she wouldn't exhibit their portraits either.

According to the clock, the time was just before 10. She remembered Michael's comment about the curfew.

The door closed. He strolled toward her, the top of his now-bare head only a palm's width from the ceiling. "Make yourself comfortable." He dominated the room.

Sarah stood her ground. "I'd have to go elsewhere to do that."

"But I want you here, and we have a number of important matters to discuss."

Sarah sighted the hearth. She held up the rolled painting. "I'll destroy it."

As if he were settling in for a pleasant evening, rather than a forced seduction, he hung up his hat and tossed his gloves onto a table. "Not tonight, Sarah."

She dashed for the fire.

He dashed for her.

He was too close and too quick, and his arms were like bands of steel.

Twisting, she tried to break free of his hold. "You cannot stop me."

Releasing her, he held up his hands and gave her a bland smile. "Nor will I try. Go ahead. Do what you must."

The canvas trembled in her hand, but she could not move her arm to throw the painting in the fire.

"Mary swore you would retaliate," he said reasonably. "And after hearing her tell the tale of Lottie and a dozen fresh haggis in her marriage bed, I believe Mary. But I do not think you will destroy her beautiful painting."

Sarah couldn't. For reprisal, she'd have Mary's face painted over her own and display the scandalous canvas at London Bridge. The idea soothed her, and she smiled. "You can be sure that Mary will get fitting wages for this shoddy work."

All patient man, he shook his head. "If you call that shoddy, the king's a MacKenzie."

Ignoring him, she asked the question foremost in her mind. "What language were you speaking to Turnbull, and what did you say to him?"

Ignoring her, he removed the glass top from a dish of candy. The smell of ginger filled the air. When she refused the offered sweet, he took one and replaced the lid.

"What possessed you to foul Lottie's marriage bed?" he asked.

How did she explain a life of caring closeness? What words could convey the unity of four siblings who constantly battled the stain of illegitimacy? *Loyalty* seemed too ordinary a word for the unique ties that bound the four half sisters.

She settled for the oblique. "The same sort of prank that led Lottie to dose my perfume with bitters."

He pulled off his neckcloth and unfastened the top button of his shirt. "Is that what she did to earn your wrath?"

Trying to stay calm in the face of a disrobing man, she put the canvas on the seat of the facing high-back chair, then moved around behind it. For something to do, save gape at the black chest hair that peeked from the opening in his shirt, she examined the doily on the chair back. She found no grease on the cloth; he obviously did not pomade his hair.

The clock struck 10 o'clock. At least Notch and William were safe with Turnbull.

Michael reached for the canvas and laid it across his lap. "Did Lottie foul your favorite fragrance?"

She couldn't help looking at where the canvas rested. His snug-fitting breeches accented his well-muscled legs. No wonder he controlled his spirited horse with ease.

"Did she?"

Sarah swallowed back shame but couldn't fend off peevishness. "Living in the same house with Lottie is reason enough." Hearing her own testy words, she softened her tone. "But I did not act alone, and Lottie deserved it. Mary and Agnes helped me. That's generally the way it was in our youth, three against one."

He raked the ribbon tie from his hair. The long strands fell to his shoulders. "I'm not surprised Notch and the other orphans take to you. You're more adept at conspiracy than they are." Easing down in the chair, he propped his booted feet on a tasseled footstool. "But you plunder badly."

His comfortable pose drove her to boldness. "Five minutes more, and I would have made good my escape."

"Five minutes later, and I would have come after you."

As if she would let him in. "You cannot keep that painting. 'Tis wrong of you in every way."

He waved it at her. "You've looked at it?"

Sarah glared at him. "You lied about the freckles."

Resting the tube on his legs, he unrolled the painting. "Do you say so because Mary didn't paint them on your likeness, or because your skin is unblemished?"

She huffed in disdain and fought the urge to look away. "As if I would tell you." If he could be secretive about his exchange with Turnbull, she could be evasive too.

"It's a beautiful work." With his index finger, he touched the canvas, tracing the curve of the model's hip.

Even viewing it upside down, she had to agree. Emulating the lush style of

George Lambert, Mary had posed the languishing Eve on an opulent chaise of tucked white velvet and set her amid a landscape full of ferns and exotic pink blossoms, nymphs and furry forest creatures. The blue sky above perfectly matched Sarah's eyes.

To Mary's credit, she'd given Sarah's waist-length hair a high sheen and richly textured waves. To Sarah's regret, Mary had omitted the simple modesty of fashioning a sheer drape over the model. Down to the darker flesh on the nipples and lower, to the shadowy tuft of curly hair, Mary had glorified the female form. The size of the breasts, however, was a debatable matter. Sarah couldn't stave off a blush.

He grinned at her dismay.

"Stop gawking! She's made me naked, for God's sake."

"To be frank, my dear Sarah" — he choked back laughter — "I don't think religion played the smallest part. Mary made you completely naked for me."

Sarah shivered. "Was that your idea?" Until now, she hadn't considered that he could influence Mary; the notion was absurd. But on second thought, he never failed to engage Sarah's emotions.

Perhaps Mary had also been swayed by him.

With the flat of his hand, he caressed the surface, his eyes alight with mischief. His overlong hair tempered the devilish aspect of his dark good looks.

When he spoke his voice was soft, beguiling. "Alas, the commendations are not for me. Mary thought it up. I only watched."

Mary was perfectly capable of that kind of scandal. They probably discussed body parts as if they were hinges on a door.

"Is that why she sent it to you rather than to the lord provost as she threatened?"

He shrugged. "I only advised her that the lord provost would not show her work the appreciation I would. Sending it with the earl of Wiltshire was her idea. I think she was anxious to be rid of him for a day or two, or at least that's what she said. He returned to London immediately."

Mary would make her decision about the engaging earl; Sarah had Michael Elliot to worry over.

Eager to put the matter behind them, Sarah feigned indifference. "Mary should paint what is in her heart. I cannot imagine why she is content to copy others."

As if he understood, he rolled up the painting and put it on the floor beside his chair. "Her talent far surpasses her mentor."

The compliment struck a soft chord with Sarah. Mary was eccentric, stubborn, and bolder than Agnes. With the stroke of a brush, she could capture a person's soul on canvas. With the scratch of a quill, she could personify the body politic in cartoon. Out of jealousy, her male contemporaries scorned her with names like Contrary Mary. Reynolds and the others of his age embraced her. London society didn't know what to make of Mary Margaret MacKenzie. The earl of Wiltshire did, for he'd vowed before the congregation at Westminster Abbey to make her his wife.

Sarah loved her dearly. Next year, they'd sit before a roaring fire, pop colony corn, and share a merry laugh over both the painting and Sarah's revenge, whatever that turned out to be.

"Would you care to share that joyous thought?"

Melancholy swamped her, but she held it close to her heart. A conversational detour was appropriate; Sarah found that she couldn't voice it. "I was thinking how constant some things are in this life."

"Namely, your affection for Mary and hers for you."

He shouldn't be so knowledgeable about Sarah's feelings. "Yes, but Mary will still pay a hefty price, make no mistake about that."

"I'd like to be a beetle under the chair on that occasion." He removed his waistcoat and tossed it on the arm of his chair. A broadside fluttered to the floor.

Needing something to do, save watch him disrobe and question her own attraction to him, Sarah picked up the paper. A name caught her eye. Keen to the subject, she read the text. "Where did you get this?"

Consumed with his own comfort, he snuggled down into the chair again. "From my mother. She brought it back from London. Have you heard of this Lucerne?"

The innocent question gave Sarah pause, an opportunity to put aside troubling thoughts of Michael Elliot. Sarah knew well the musician Lucerne; her half sister Agnes traveled as companion and bodyguard to the young composer.

Was Michael fishing for information? His curiously bland expression appeared honest. He'd been in India for 15 years. That would explain a guileless query about Vicktor Lucerne; the virtuoso was only 12 years old, and he did not travel farther by boat than London. But he refused to perform there.

"Have you?" he asked.

"Lucerne is all the rage in Europe. At the age of three, he built a ladder and sat upon it to master the harpsichord. He composed his first opera as a tribute to himself on his sixth birthday. It's said his violin sonatas are truly inspired, and his minuets the most popular of the day."

"How do you know so much about him?"

She wouldn't tell him about Agnes yet, not until she'd heard everything he had to say on the subject. "I enjoy learning, no matter the topic. Why do you ask?"

"My mother has arranged for him to give a concert in Edinburgh."

His mother? If Lady Emily were involved, Henry must be too. That spelled trouble. If Henry dared to use Agnes as a pawn to get Lucerne to Edinburgh, and Agnes found out, Henry would regret it for the rest of his life.

For lack of anything better, Sarah said, "How interesting. How did that come about?"

"Happenstance, actually. A thief cut Mother's purse in London, and a lady friend of this fellow Lucerne recovered it."

An unholy suspicion gripped Sarah. "Another musician found your mother's property?"

"No. That's the oddity of it. A noblewoman brought it back."

"A noblewoman?" Drat her warbling voice. "Who was she?"

"Mother could not remember her name — only that it was Scottish. She was also quite taken with the woman's pink jade necklace and her Oriental servant."

Sarah knew who the woman was, and she also knew how adept Agnes Elizabeth MacKenzie was with her hands; she could snatch a purse with an ease Notch would envy. But even if Agnes hadn't taken the reticule herself, which was entirely possible, she was clever enough to see it done intentionally to facilitate an introduction to Lady Emily.

Yes, Agnes must have instigated the meeting; the coincidence was too great. The pink jade necklace was too rare. Auntie Loo, the servant from Bangkok, was unforgettable. Since Agnes was in London, she and Mary had probably cooked up the concert scheme together. But to what end, Sarah wondered? And how could she glean more information from Michael without rousing his suspicions?

She smoothed out the doily. "I'm surprised your mother had time for anyone but poor Henry."

"According to Mother, she and the woman became friends. The woman was quite eager to make the acquaintance of another Scot."

Agnes could leach a secret from a person before the poor soul realized he, or in this case she, had revealed it. But Henry was involved, and he was Sarah's problem. Did he know about the meeting between Lady Emily and Agnes? "I assume Lady Emily mentioned Henry."

Michael smiled, but the expression

lacked fondness. "As Mother tells it, the good samaritan couldn't ask enough questions about Henry and the Elliots."

If Agnes was up to meddling, Sarah would have her head on a pike. But what if this were Agnes's noble way of coming to Sarah's aid? Agnes didn't know the truth about Sarah's parentage, not that it would matter to Agnes. They'd been raised as sisters, and pranks aside, they were fiercely loyal. Lack of a blood tie would not change that. But Sarah wasn't ready yet to face Agnes and tell her the truth.

In any event, Sarah needed to know if Agnes had truly kept her identity a secret from Lady Emily. "Are you certain your mother doesn't remember the woman's name?"

"She didn't. She mentioned Anne, but tossed it out as faulty recollection. Do you know the woman who travels with Lucerne?"

13

Sarah strove for lightness. "Me? I haven't a dot of musical talent or appreciation, and I assure you, I do not move in the same circles as Vicktor Lucerne. It is an interesting story, though, and I'm delighted that your mother has made a friend." He couldn't know how false that statement was; befriending Agnes MacKenzie could spell trouble for Lady Emily.

"Then the Elliots can count on you for the price of an admission?"

Removing his outer clothing made him more brazen than ever. Sarah was undaunted. "You'll pardon me if I decline. I'd sooner toss a handful of shillings down the nearest privy."

"What if the proceeds free my brother?"

That brought up another question. "Does Henry know about the concert?"

"No. It's to be a surprise."

A comforting bit of information. During his only visit to Rosshaven Castle, Henry was given a lengthy discourse by Lottie on the accomplishments and locations of all of the MacKenzie sisters. Through Lottie's tales, he knew of Agnes's unusual vocation and the reason behind it. Pray Lady Emily kept her secret; if Henry learned that Agnes was involved, he'd try to foil her plans, whatever they were.

A bright spot in the dark tragedy would come later when Sarah shared with Rose the story of Agnes's friendship with Lady Emily. The maid would laugh herself to tears.

"Sarah? What will you do if Henry is freed?"

"I'll wish him to hell in a hop cart and thank the devil for taking him in."

"Come now, are you sure you won't attend the concert to benefit poor Henry?"

At his sarcasm, Sarah relaxed a little. She knew the players in the event. Michael did not. "Your brother can rot in King's Bench Prison for all I care."

"Yes, well . . . I'll make you a trade, Sarah — this painting for the truth. Tell me why you betrothed yourself to hell-bound Henry."

During one of their many discussions on the subject, Michael had said he believed that marriage to Henry was merely the means to an end for Sarah, the end being her desire to come to Edinburgh. He was off the mark, but even if she told him the truth, he wouldn't believe her now.

She snatched up an excuse she thought would pacify him. "Henry agreed to let me build an orphanage in Edinburgh. Many husbands would not have been so generous."

"Ah, the infamous stipulations, but I'd hardly describe Henry as generous."

He didn't look convinced. "There's nothing wrong with a woman looking after her own interests. Your mother was so envious of the document, she added her own conditions to the page, not that they are legally binding, but I suppose you know that."

"No, but I'm wildly curious." He crossed his arms over his chest. "What did the countess demand?"

Sarah couldn't stop staring at his arms and admiring the way his muscles strained at the fabric of his shirt. Her gaze moved lower, to his lap and the manly bulge in plain view.

"Care to sit down?"

At his provocative words, she looked at her hands and returned to the moot subject of Lady Emily's stipulations. "Your mother demanded the construction of an entire wing of her own at Glenforth Manor and an allowance of one penny greater than mine. I told you she fears being packed off to Fife, and Henry has sworn to move her there. Her life and her friends are here."

Michael whistled in mock astonishment. "An inventive excuse, my dear, but not the primary reason you agreed to wed my brother." He stretched out his long legs, languishing like a dark conqueror among the vanquished.

"Try again," he murmured. "And get to the heart of it this time."

Unable to stand still, Sarah marched across the room and stood over him. "Wipe that smug look off your face, Michael Elliot. I did not have to go a-begging for a husband, if that is what you want to hear."

"Did I say that?"

"Nay, but you insinuated it. And why belabor the point? Why should you give a bent carpenter's tack why I agreed to wed your brother?"

Rather than tell her she was a prize even a king would cherish, Michael told her something she already knew. "Because I want you for myself."

She folded her arms and huffed beautifully. "So you've said before. Forgive me, but with twenty thousand pounds as inducement, I'm sure you'd put me up for sainthood."

"Oh, I'd never do that. No one would believe me — not after ten minutes in your company."

Her eyes narrowed, the lashes so long they shadowed her cheeks. Even garbed in servant's clothing, she looked like a princess.

"You're lower than a toad's belly, and since honesty is your watchword tonight, tell me why you'd spend nine thousand pounds to refurbish the orphanage when your brother needs the money to get out of jail."

"The answer to that . . ." He let the sentence trail off; interest in Henry was the last subject on his mind. Discussing his finances was the next to last.

Basking in Sarah's presence was foremost on his list of pastimes. She was meant to be in firelight. Were her breasts as lush as Mary had depicted, or did Sarah employ artifice?

"Have you lost the gist of the conversation?" she asked.

"Not at all. Since you broached the topic of bellies, I should tell you that Mary gave you a nice one. Gently rounded and begging for a man's touch."

"I hate you."

"No, you don't. You like me, and were it in your power, you'd change my name to Munro or Brodie or some other clan you favor."

Her gaze again flitted to his groin. "You know what Shakespeare said about roses and names. 'Tis for certain all of the Elliots smell alike."

Her nearness sent his desire soaring, and if she continued to peek at his lap, she'd soon have an eyeful. "Oh, come now. Be merry, Sarah." *Be naked,* he silently urged, *and wanton in my bed.*

"How can I enjoy myself when you insist on keeping that painting?"

"You know my terms." The little general in his breeches knew them, too.

Arms still folded, she strummed her fingers on her elbows. "How can I keep them straight? They keep changing. First you tell me I can have the painting if I offer you a like-clad substitute. Then you say —"

"Stop right there."

"Why?"

The squeak in her voice gave her away. Michael pounced on her momentary vulnerability. "I'll take the substitute over the confession, so long as you are the proxy."

"After all that's happened, you couldn't possibly want me."

"Then your intellect has failed you." He patted his thigh. "Sit here, and we'll discuss the intimate details of why I want you and what can be done about it."

"Oh, no. I'm perfectly comfortable where I am." To prove the point, she dropped her arms and gazed about the room, as if she were having a jolly old time.

The clock struck the hour of 11.

Sarah started, revealing her true state of mind.

Michael glanced pointedly toward the bedroom. "There are other locales to be considered."

She gave him that huff of disdain. "I assure you, my wits and my scruples haven't taken a holiday. But you have forgotten your pledge to comport your-self honorably."

"Honoring you holds a prominent place on my list of proper comport-ment."

"Honoring me? I'm acquainted with the post of mistress. It's been offered to me before."

Jealousy simmered beneath the sur-face of his desire. "By whom?"

She presented him her profile. "If you're done with tiresome questions, Michael, I'll take my leave."

Not yet, she wouldn't. "Then I assume you do not kiss and tell?"

"Where you are concerned, neither kissing nor telling holds any appeal for me."

"You lie with as little skill as you burgle. Unless you've changed your mind about acquiring the painting."

Raising her bonny blue eyes to the beamed ceiling, she gave life to the term, tiresome. "I won't be caught at this inn and trapped into marriage over that canvas. And that is precisely what will happen if anyone finds me naked with you in this room."

After the fact, perhaps, for once he had Sarah naked in this room, an army of angry fathers wouldn't stop him from making love to her. "Marriage to one man and a betrothal to another? You *are* modern, Sarah MacKenzie."

Too late she caught the slip of her tongue; the stain of embarrassment blossomed on her cheeks. "You're a beast, Michael Elliot."

"Yes, well . . ." He peered at the carpet through the rolled-up painting. "You are promised to my brother. I'd say that's tit for tat."

Sarah glanced at the exit door. "I'd like to go home now. Will you excuse me?"

"Not just yet." He stood the rolled painting on end, his palm resting on the top of it. Whether or not the betrothal stood, a marriage between Henry and Sarah was out of the question, and not just because Michael had sworn to have her. Henry would stay in jail until he apologized publicly to Richmond. That would never happen; Henry had too much pride to humble himself.

"What else do you wish to discuss?" she asked. "And if you try to forswear the oath you made to Notch, I'll scream down the inn and have you thrown in jail for a common nuisance."

The presence of the magistrate would force an exchange of marriage vows, but reminding her of that logic would only anger her more.

"There is another matter," he said. "Obviously you haven't written to the duke of Ross. Is it because you also cannot find him?"

Her eyes twinkled with awareness. "Also?"

"Henry's solicitor sent a man to both of the duke's estates. Lachlan MacKenzie is nowhere to be found. Even his enemies do not know his location."

"I haven't an inkling. The comings and goings of the duke of Ross are his own affair, and if you'd met him you'd understand that."

"I think it's odd that he would disappear when one of his flock is in trouble."

"I do not need his help to escape the Elliots."

"But he's a family man and a protective father. I doubt he'd ask your permission to act in your best interests."

"Then by your own admission, you know he will not stay away for long."

"He's been gone for three months, and his duchess is not concerned."

Sarah struggled with the contradictory statement. Lachlan gone three months? That meant he had dropped from sight shortly after penning his last letter to her. She'd wager her fondest memories that Juliet knew exactly where Lachlan was.

Whatever the outcome, Sarah knew she must make light of the situation. "If Lady Juliet accepts his absence, so should you."

"You're quite right, I'm sure," Michael said. "My mother and Henry have given up searching for his grace of Ross. Perhaps he is simply waiting them out in a favorite hideaway?"

Sarah chuckled. "He's no coward, the duke of Ross, if that is what you are implying. Believe this, Michael, the battle has yet to be struck that Lachlan MacKenzie will run away from."

"I'm sure his courage is legend. But where is he? You haven't a notion. Mary hasn't a notion. Both of you are being coerced into marrying men you swear you do not want. What concerned father would turn his back on the very children he professes to love? Not to mention spoils beyond redemption."

Her stubborn nature roared to life. "I am not spoiled."

He laughed and indulged in another piece of candy.

Sarah was tempted to tell him that she wasn't Lachlan's daughter, but intuition told her to save that revelation for the countess of Glenforth.

Instead, she said, "The duke of Ross cannot be held responsible for the lamentably poor choices of men Mary and I have made."

He laughed again, this time so hard his shoulders shook.

She moved to the door. Like a cat, he lunged to his feet and approached her. Without the waistcoat, his hips and flanks looked lean, almost too narrow to support his broad chest and neck.

"Don't touch me," she said.

"Why not? Are you afraid you'll remember how much you like the feel of my arms around you? How you sigh and press your breasts against my chest when I kiss you?"

She'd heard such bold remarks before, but never from a man who spoke the truth. But Sarah MacKenzie had learned boldness side by side with three sisters who made fool's play of the courting game. She borrowed and expanded upon one of Mary's most brilliant rejoinders.

For effect, Sarah looked him up and down. "The pleasure I took in your embrace is just that — a moment's enjoyment. Do not glorify it or misconstrue it into a license to paw me again."

He went very still, and she had the eeriest feeling she'd underestimated him.

His gaze rested on the shoulder of her borrowed gown, which again felt scratchy against her skin.

"Sarah," he said ominously, his gaze sliding ever upward. When their eyes met, his voice dropped. "The pleasure *you* took in *my* embrace is a harbinger of the passion to come between us. We will cherish each other and bestow upon our children the ability to find their own abiding loves. Lie to me now to save your pride if it suits you, but do not lie to yourself." His words were all the more dangerous because he didn't move to touch her. His winsome smile intensified Sarah's confusion, for she felt at once captured by him and freed. "Have you a cloak?" he asked.

With effort she rose above his seduction. "No."

He donned his own cloak and performed the exceedingly romantic gesture of wrapping her in his tartan plaid. Still smiling, he said, "In spite of it all, my dear Sarah, and as regrettable as it is for me to say, you flatter the colors of the Elliot plaid. Hamish would have carried you off without a proper introduction had he seen you in the cloth of our clan."

Disarmed, she opened the door. "I'll return the tartan to you tomorrow."

"No, you will not. I'll see you home." Commanding both her person and her emotions, he led her down the back stairs and to the stable, avoiding the public spectacle of the common room. The small and unexpected kindness went straight to Sarah's heart. Holding her arm in gentlemanly fashion, Michael called for the inn's best carriage.

As the attendants readied the conveyance, the farrier came forward. "Lord Michael. The streetsweeper, Cholly's his name, is lying in wait for you in the mews of Carter's Close. He's madder'n an Englishman without a bucket o' gin."

Michael looked exasperated. To the stable at large, he said, "Who is this damned Cholly?"

Sarah had no answer; her mind spun with visions of children and abiding love.

As he handed her into the carriage and tucked her to his side, Michael murmured, "Why does a bloody street-sweeper champion your causes?"

The weight of his arm across her shoulders was more than noteworthy, for Sarah knew he was sending her a message: in the game of domination, he would stand as the victor. To her dismay, she was beginning to covet the spoils of the vanquished. "What will you do?" she asked, anticipating the fun he would make of the benign statement.

"Since I cannot have you at the moment, I'm feeling rather testy. Once I've seen you home, I'll find out if this Cholly is worth the bother."

14

"Happy birthday!"

Stunned, Sarah stopped on the threshold of the customs house.

Notch, the Odds, William, and Sally jumped into the air. Rose whistled, and Helen Lindsay clapped her hands. John Lindsay, garbed in full Highland regalia, stood in the midst of the chaos, wailing away on the bagpipes.

Happiness swelled in Sarah's chest, and tears came to her eyes. Now she knew that Rose had feigned illness this morning. When Sarah had returned from church service, she'd found a note from the fully recovered Rose, saying she'd see Sarah at the customs house.

"There's cake and cider." Notch took her arm and dragged her down the hall to the library.

One of the tables was covered with a starched cloth. Upon the bed of white linen sat a cake, a bowl of fresh oranges and cherries, and an enormous bundle of rare white heather. A wave of home-sickness washed over Sarah. In harmony with the loneliness beating in her chest, the skirl of the bagpipes ebbed in a slow, whining sound.

A teary-eyed Rose pulled two handkerchiefs from her wrist bag and gave one to Sarah.

"Lang mae yer lum reek," said the smiling maid.

Good luck was just what Sarah needed. "Thank you, Rose. But how did you manage to get everyone to keep the secret? No one said a word — not even the children."

"The children didn't know until this morning."

"Very clever. Did you bake the cake?"

Striking a sassy pose, Rose chirped, "Who else could?"

"Mistress Rose says the cake has golden butterflies inside." William appeared at the maid's side. "Is it true, Lady Sarah?"

"Yes, a dozen of them about this big." She held her thumb and index finger an inch apart. "If your piece of cake has a butterfly inside, Rose will give you a shilling."

He frowned. "That much gold's worth

more'n a shilling, ain't it, Notch?"

"Aye, the goldsmith at Luckenbooths pays fair prices."

These children were strangers to family traditions; mere survival from one day to the next had long occupied their lives. But no more. They now had a home with comfortable beds, food aplenty, and people who cared. Guiding them came natural to Sarah. She addressed their leader. "If you sell the butterflies, what will we put in your cake when your birthday comes?"

Notch frowned. "Sally's the only one with a birthday. Right Odd saw her bein' born."

Every time she thought she truly understood them, Sarah faced another surprise.

"Then each of you shall pick your very own day," said a familiar authoritative voice. Michael stood in the doorway, a bouquet of roses tucked under his arm. "Happy birthday, Sarah."

Her spirits soared. For months her life had been a tangle of uncertainty, but with the help of these people she had made a place for herself, and her future loomed as bright and precious as the golden butterflies. Much of the credit went to Michael Elliot; without him, the orphanage would still be a dream.

Before his trip to Fife, she had asked him to teach the children world history at her Sunday school. "You remembered the lesson," she said.

He dodged the excited children as he moved across the room. "I always keep my promises, Sarah. For you." He handed her the flowers.

Overnight he'd changed from the reckless and intimate rogue to the gallant and generous friend. Watching him fend off questions from the others in the room, Sarah admitted that she cared deeply for this beguiling man with his military air and commanding presence.

Her voice trembled with joy and hope. "Thank you for remembering — everything."

Notch stepped between them. "Cholly said you didn't tarry overlong in returning Lady Sarah to her home last night."

Only long enough to capture her heart and soul. And watching Michael and Notch together, she now understood why she often linked them. Neither had experienced parental love. Both of them thrived in spite of it.

"Lord Michael was testy when we parted," she said.

His gaze turned hungry, devouring. "Yes, well . . . after saying good night to you, another brawl with a street-sweeper lost its appeal."

A confused Notch scratched his freshly combed hair. "Cholly tells a different tale. He says he decided to spare you a bloody nose and busted ribs, and that was after I told him you gave me 'n' Pic your word to treat Lady Sarah kindly."

Michael laughed, but Sarah suspected a dent to his pride fueled his humor. She knew he was too much the gentleman to continue the subject with the impressionable Notch.

To aid them both, she put her hand on Notch's shoulder. "Shall I cut the cake?"

He nodded, and a rare smile of pure boyishness blossomed on his face. "I'll get the most butterflies in my slice o' cake."

"I will!" Pic declared, which set off a chorus of declarations from the other children.

After the cake was served and eaten and the rewards distributed, Michael took Sarah's arm. Drawing her into the sitting room, he said, "Have you any last-minute advice before I begin the lesson?"

"Why? Do you think you'll need it?"

Michael thought she looked happier than he'd ever seen her, her eyes sparkling with joy and her mouth curled in a constant smile. If she missed having her family present for the occasion of her birthday, she disguised it well.

Michael tamped down his own trepidation. "My teaching experience begins with absolute obedience and ends with military tactics."

She laughed. "Perfect methods for keeping the lads and Sally in line. Just be sure to separate Notch and Pic. Pic is the best reader, and he's quick to volunteer, but Notch will tease him into silence."

She spoke as if she wouldn't attend the lecture. Troubled by that, Michael said, "Where will you sit?"

Her expression grew pensive. "I have an errand."

"Can it wait?"

A sigh lifted her shoulders. "Nay. It's waited for twenty-three years."

Raising his brows, he silently encouraged her to explain.

Blinking away the momentary distraction, she gave him a knowing grin. "There is one thing. You have crumbs on your face."

Whatever her serious mission, she would keep it to herself. Michael wanted to protest and offer to accompany her, but she was smiling again.

He said, "I *can* think of a very pleasant way of removing crumbs, especially from the lips, but it will require your cooperation."

She raised her gaze to the ceiling in mock exasperation. "I'm sure you can. Good luck with the class."

When she started to move away, he couldn't let her go. "How long will you be gone?"

Pensiveness again captured her. "I do not know."

"How will you get there?" He couldn't offer her the carriage; he'd sent Turnbull to Glenstone Manor to deliver the promised money to Lady Emily.

"I'll hire a sedanchair."

She returned to the library and took a single rose from the bouquet. Then she spoke quietly to her maid, who nodded in agreement and helped her with her cloak.

As Michael watched Sarah leave, he felt the room turn decidedly cold. But soon the children demanded his attention, and he spent the next hour explaining the complex cultures and the history of the people of India.

Disciplining the children proved considerably easier than gleaning Sarah's destination from Rose. When the maid finally yielded the information, Michael hurried to join her. Twenty minutes later, he stepped from the confining sedanchair that had jostled him incessantly during the journey across Edinburgh. The surly chairman held out his hand for the fare. Michael realized he'd used all of his money to buy back Sarah's golden butterflies.

From across the lane, someone called out, "I'll settle your fare, Elliot. Help the lass."

It was Cholly, the streetsweeper. He sat on the ground and leaned against a lamppost, his arms clutching his broom. Something about the laborer's pose told Michael the man had been there for a while.

Help the lass.

Was Sarah in trouble? Fear ripped

through him and set his feet into motion. He ran around the sedanchair and raced along the stone wall that surrounded the Hospice of Saint Andrews. Once inside the gate of the ancient structure, he leaped over the trimmed shrubbery and hurdled a stone fence built by masons in the Dark Ages. A flock of greenfinches noisily took flight. Squirrels scrambled into the oak trees.

Rounding the back corner, he slowed his pace.

She sat in a small cemetery, her pink dress vivid against the gray stone markers, her dark blue cloak spread out for a pallet. In her hands she held the rose.

Catching his breath, Michael read the words on the gravestone nearest to her.

Here lies Sarah's beloved mother,
Lilian White,
Taken by her master
on the 20th day of June, 1762.

Rather than a tribute to the dead, the words were an outpouring of affection from a devoted father to his treasured daughter. Michael decided the duke of Ross was as complex as he was elusive.

But where was he?

Glancing over her shoulder, Sarah spied Michael.

"Have you run all the way?" she asked.

"No." He searched her face for signs of distress. Traces of tears still lingered around her eyes, and her nose was red from crying.

"How did you get here?" she asked. "How did you find me?"

Too relieved to stand, Michael dropped down beside her. "A sedan-chair and Rose."

Sarah looked down at the flower in her hand. The stem was now free of thorns; she'd raked them off with her thumbnail. In her words, she'd waited twenty-three years to visit her mother's grave.

He glanced again at the marker. "It's a lovely stone."

Setting her jaw, she lifted her face to the wind and breathed through her nose. As he watched, she battled sorrow and won.

She had told him that her mother died in childbirth, but hearing the words and seeing the grave were two different matters, one emotionally telling and the other deeply touching. Peace had come to Sarah MacKenzie here; she had gained strength sitting by this well-tended grave. Michael could feel her courage.

"Has something happened at the orphanage?" she asked.

He held up his hands. "I survived, and without a mark on me."

Deep-throated laughter further evidenced the tears she'd shed.

"Tell me about your mother."

She twirled the rose. "She was an orphan from the Virginia colony. Lachlan met her at court."

Michael wanted to ask why the duke of Ross hadn't married Sarah's mother, but the answer was none of his business. "Do you favor her?"

"When I was young I did." She sniffed. "But now they say I look like my father."

"They?"

"My Aunt Juliet, she's Lachlan's duchess. He agrees."

He remembered Sarah's story of a governess who won the love of a duke. "Where is he, Sarah?"

She placed the rose on the grave. "I do not know, but I'll find him, now that I'm ready."

A sense of rightness filled Michael. He

got to his feet and held out his hand. When her fingers touched his, he lifted her slight weight effortlessly.

"You must be chilled," he said.

"A wee bit." She shook out her cloak.

Michael helped her on with it. "The inn's close by. Will you join me there for a tankard of mulled wine?"

"Will you give me the painting — free of conditions?"

Caught off guard by her frankness, Michael paused.

"And if you preface your answer with 'yes, well,' I'll ignore you."

Michael couldn't remember the last time a woman had been so straightforward with him, but there was only one Sarah MacKenzie. "Do I do that?"

"Always, when you do not choose to reply." She threaded her arm through his and started down the path. "Then you change the subject or ask a question yourself. It's the way you avoid answering troublesome questions."

Complimented to his bootflaps, Michael wanted to kiss her then and there, but propriety stopped him. "Since you know me so well, I'll consider returning the painting to you."

She lifted one brow.

Grudgingly, he said, "Without conditions."

"You are kindness itself," she said, meaning anything but.

As they exited the hospice grounds, Michael looked for the streetsweeper, but the lane was empty.

"Who collected the most shillings?"

"Who do you think?"

"Notch." She smiled in honest query. "Do I get a shilling?"

Several benign replies came to mind; Michael discarded all of them. "I had a sweeter reward, of a more personal nature, in mind for you."

A blush stained her cheeks. "I can imagine what it is."

"Yes, well —"

"Aha! I told you so."

Properly chastened, Michael suppressed the need to defend his conversational habits. Today was Sarah's day.

They walked the short distance in companionable silence. Fat pigeons strutted in the lane and pranced on the ledges of buildings. Few merchants opened their shops on Sunday afternoons, and the craft guilds were closed up tight. The wagonways were deserted, and only carriages and sedanchairs shared the lanes.

The day was comfortably warm; only an occasional cloud cast its moving shadow over the town. Michael had left the customs house in such haste, he'd forgotten his cloak, but he did not miss its warmth. He remembered how chilled he'd been upon arrival in Scotland, and decided his affection for the woman beside him wasn't the only change in his life since leaving India. The climate of Edinburgh now suited him as well.

The doorman at the Dragoon Inn hastened to let them inside. Michael halted, temporarily blinded in the darkened room. When his eyes adjusted, he saw that the chairs and benches were upended on the tables and the bar. A scrubmaid sloshed her mop across the worn plank floor. The pungent odor of lye soap permeated the close air.

Sarah waved her hand in front of her nose. Michael helped her off with her cloak. "Will you join me in my room?"

Her gaze snapped to his.

He quickly added, "Just until the maid's done, and the air is breathable again."

"Stop trying to look innocent, Michael

Elliot; your boldness spoils the effect."

He smiled, and led her toward the stairs. "Seems strange, not having William on the steps to trip over or Notch —"

"Lord Michael!"

Turning, Michael saw the owner hurrying toward them.

He held out a small blue box. "Someone left this for you."

Beside him, Sarah gasped. "Who?" she demanded sharply.

The man shrugged, and as propriety dictated, spoke to Michael although the message was meant for Sarah. "The doorman brought it. Said a stranger gave it to him."

"Bring up two tankards of warm wine — straightaway."

"Aye, my lord."

Eager to get her away, Michael took the box and ushered her to his rooms.

Moving up the stairs, Sarah walked on leaden feet. Only moments ago, she had made her personal peace with Lachlan MacKenzie. As if he'd heard her very words, he'd sent the one possession that best symbolized the estrangement between them: the necklace from Neville Smithson. The box and the necklace were a birthday gift from her real father.

Just as she sat in one of the comfy chairs, Michael handed her the box. "I believe this is yours."

Her hand shook as she released the clasp and lifted the lid. Resting on the satin lining was a folded note. Beneath it lay the golden beads, some broken, all unstrung as she had left them. The cruelty of Neville Smithson still ached like a raw wound. She had forgiven Lachlan MacKenzie. His words of explanation and defense rang in her ears. *I would not have given you up, Sarah lass.*

She closed the lid.

"Is it yours?" Michael asked.

"I do not want it. You take it. Give it away. Throw it in the rubbish bin."

"Come now, Sarah. You're too brave to run away from a piece of paper and a handful of beads. Read the note."

The command in his voice startled her.

A fierce knocking sounded on the door.

"Read it now." Michael moved to see who was there, while Sarah opened the box and took out the paper. There, in the duke of Ross's distinctive hand, were the words

Come back to us, Sarah lass, for without you, we are as these beads, broken.

The plaintive note sent tears streaming down her cheeks.

Michael knelt beside her, a steaming tankard in each hand, his gaze fixed on the note. "I'll trade you," he said, a tentative smile beginning to glow in his eyes.

She exchanged the box for the wine, and as her hands curled around the warm mug, her heartache eased. She had behaved like a coward these last few months, never considering the pain her family suffered.

And they *were* her family, the Mac-Kenzies. Their blood did not travel in her veins, but their love dwelled in her heart. She'd spent her life among them, rejoiced at the birth of each new sister and brother, grieved at the loss of dear Virginia.

At the remembered pain of that tragedy, Sarah knew that her desertion had dealt her family another painful blow.

They did not deserve cruelty, not from a prideful woman who'd been raised with love and kindness.

She choked back a sob.

The mug was taken from her hand; then Michael lifted her from her chair and pulled her to stand in his embrace.

"Shush," he soothed, patting her back and rocking from side to side. "All will be well, Sarah."

How could it be? She'd stormed from Rosshaven Castle, too consumed with self-pity to notice the destruction she'd left behind. Her younger siblings wouldn't understand. Juliet surely blamed herself, and with sinking dread, Sarah knew her stepmother did not carry that burden alone.

Where was Lachlan?

"Oh, Michael. I've been such a fool."

"Impossible. You could never be that."

"I'm selfish. Even you said I was spoiled."

"I exaggerated. You're headstrong and determined."

"I'm reckless. I've hurt them so."

He pushed a handkerchief into her hand. "Not apurpose, you didn't. You haven't the heart for cruelty, especially to the MacKenzies."

"Oh, I do. Pride drove me away from them."

"Why?"

"I felt as if I were in the way. Mary and Agnes were off on adventures. Lottie wed years ago to a man she has loved since childhood. Lachlan and Juliet have another family."

"You thought they didn't need you."

" 'Twas that and worse. I wanted my own family, and I wouldn't listen to Papa. He knew Henry was wrong for me."

Michael held her at arms' length. Even through teary eyes, his concern was plain to see.

"Have you committed murder?" he demanded.

A yoke of misery weighted her shoulders. "Nay."

"Have you compromised the sovereignty of the realm?"

She took a deep, shaky breath.

"Have you? Answer me, Sarah."

She ducked his gaze. "Nay."

"Have you stolen anything other than my heart?"

15

Sarah's pain ebbed, leaving a spark of hope. But she could not address his admission now, for too many things were left undone. Hoping he understood, she said, "I tried to steal the painting."

In mock reprimand, he replied, "You're a wretched failure at thievery."

"You're a knave for taking advantage of the moment. You know I'm too miserable to mount a defense."

He grinned like a sailor home from the sea. "Guilty as charged. Why did you ask Henry to marry you?"

Drawing in a deep breath, she stared at the gold braid on his coat. "You will not believe me. My reasoning will sound too simple, which it truly is. Too much has occurred between us."

"Enough has occurred between us for you to know that I am a man who makes up his own mind — when I am afforded the opportunity."

His eloquent words answered all of her reservations. "I proposed to Henry because he was the first man with all of his teeth who could even read my stipulations."

A smile danced in his eyes. "And he agreed to them."

"Yes. You see, I must have money and means of my own. I'm far too —"

"Stubborn."

"Any man who refuses me a voice of my own is —"

"A fool." He pulled her to his chest. "You're better off without him."

Like a kindred spirit looking for his match, he melded her to him. His strength of will seeped into her, urging surrender, demanding that she see the truth that was in his heart.

She languished in his arms and reveled in the feel of his power, for she knew without doubt that Michael Elliot was constant in his desire for her and honorable to his soul. He had not tried to stifle her with arrogant male authority; he had, at almost every turn, employed patience and understanding.

And seduction, she had to admit.

Cupping her face in his hands, he pressed his lips to her eyes and cheeks and kissed her tears away. With a gentle smile, he turned to the side and moved his lips a touch away from hers. He smelled of exotic places, and he embodied her every dream of chivalry.

On a breathless sigh, she said, "You're seducing me."

"Only as a prelude to ravishment." His mouth settled on hers, and he breathed the words, "By my oath, I love you, Sarah MacKenzie."

Desire poured over her, and as he deepened the kiss, she let his vow spin round and round in her mind, until she grew dizzy with need of him. As if in answer, he slid his hands down her back and drew her forward, showing her the fierceness of his desire. She clung to him, wanting more, struggling to get closer, to put out the fire that raged between them. But the flames soared, and his tongue thrust into her mouth, fanning the inferno, feeding her wanton cravings, and sending her delving after the greater joy that was sure to come.

His hands kneaded her, his hips ground against her, and when the cadence of his movement slowed to a steady, constant rhythm, Sarah couldn't hold back a moan.

He swept her into his arms, as if she were thistledown. "Hold on."

"As if I'd let you go," she murmured, resting her head on his shoulder.

A chuckle vibrated deep in his chest, and the furnishings in the room sped past in a blur. Once in the bedroom, he again set his mouth to hers in a kiss that went beyond bold, past seduction, for it held a promise too precious for words.

Relaxing his arms, he let her legs slide slowly to the floor. Her knees wobbled, and the room whirled like a spun top. With suspiciously expert movements, he loosened the intricate fastenings at the back of her dress and worked it down to her hips.

The cool air teased her naked arms and turned her skin to gooseflesh, but the touch of his hands on her breasts obliterated any notion of a chill. Her own aggressive nature came to the fore, and taking his lead, she unbuttoned his waistcoat and tunneled her fingers beneath the satin lining. When she tried to ease the garment from him, he shrugged, sending it to the floor.

Her thumbs and fingers fumbled with

the buttons of his shirt, and noticing her dilemma, he broke the kiss long enough to grasp the front of his shirt and rip it off.

Buttons clattered against the wall.

Sarah gasped at the sight of his thickly muscled chest and arms. Broader and stronger than she had imagined, Michael Elliot loomed before her, filling her mind with contradictory impressions: power and gentleness, elegance and might.

He grew still. "Have I frightened you?"

Never could she fear him; his strength enchanted her every feminine illusion. "No. You're . . . beautiful." She could have told him he had warts on his chin, so anguished was his expression. She quickly added, "In a perfectly masculine way."

"I'm relieved, then." He pulled off his boots. "But you have on too many clothes."

Sarah's gaze followed the narrowing line of jet black hair on his belly to where it disappeared beneath the waist of his velvet breeches. His hands moved to the placket there but stopped.

Glancing up, she saw him watching her.

Haste forgotten, he moved toward her, and Sarah's heart began to pound like the drums at All Hallow's Eve. Locking his gaze to hers, he grasped her waist and lifted her until they were nose to nose. Holding her there, seemingly without effort, he resumed the kiss. Again, his strength beckoned, and she sent her hands roaming his arms and shoulders and neck. He felt rock hard and robust; yet beneath his manly exterior thrived a gentle, loving soul.

Dragging his mouth from hers, he lifted her higher, and when his lips touched her breasts, Sarah teetered on the edge of a swoon. Her head fell back, and her hands cradled his head, pulling him closer, glorying in the feel of his silky hair sliding between her fingers. The drag of his tongue on her nipples and the soft suckling of his lips sent shafts of desire to her belly and lower. She grew damp in hidden places, and as he continued his loving assault on her senses, she discovered an odd feeling of emptiness deep in her woman's core.

The rush of his heated breath against her skin made her shiver with longing. Her toes curled, and her legs hung useless and dangling in air. Seeking purchase, she tried to wrap herself around him, to clutch his hips with her knees, but her bulky skirts were in the way.

He tore his mouth from hers, and when their eyes met, she saw her own passion reflected in his fierce gaze. Gasping in ragged breaths, they spoke without words in a language springing from want and need and soul-deep longing.

How do you feel, love? his expression seemed to ask.

Safe with you, her heart answered.

He smiled and lowered her to the bed. Looming over her, he worked her remaining clothing over her hips and tossed dress, petticoats, and chemise to the floor. Then his hungry gaze embarked on an intimate roaming that began at her breasts and ended at her loins.

The air in her lungs turned to fire, and anticipation filled her, but her hands tingled with the need to hold him again. She lifted her arms in entreaty. Smiling, he took her wrists, turned her hands over, and kissed her palms. Her eyes drifted shut, but he said her name in a whisper, compelling her to observe.

With maddeningly slow progress, punctuated by hums and groans of approval, he tasted and savored her from the tips of her fingers to the soft, sensitive skin under her arms. When his mouth moved over her ribs to her navel, she felt a great well of need open inside her. When his hands eased between her legs and spread her to his view, she gasped in shock.

Giving her a devilishly daring grin, he lowered his mouth to her most intimate place.

Sarah jerked and scooted out of his reach. Too mortified to speak, she shook her head. What he had in mind went beyond debauchery, and in her befuddlement, she couldn't fathom an intimacy so great.

"Oh, very well, my prim Sarah," he said, and peeled off his breeches.

She stared, puzzlement turning to absolute shock. His legs were more than well formed, as she had suspected, but his masculinity, boldly jutting from his loins, made her rethink a lifetime of girlish notions. A lump of appreciation swelled in her throat. She swallowed loudly.

Watching her, anticipation in his eyes, he said, "Would you care for a glass of brandy?"

Refinement in the face of so much palpable desire brought a smile to her lips. "Not if you have to go past arm's length to fetch it."

With that, he moved over her, tunneling his arms beneath her shoulders, carefully taking his own greater weight. Spreading her legs to accommodate him, she felt his maleness brush her inner thigh.

He sucked in a breath and drew back. Then he shifted his weight and eased a hand between her legs. At his touch, she gasped for breath, which drew an anguished groan from him. As if exhausted, he dropped his head to her shoulder, and she felt the tickle of his long hair against her skin, but the sensation came from far away; her mind stayed fixed on the havoc his agile fingers were creating.

Of their own accord, her hips moved in harmony with the motion of his hand, but as he prolonged and expanded his ministrations, she felt as if she were soaring toward some divine circumstance. In an explosion of sheer ecstacy, she burst into an event so spiritual, she felt thrust into heaven itself. Languishing there, she concluded that passion was indeed a sound, for it echoed through her body in little joyous whispers.

He moved up and lifted her hips, wedging himself into her loins. She felt his desire nudging forward, and she shifted to accommodate him.

"Be still, Sarah," he rasped. "I have no personal knowledge of virgins, but I've heard the pain is brief and better done without resistance."

His admission that she was his first innocent charmed Sarah. "I ceased resisting when you took off all of my clothes."

"Not entirely." He pushed into her. Breathlessly, he said, "You balked at certain pleasures I wanted to give you."

"Any decent woman would refuse such a thing."

"Yes, well . . . not the second time. Now, I want very much to make you mine, sweetheart, and if what I see in your eyes is a sign, I believe you are ready to be free of this maidenhead, which is tickling me in an unmentionable place."

"Unmentionable places are not allowed."

Tried patience narrowed his gaze.

Sarah felt bound to say, "But I'm talking too much, aren't I? Going on about nothing."

Against her belly, she felt laughter rumble through him. "Sarah, darling. You 'go on' delightfully, but when a man is primed to love a woman, he —"

"Of course. He must get on with it. But do not think I believe it a duty to be suffered by a wife."

He sighed loudly. "You know a great deal about the subject?"

"Everything except those 'certain pleasures' you tried to foist off on me."

"Yes, well. I have another pleasure in mind at the moment."

"But not if I keep nattering on."

She looked beautifully abashed to Michael, and yet provocatively daring at once. "You will forgive a wee bit of pain when I make you mine?"

" 'Tis only delays I cannot abide."

He took her quickly, completely. The message in her eyes screamed surprise and distress, and he soothed her with soft words and long, deep kisses.

Now that the pain had eased, Sarah

became the aggressor, finding the cadence that produced his deepest groans and heightened her own need. He thrust deep, capturing her completely, only to draw back, and like a fierce, dragging tide, he seemed to pull her desire and stretch it taut. When the pressure grew too great, she felt the rapture engulf her. Knowing her pleasure was at hand, he took her mouth at the moment she cried out, and a heartbeat later, he returned the sound in a roar of male contentment.

Feeling deliriously complete, Sarah clutched him in her arms until their breathing slowed, and he rolled to his side, pulling her with him.

Details of the room sharpened into focus; the lamplight glowed brighter than before, and the clock ticked in a steady cadence. She noticed his neatly stacked clothing trunks against the wall, and on the vanity, his combs, brushes, and shaving tools were lined up like soldiers on parade.

On the table by the bed, a decanter and glass stood no more than arm's length away. He had offered her the wine, but she'd been too entranced by him and the loving to come to give the offered refreshment more than a passing thought.

A glass of water sounded divine, but at the prospect of leaving his embrace, her thirst declined.

With a swift smack of a kiss, he threw the bedcovers aside and moved to leave the bed. As quickly, he stopped and covered himself. "Sarah?"

"Um, yes?"

"I must get up and see to a few things for —"

"Of course," she blurted, suddenly self-conscious. "Do what you must."

Patiently, he said, "But I haven't anything to wear within reach except the suit of clothes I was born in."

"I'm also wearing that."

He gave her a smile rife with pure male serenity. "Gloriously so, I must confess."

Her unease fled. " 'Tis better than sackcloth."

"Just so, and I wondered if you would be embarrassed now with my nakedness."

His thoughtfulness pleased her, and she knew that consideration for others came naturally to him.

"No," she said. "I rather enjoy looking at you."

He jiggled his eyebrows in a mocking leer. "Look your fill, my dear."

"But if you discover a robe or two, you might leave them within arm's reach."

He padded, bare of foot and everywhere else, across the room to the high chest of drawers. Pouring water from a pitcher, he wetted a soft cloth and returned to the bed. In naked awe, she watched him perform the gentle task of bathing her most intimate places.

Completely uninhibited, he smiled as he worked.

"Thirsty?" he asked.

"For water," she said.

He placed a pair of robes at the end of the bed and poured her a drink of water from a corked bottle. When she'd had her fill, she slid beneath the covers. He lowered the flame of the lamp, climbed into bed, and nestled her against his chest.

The ticking of the clock grew loud.

"I will not sleep," she said.

"I know." He rubbed her arm.

"I've never been in bed with a man before."

He chuckled and kissed her forehead. "I *know*."

"We're to sleep na-naked?"

"The notion appeals to me."

"I've never been —"

"Ravished twice in one night, if you do not go to sleep."

She walked her fingers down his chest. "I told you that I left Tain for adventure."

"Adventure," he repeated thoughtfully. "Much more of your teasing, Sarah, and you'll think war is a lightsome moment."

His thick black hair tickled her palm. "Are you tired?"

"Not in the least."

With a fingernail, she traced the edge of the bed sheet. "I could dance a jig."

His hand covered hers. "There was a little blood. You'll be sore."

Peering up at him, she looked deeply into his eyes. Desire smoldered there. Lowering her gaze, she said, "Just my feet will be sore — if we dance."

His groan of indecision vibrated against her cheek. She asked, "Do you know the twosome reel?"

"Only the recumbent kind."

She giggled and hugged him.

He squeezed her, then turned her to face him.

Only soft cloth and his sense of honor separated them.

Feeling warm and cozy, she laid her hand against his jaw. The stubble tickled her palm. "But if you don't want to —"

He growled, his gaze sharp, his grip like steel. "Send your other hand exploring, my little adventurer, and you'll discover a new land of 'want.' "

"Yes, well —"

"Sarah! Teasing will be returned in kind."

"You said you wanted me to act the wanton in your bed. But I'm not acting. I feel deliciously debauched. And *deflowered* is a seriously flawed word to describe what has occurred here."

Michael couldn't decide which he loved more, her lush body or her bright mind. When her hand slipped below the covers and touched him, he cast off all notions of chivalry and made love to her again.

Later, too exhausted to move, he nestled her against him and drifted to sleep, his soul at peace and his body content.

He was awakened by the sound of his mother's voice. He opened his eyes. Sunshine flooded the room.

The countess of Glenforth stood at the foot of his bed, a flutter-fingered Turnbull at her side.

16

"Wake up, Michael!" his mother said. "You must get up. The most wretched thing has happened —" She sucked in a breath and looked at Turnbull. "You said nothing about a wo-woman in Michael's bed."

The valet's mouth worked, but he made no sound.

Offended beyond good manners, Michael yanked the covers higher to conceal his nakedness and Sarah, who was cuddled against his chest. She ducked beneath the blankets.

As still as a statue, his mother continued to glare. "Oh, goodness, the magistrate will be —"

"What are you doing here?" Michael demanded.

A befuddled Turnbull wrung his hands.

His mother waved a piece of paper. "Richmond has ordered Henry transported to a prison in Botany Bay — 'tis a penal colony across the ocean. We must do something! They'll send him away in chains."

"He deserves it," Sarah murmured against Michael's shoulder.

His mother's gaze flitted from the clothing strewn on the floor, to both occupants of the bed. "Is that woman Sarah MacKenzie?"

"This woman is none of your affair, Mother. Turnbull, wait in the hall. Mother, go into the sitting room."

Sarah said, "I hope the sitting room's in Glasgow."

"What did she say?" his mother demanded. "I will not allow her to cast further aspersions on the Elliots."

Struggling to keep a tight rein on his temper, Michael held up his hand for silence and began counting to 10.

Turnbull made a speedy exit.

At the count of six, Michael heard his mother say, "If that strumpet is speaking lies about me, or if she had anything to do with poor Henry's being transported, I'll have her thrown in jail for peddling her tawdry wares among the gentry."

He heard Sarah emit a low, feminine growl.

Michael gave up. "Mother!" he snapped. "Take yourself into the other room. Do it now! I'll join you there in a moment."

"Something will have to be made of this muddle." She whirled and sailed out, pulling the door closed behind her.

Michael threw back the covers and donned one of the robes, tossing the second to Sarah.

She looked beautifully disheveled, her thick blond hair falling to her waist in a tangle of waves, her skin slightly flushed with anger. Or was it shame?

"How do you feel?" he asked.

She slid him a sidelong glance. "Betrayed."

"By whom?"

Taking the robe, she thrust her arms into the sleeves, but the garment was so big, her hands were completely concealed. As she fumbled to work her fingers free, the motion set her breasts to bouncing.

In spite of the trouble awaiting him in the other room, Michael couldn't stave off a new rush of desire. He had hoped to lounge in bed all day long with her. He had planned to order up a meal, after he'd first feasted on her. But if her jerky movements were an indication of her mood, Sarah was not the least bit interested in making love with him again.

He got to his feet and held out a hand to help her from the bed. "Talk to me, Sarah. Tell me what's on your mind."

She shoved her hair out of her eyes, which now blazed fire. Ignoring his offer of assistance, she scrambled from the bed and started snatching up her clothes.

Hoping to give her a little time to settle down, he moved to the door. "I'll only be a moment."

To his astonishment, she preceded him into the sitting room and marched up to his mother.

"An admirable performance, Lady Emily," she said. "But I'm not fooled."

"Fooled?" his mother said, looking Sarah up and down. "Ha! I should have expected low behavior from a Highland by-blow."

"Then I have news for you. The duke of Ross is not my father. He only took me in when my own father would not."

Michael could only stare, wondering how many more shocks awaited him.

Was this the payment for a blissful night of love?

His mother's gaze darted from him to Sarah.

At length, Lady Emily said, "I had hoped for better for Michael, but there's nothing else to be done about it now."

"Hoped for better?" Sarah challenged. "You've treated him abominably, and that's when you even thought of him at all. Henry is all you care about. Michael was only a babe, and you left him in Fife for the Lindsays to raise."

Stiff with indignation, his mother stared at her own hands. "He'll be allowed to wed you, but not for fifteen thousand pounds." Looking up, she drilled Sarah with a steely gaze. "We'll need thirty thousand pounds if you expect Michael to marry you — a commoner."

Sarah crossed her arms and huffed. "There is no dowry; I am not Lachlan MacKenzie's daughter."

"When did that truth come out?" Lady Emily asked.

"I was told of my parentage on the day before I arrived in Edinburgh."

Michael believed her, and he now knew why she had refused any communication with Lachlan MacKenzie. She'd been hurt and confused.

"The duke of Ross signed the betrothal," his mother argued. "I've a writ authorizing release of the funds you deposited in Mr. Coutts's bank."

"Are you daft?" Sarah's voice rose. "I've read the law, and you cannot claim my dowry. No court will find in your favor."

At that revelation, his mother's demeanor changed. Tense with stubborn pride, she said, "I doubt we'll need it. I've arranged for the great Lucerne to perform a concert here. The admissions will free Henry."

Sarah's temper cooled to simmering scorn. "The arrangements you speak of, were they made with a noblewoman you met in London? The one with the pink jade necklace and the Oriental maid?"

Suspicion pinched Lady Emily's face. "What about her?"

"She happens to be Agnes MacKenzie. We were raised as sisters, and she is a true daughter of the duke of Ross."

Michael cursed.

"Nonsense."

Through gritted teeth, Sarah said, "Listen to me, Lady Emily. If you ever again accuse me of speaking nonsense, I'll yank off your wig and toss it in the nearest slop bucket. I do not speak nonsense!"

Seeing her hopes of freeing Henry dashed, Lady Emily softened her tone. "I doubt that woman is your sister, but even if she is, you have no right to interfere in the plans for my concert."

Michael felt as if he'd stepped into a nightmare.

But Sarah wasn't done. "Don't you see, you thickheaded Elliot? *Agnes* approached *you.* She probably pinched your purse herself. Agnes MacKenzie bamboozled you in retaliation for the wretched way you've treated me."

"How do you know? Unless you put her up to it?"

"Has the word *loyalty* ever entered your limited vocabulary?"

"If what you say is true, and she's not really your sister, why would she be loyal to you?"

Sarah threw up her hands and stomped from the room.

Michael opened the exit door and shouted at his mother. "Out!"

Sputtering in disbelief, she planted

her feet. "No. You cannot order me out. I let Henry throw away his life. I will not allow you to do the same."

Frustrated to the point of rage, Michael slammed the door and began to pace.

"If it takes all of my strength," she went on, "I'll keep you from those wretched gaming houses. You'll not go dallying off to London whenever the mood strikes you."

"Mother!" he wailed in frustration.

"You will make something of yourself."

Balling his fist, he pounded the mantel. The clock banged, and his collection of boxes tumbled to the floor. "I have already *made* something of myself, Mother. You would know that had you bothered to ask."

Caught up in giving edicts, she didn't hear. "No matter what Lady Sarah says, you must believe that I never wanted to send you to Fife. 'Twas your father's doing. He forbade me to 'coddle another of his sons,' as he put it. I was only six and ten when you were conceived and too naive to challenge my husband."

Sweet Lord. She'd been no more than

a child when she'd given birth to Henry. A child raising a child. Why had Michael never known her age?

Because his earliest memories were those of a five- or six-year-old boy, riding his pony for his snowy-haired father and demonstrating his skill with a bow and arrow. Lady Emily had been a small shadow on the edge of the images, or not there at all.

"No packing off *your* children to Fife," his mother declared. "We'll raise them here."

"Raise my children? I must beget them first!"

Her face blushed crimson and she glanced at the bedroom door. Catching his own absurdity, he struggled for control of his anger.

"Mother," he began patiently. "I love Sarah MacKenzie, and I intend to make her my wife. But if you do not leave before she gets on her clothes and marches through that door, there will be no marriage."

Lady Emily's expression smoothed out. "Of course she'll wed you. You have the Elliot good looks. You haven't been ruined with gaming, and with her temper, she's more than a match for you. You're like your grandfather, you know. All domineering and have-it-your-way —"

"Mother!"

"Oh, Michael. Do not bluster so. She cannot possibly dress herself alone."

On that erroneous declaration, the bedroom door swung open. Righteously angry, a still-disheveled Sarah burst into the room.

"I told you so," his mother whined. "Her dress is hooked all wrong. Just look at her hair. She'll need some work before we summon the parson to marry you."

"Marry us?" Sarah chortled with glee. "Never. I've had enough of the Elliots."

"What else is there to do?"

"I'll show you." Head held high, her hastily done up hair falling around her shoulders, Sarah headed for the door.

"Stop," Michael snapped in his general's voice.

Deaf to his words and blind to all but her escape, she didn't break stride.

"One more step, Sarah MacKenzie, and I'll drag you back."

She bulled, tucked her slippers under her arm, and grasped the handle.

"I mean it, Sarah." Michael ran to the

door and threw the bolt. "You're not going anywhere."

Her foot slammed into his shin.

She winced. "Open that bloody door."

Hobbling himself, he grasped her arm and pulled her back. Facing his mother, he said, "Out!"

Agog, the countess stared at Sarah. "You will not hurt her — above ruination."

Sarah quivered with rage and spat, "Ruination? You're just afraid he'll damage the goods."

His mother stepped back. "I never truly disliked you, Sarah MacKenzie."

Sarah wilted in mock relief. "You cannot fathom how happy that makes me feel. You're a selfish and cruel woman who wouldn't know like or dislike if they crawled under your silly dusted wig."

Unreality gripped Michael.

Drawing herself up, Lady Emily said, "You insisted Henry send me to Fife."

"That's a wretched lie. Henry hardly mentioned you. Henry never talked about anyone except *Henry*."

Michael felt as if he had a pair of angry Bengal tigers on his hands.

His mother spat, "You only saw Henry

three times before you sent that agreement."

"Then four must be my lucky number," Sarah railed. "I rue the day I set eyes on your son." She glared up at Michael. "*Sons!* Let me go."

He tightened his grip. "Calm down, Sarah. You're not truly angry with me."

"Then you're as daft as she is. You seduced me and arranged for her to find us together. Now get your hand off my arm. I'm leaving."

His mother moved toward the door. "No. Someone must fetch the clergy. I'll be the one to go."

Michael pushed Sarah behind him. "Yes, Mother, you will leave, but Sarah and I will notify the church."

The moment he unlatched the door, Sarah shoved him back and darted into the hall. Lady Emily went after her. In his haste to get to the door, he almost knocked his mother down.

When he at last set her aside and moved into the hall, he stopped in his tracks.

William, Turnbull, the Odds, and the blustering magistrate stood on the landing.

With Notch on her heels and the maid

Rose at her side, Sarah ran out of the inn.

Tears of shame and regret streamed down Sarah's cheeks and mingled with the water in her bath. Michael's arresting and masculine odor lingered around her, and no matter how many times she lathered her skin or how much fragrance she poured into the water, she could not obliterate the heady smell of him.

Just as his scent stayed with her, so did the memories of his loving fill her mind. She shivered and slipped deeper into the tub.

Not only had she betrayed the MacKenzie family love and loyalty, she'd ruined any chance for a loving marriage or a respected life in Edinburgh. She would be branded a wanton and deemed unfit to supervise the orphanage. Her pride and stubbornness had led to her own downfall and seduction.

Outside, the bells of Saint Giles chimed the meridian. As soon as she mastered her emotions over the disastrous encounter with Lady Emily, Sarah intended to pen the brief that would negate the Elliots' attempt to steal her dowry. But how could she concentrate on rescuing money from the bank when she couldn't stop crying? Burying her face in her hands, she gave way to the agony and sobbed. Why anyone ever named her Sensible Sarah, she did not know. *Foolish Sarah* better suited her actions of the last six months.

But the folly of the night before made pettiness of her other mistakes. She had given her heart to Michael, and when she most needed his support, he had behaved in true Elliot form.

Her stomach soured when she recalled the insults and lies his mother had told. But Sarah's own outrageous behavior stunned her more. Wearing only a man's robe and coming straight from a bed of sinful pleasures, she had flaunted her sin and railed at the city's biggest gossip.

What had she been thinking? She hadn't; Michael and their shared passion had wiped out all sense of propriety.

Even knowing the truth, Sarah couldn't help wishing she were wrong. Her heart ached at the memory of his loving declaration and her own yielding response.

Had he meant those words of affection? Had his vow of love been true?

Perhaps, but no man would willingly take a shrew for his lifelong mate.

The pain of loss and disappointment stabbed like a knife, and she clutched her belly, hoping to soothe the ache. She remembered the feel of his hands caressing her, his mouth tasting her in places that couldn't be named outside the marriage bed.

The marriage bed. She cried harder. In the light of day, their glorious hours of passion seemed like a nightmare. Word of the entire wretched affair would spread like the plague.

Sarah, discovered in Michael Elliot's bed. Sarah, screaming like a fishwife at the countess of Glenforth. Sarah, in complete disarray, dashing from inn to carriage. Sarah, the topic of conversation in every gin shop and drawing room.

Lachlan MacKenzie would suffer for her dishonor. Just when she'd made peace with her past, she'd wrecked her future. Even if Michael forgave her, Sarah couldn't forgive herself.

Bold and reckless. She was all of those things and more. The need to run away drove her to finish her bath and dress. In the quiet confines of the bedroom, she ordered her thoughts and penned a rebuttal to the Elliots' claim on the money she'd deposited in the Bank of Edinburgh.

Fighting back another bout of shame, she ordered a carriage. But when she arrived at the bank, she discovered that Lady Emily had not presented a writ, but Mr. Coutts assured Sarah that he would not have released the money if he had received such a paper.

From a clerk, she learned that Lady Emily had left on a hastily arranged trip to London. Word of Sarah's downfall was on its way to the Court of Saint James.

Too distraught for any company other than her own, she returned home and began the letters of explanation and apology to her family.

Sometime later, Rose burst through the door. "Come quick, Lady Sarah. Notch says Cholly and the general are fighting in Pearson's Close over what happened last night."

As if the hounds of hell were on her heels, Sarah raced through the streets of Edinburgh. She couldn't bear the thought of Michael disgracing himself in a public brawl, not when she was the cause. And the streetsweeper. What had moved the stranger, Cholly, to rise in her defense? His misplaced gallantry would land him in Tolbooth, for the magistrate was duty-bound to bring down the law on any common laborer who attacked a member of nobility. For Cholly's plight, too, she felt remorse.

At the corner of High Street and Pearson's Close, she encountered the fringe of the crowd that had gathered for the occasion.

"Ten quid more on the streetsweeper," someone called out. "He's busted the general's lip."

"And why not? The general called him a meddling old fool."

"Only after Cholly said the general was a toad-kissing Lowlander."

"My money's on the general. He's too quick for the likes of ol' Cholly."

"Open your eyes, man. Cholly ain't old."

Feeling more ashamed with every step, Sarah elbowed her way through the crowd of cheering onlookers. She spied Notch and his friends across the

411

way. From atop the shoulders of Right Odd, Sally stared, eyes agog, at the spectacle.

Hemmed in by the jeering throng, the two men were locked in combat. Michael was facing in her direction, but Cholly's broad back blocked her view. Michael feinted left to dodge a blow.

Now that he was in full view, Sarah looked for injuries. Blood from his cut lip stained his white neckcloth. His waistcoat and breeches were soiled and torn. A swelling high on his cheek made his fierce countenance all the more menacing. Her heart tripped fast with worry. What if he were permanently lamed or killed? That outcome was certainly possible, for his opponent was obviously skilled with his fists.

Without the blanket cape, the street-sweeper did look younger to Sarah. His back was broad, and his dull, unkempt hair gave proof of his lowly station in life. Did his face bear the marks of the fight? If he turned to face her, she'd have her answer.

His teeth gritted, Michael came on with a flurry of punches. She winced, knowing his opponent would suffer a black eye from the ferocious blows.

"Eh, mates," the man beside Sarah shouted. "Lady Sarah's come to watch."

Cholly roared a common Scottish curse and drew back his fist. Michael ducked, but the next punch caught him square on the chin. His head snapped back. He staggered. Seizing the moment, the streetsweeper crouched and charged like an angry bull, forcing Michael into a door. Wood splintered and the door gave way. Locked in combat, the men disappeared over the threshold.

Before the crowd could close in, Sarah dashed after the fighting men. Once inside the darkened space, she grasped the door, which hung crookedly on its hinges.

"Get back, all of you!" she yelled.

A reply came in the form of boos and protests.

Crashing noises sounded behind her. The nearest spectators craned their necks to get a peek at the ongoing fray.

Sarah was just as determined to end it, and from the frenzied expressions on the faces of the crowd, none of them would help her. They were strangers.

She sighted Notch. "Get the magistrate," she screamed. "And find Turnbull."

Bless the lad, he nodded and dashed away.

Putting her shoulder into the damaged door, she wrestled at getting it back into the jamb. The sprung hinges protested. Sarah would not be denied. With a last push, the door fell into place. She slammed the bolt home.

Grunts and hisses filled the air. Pottery exploded to the floor. Whirling, she searched the dimly lit room. The shutters were drawn, allowing only bars of sunlight to penetrate the shadowy space.

"Michael! Stop it!" she yelled.

Another, louder grunt sounded. Other noises followed.

Desperate, she moved to the shutters and threw them open. The furnishings took shape; she saw a tapestry fire screen, and on a marquetry table, an array of pipes and a tobacco jar. She had a moment to notice the familiar items just before the brawling men careened into the smoking stand.

Clutching the streetsweeper's shoulders, Michael yanked him up off the floor and threw him into a chair. Light fell on the man's face, and she recognized him. Lachlan MacKenzie.

"Papa!" she screamed.

Drawing in a breath, he turned to her. In that moment, Michael's fist crashed into his face.

"Michael!" She ran across the room and grabbed his arm. "Please stop. You must stop. Get away from him."

Dazed, his chest heaving, his hands still knotted for battle, Michael shook his head.

Tugging on his arm, she said, "You're going to kill the duke of Ross. That's no streetsweeper. He's Lachlan MacKenzie."

Blinking, struggling for breath, Michael finally noticed her. "What did you say?"

She dropped to the floor beside the chair containing a very still duke of Ross. "He's Lachlan MacKenzie."

To her astonishment, Michael threw back his head and laughed.

The duke groaned and lifted a hand to his bruised cheek. "Sarah lass?" he said, in a groggy voice.

"I'm here, Papa," she crooned, pushing his hair out of his eyes and searching for a life-stealing injury. But tears blurred her vision. Lachlan MacKenzie had been in Edinburgh for months. In the guise of streetsweeper, he'd watched over her.

Love squeezed her chest. "Say something, Papa."

"Oh, Sarah lass." He put his hand over hers. "I never thought to hear you address me so again."

"I'm so sorry, Papa. I've brought you nothing but shame and dishonor."

"Nay, 'tis me who is sorry. I should have come to you yesterday, in the cemetery, but I thought you loved that rounder."

"She does love me, you interfering fool."

Lachlan's eyes narrowed. "You'll pay for that, you despicable rake. By God, if Hamish were alive today, he'd help me bring you low."

"Bring me low? You're the one who cannot get up."

Relief sapped Sarah's strength.

Lachlan tried to rise from the chair.

"Cease this instant," she said, pressing a hand to his chest to keep him down.

Looking up, she said, "Michael, find a damp cloth. You've made a mess of his

416

face. Juliet will never forgive me."

Lachlan grinned, but winced with the effort. "Elliot's lost some of his comely looks today, I'll wager. With that face, he won't be ruining another lass any time soon."

"Hush, Papa."

"That's right, Ross," Michael said, touching Sarah's shoulder in a possessive way. "Because I'll be marrying Sarah just as soon as she's tended your battered face."

"A Stewart will again sit on the throne at Westminster Abbey before I give her to you, you foosty scunner."

"Sweet Saint Mary," Michael cursed. "Are all of the MacKenzies as stubborn as the two of you? I wonder why they allow you into civilization at all."

Michael did want her for his wife. In spite of the spectacle she'd made of herself, and even though she wasn't of noble blood, he wanted her.

Delightfully happy, she dried her tears and gazed lovingly at the man who had donned tattered clothing and swept streets to watch over her.

Lachlan must have sensed her joy, for he said, "Do you truly want that brawling Elliot for your husband?"

Michael growled a warning. "Much more of that, your grace, and I'll bar you from the ceremony."

"Oh, please, stop squabbling," Sarah begged.

"It'll take more than a quick left fist to keep me away. But what about the rest of the Elliots?"

The events of the morning came rushing back, and Sarah grew melancholy again. She craned her neck to look up at Michael. "I'm very sorry for the things I said to your mother."

"I'm sorry for not getting between the two of you sooner than I did. She deserved your wrath. She also sends her apologies to you."

"You have conveyed her false apologies before — on the day I met you."

He slapped a hand over his heart. "On my honor, she spoke her regrets to you."

"Honor," huffed Lachlan. "What would an Elliot know about honor?"

"Hush, Papa."

"Why did Lady Emily go to London?"

"To repay Richmond."

"But how? Mr. Coutts refused her my dowry. Where would she get that amount of money?"

Looking suddenly sheepish, Michael pressed the cloth to his bruised cheek.

Lachlan chuckled. "Will you tell her the truth, Elliot, or shall I?"

Baffled, Sarah glanced from one man to the other. "Tell me what?"

"I gave her the money," Michael admitted.

"There's more, Sarah lass, but make the scunner squirm when he tells you all of it."

"All of what?"

"I made a tidy sum over the years, investing in the East India Company."

Chuckling, Lachlan said, "To hear our friend, Cameron Cunningham, tell it, the only time Michael Elliot lost a quid in the company was a shipment of tea that set off a rebellion in Boston Harbor."

Sarah didn't know whether to admonish him for keeping secrets or fly into his arms. She settled on logic. "All of the money in the world will not free Henry if he doesn't apologize."

His expression turned sad. "True."

"I know Richmond well," Lachlan said. "He wilna let the slight go, and perhaps New Holland's the place for Henry. Then the title will pass to you."

Pride filled Sarah. "He doesn't want it, Papa. He wants to stand on his own for the House of Commons."

The duke of Ross flexed the fingers on his right hand, then held it up to Michael. "You'll need that sort of gumption to manage my Sarah lass."

She huffed.

Michael helped the duke to his feet. "I do have one question. If you are not her father, who is?"

Lachlan pressed his hands to the small of his back and stretched. "You tell him, Sarah."

Michael draped an arm over her shoulder and pulled her to his side. "Yes, you tell me."

Secure in Michael's love and reunited with the only father she'd ever known, Sarah told him about Neville Smithson.

When Sarah had finished the story, Lachlan cleared his throat. "I'm deeply sorry, Sarah lass, for the way in which I told you." Sorrow wreathed his face. "But I couldn't see past the loss. He was my friend."

More like brothers, folks often said. With that admission, healing came to Sarah. Sensing it, Michael pushed her toward Lachlan, who held out his arms.

She basked in the embrace, a renewal of a lifetime of loving concern.

"Neville would have claimed you Sarah, but I could not let you go."

A crash sounded behind her.

"Good Lord!" Michael exclaimed. "Who is that?"

Lachlan looked past Sarah, his blackened left eye wide with shock.

Sarah turned around. And groaned.

There on the threshold stood a very angry and extremely dangerous woman. In each of her hands she held a primed pistol.

"Michael," Sarah chirped. "May I present my sister, Lady Agnes MacKenzie."

Epilogue

One month later

Sunlight streamed through the vaulted stained-glass windows of Saint Margaret's Church, casting a brilliant shower of jewel-like colors over the flagged stone floor. Standing in the vestibule, Sarah tilted back her head and gazed up at her husband.

He grinned down at her. "No second thoughts?"

"I've given up thinking today. I'm only feeling, and deliriously happy is my watchword for the moment."

"Good, because Lachlan MacKenzie swears he will not take you back."

As if she would consider leaving Michael Elliot. "That's because you broke his nose. Juliet will not stop teasing him. She has the entire family and the population of Tain making fun of him."

Sudden vulnerability wreathed Michael's features. "He's a wonderful father, Sarah. Will you forgive me if I do not succeed as well with our children?"

Love filled her to bursting. "Oh, I think you'll manage admirably, Michael. Unless you think the MacKenzie brood is perfect."

His laughter echoed off the ancient walls, mingling with the sound of dozens of conversations going on in the nave of the church. In a few moments, Sarah and Michael would formalize their spoken vows by signing their names in both the Book of the MacKenzies and the family Bible.

"Behold the harmonious Clan MacKenzie." He cupped a hand to his ear. "Hear them?"

Sarah thrilled at the familiar sound, and if she concentrated she could separate Agnes's sultry tone from Lottie's sophisticated speech. Lachlan's hearty laughter floated above the din as he assumed the role of proud father.

All of the MacKenzies had come to Edinburgh for Sarah's wedding. Sketchpad in hand, Mary now stood near the altar, preserving the event for generations to come. The tenacious earl of Wiltshire dogged her heels. Notch and the other orphans hadn't moved more than a step away from Agnes, who drew the young ones to her like sunshine to summer. Since the loss of dear Virginia, watching over children had become her special quest in life.

At the opposite end of the church, in the apse, Lady Emily conversed with Vicktor Lucerne, who had composed a stirring wedding march for the occasion. Michael's mother had at last seen Henry for the selfish, prideful man he was. That stubbornness had earned him a sentence of transportation to the penal colony at Botany Bay. Aside from fawning over the young Lucerne, Lady Emily put her efforts into convincing Michael to assume the earldom of Glenforth.

The Smithson family had also descended on Edinburgh for Sarah's wedding. Clutching Michael's hand and kneeling before the altar, Sarah had made her peace with Neville. Although she knew she would never truly think of him as her father, he held a special place in her heart.

Other guests, friends of Michael, had come from London and Glasgow. Members of the Complement had hosted a reception the evening before. The arrival of one guest in particular had taken Sarah by surprise. Lord Edward Napier, earl of Cathcart, was considered the most respected statesman and scholar of the day.

"Sarah?" Michael whispered. "Are you my sweetheart?"

A sense of harmony thrummed through her. "I'm your wife."

Dots of color from the windows played across his noble features. "You did not answer the question."

Baffled by the request, she murmured. "Yes, I'm your sweetheart."

"Good. Now close your eyes and cup your hand."

"Why?"

"Because your husband *asks* it of you."

The command in his tone begged for a challenge. "You have an odd way of phrasing a request."

He made a desperate face. "Please?"

She did, and when his lips touched hers, she felt something cool and heavy fall into her palm.

He pulled back, and looked pointedly at her hand.

She looked there, too, and saw her golden beads, intact and resting in her palm. The irony gripped her; with thoughtfulness and love, Michael had helped her heal the rift with her family. Thanks to him, the MacKenzie family unity, like the necklace, had been restored.

"See?" he said. "Jewels do fall from the sky when I kiss my sweetheart."

Happier than any woman had a right to be, Sarah threw her arms around him and thanked God and all of His angels for the gift of Michael Elliot's love.